MICHAEL L. CLARK
I0695211
The RedRaven

Published by: Historic Traces Publishing

Pensacola, Florida 32534

PAPERBACK ISBN: 978-1-965756-03-4

HARDBACK ISBN: 978-1-965756-04-1

EBOOK ISBN: 978-1-965756-05-8

Dedicated to Swashbucklers Everywhere!

Chapter 1

A New Beginning

Bristol, England – 1702 - It was bad, really bad. In fact, it couldn't have been much worse for the residents of the area in Bristol known as Water Fort. The streets were lined with filth; bodies had been brought out and left to be picked up like yesterday's garbage. Victims of measles, dysentery, fever, and the like who had succumbed to their illness were buried in mass graves at the cemetery. Manure from horses and other livestock had been piled up on the curbs of the streets, where waste from residential chamber pots was also dumped. Then, when heavy rains arrived at Water Fort, everything was washed away into the River Avon, contaminating the waters.

Parentless children wandered the streets begging for and stealing whatever they could get to sustain them from day to day. Many traveled in gangs to attack honest citizens and relieve them of whatever they might be carrying. Or, they would break into homes and ransack them, searching for anything of value that could be traded or fenced.

Press gangs wandered the streets near the docks, searching for anyone they could press into service onboard a sailing vessel, either His Majesty's naval ships or one of the merchant marine vessels. Men often hid in attics or closets for days to avoid being pressed into service. If captured, they would be forced to serve aboard one of the ships until their voyage was complete. It might be months, but more likely years. To serve on a naval vessel was more insufferable than on a merchant marine vessel. The pay was much less, and discipline was much harsher on a naval ship. A man might receive thirty lashes for sleeping at his post or even be put to death if captured from desertion.

When word spread early this Saturday morning, men and boys scrambled through the streets and alleys, searching for a hiding place. The Press gangs moved through the streets carrying clubs, searching for any able-bodied man they might seize into service. Both the navy and merchant marines well paid the Pressers and their pay was based on results. So, the more captives provided, the higher their income.

When John Ashworth heard that the Press gangs were coming, he took a different approach than most. John had served on merchant marine vessels before. He was an experienced seaman who knew his way around a ship. Unfortunately, he hadn't served as of late because his wife had fallen ill and only recently died.

John grew up in Bath, about eleven miles from Bristol. What he lacked in education, he made up for in experience. His mother taught him to read and write at an early age before she died of consumption when he was ten. John never knew his father. John's mother said that his father had been killed while serving onboard a merchant ship during a hurricane. She always told him he looked just like his father with his auburn hair and freckled complexion.

After his mother died, John walked to Bristol and searched for work onboard a ship like his father had. He knew nothing about sailing or the seas, for that matter. But he was strong and big for a boy of only ten.

When John arrived in Bristol, he was shocked to see how much larger it was than his home in Bath. The people were always busy and noisy along the streets leading to the docks. For the most part, everyone ignored John. However, a group of young thugs not much older than him spotted him right off. The group leader tried to lure John off the main streets by telling him they had a place to put him up for the night. John was suspicious of the group and told the young man to "shove off!". When the boy continued to harass John, the boy quickly discovered John wasn't an easy target. The boy grabbed John by the arm to force him into an alley, but John swung his fist, hitting the boy in the ear and making him fall to the ground, crying in pain. John looked at the rest of the gang, who were watching from a distance, and he watched as they all disbanded and ran away.

John found work as a ship's boy on a merchant ship called the *Lazy Queen*. He found the work to his liking and spent several years working his way up through the ranks, eventually moving to other ships and working as a helmsman.

He met a young woman named Martha Allen in Bristol who worked in a dry goods store. Over time, they became quite close, and John finally asked her to marry him. Nine months later, a child was born. When the child was seven, Martha began showing signs of failing health. She suffered through aches, pains, and bleeding from her mouth and nose for years before finally succumbing to her illness.

John was left to care for his only child. He could not depend upon his relatives to care for the child in his absence, so the twelve-year-old would have to come along as John sought a vessel to sign on with.

"Do you have everything, Richard?" John asked the child.
"Yes Papa."

"Then lets get going. We need to find a suitable vessel who might need a ship's boy as well as a helmsman."

John wasn't tall, only about 5' 9". Richard was tall and lean for a twelve-year-old, 5' 6". Richard had dark red hair that usually curled over his ears and down the back of his neck. Today, Richard tied it back with a bit of ribbon and wore a knit cap to keep his head warm. He wore a blue woolen coat over his red and white striped shirt and brown knickers.

John led the way as he and the child snuck through the alleyways and streets leading to the docks. John didn't want to be found by the Pressers for fear that they might separate him from Richard and have them on separate ships. John peeked around every corner before going from one street to the next. In the distance, men could be heard screaming and shouting as the Pressers found their prey hiding in various locations.

Half an hour after leaving the squalor they called home, John led Richard to a gangplank leading to a merchant vessel of considerable size. It was a square-rigged ship displaying three tall masts. A tall, rough sort of a fellow stood at the top of the gangplank of the five hundred-ton ship named *Destiny*. The man eyed John and the boy as they slowly made their way up the plank.

"What can I do fer ye?" he asked in a dialect and manner befitting a seaman.

"Might you be needing a good helmsman and a ship's boy?"

The sailor looked them over, asking, "What experience might ye have?"

John replied, "The boy has never sailed, but he is well educated. He can read and write and do sums. I have been sailing since I was a wee lad. I served as helmsman on my latest vessel, The *Ocean Seeker*, until a year ago. The boy's mother fell ill and I've been tending to her since I came back ashore last winter. She died, bless her soul, a week ago. I have no one to leave the boy with, so I need to sign on with a ship that needs the both of us."

The burly man replied, "The *Seeker* I hear tell, went down in the Caribbean five months ago. I guess it be lucky you were not aboard her."

John said, "Really! I guess you're right."

"What be yer names?"

"I'm John Ashworth, and this is Richard."

"I'll be the first mate of this vessel. My name is Mr. Faulkner. The captain and I run a tight ship so be warned. It just so happens that we lost one of our helmsmen on the last voyage. And, we can always use another ship's boy. Welcome aboard! You can stow your belonging below."

Faulkner turned to a young man and called, "Jamie!"

A boy of about fifteen quickly approached the first mate and awaited his orders. "This is Richard Ashworth and his father, John. Show them where to stow their gear. Richard will be helping you. So, show him what to do. John is the new helmsman. Introduce him to Mr. McGuire."

"Aye, Mr. Faulkner!"

Jamie led the two sailors below decks where they could stow their gear. Richard had never been aboard a ship before. There were two levels below the main deck of the *Destiny*. The mid-level deck was where the ship's supplies and the crew's quarters were. Jamie showed John and Richard where they could stow their gear. Hammocks hung from beams of the upper deck. The Ashworths chose beds beside each other, although they likely wouldn't sleep during the same shifts. John, as helmsman, might be on duty late at night, while Richard would more likely sleep during regular hours of the night. They would both be expected to work long hours and be at the beck and call of the Captain whenever he wished.

Richard noticed a hatch in the floor and asked Jamie, "What's that?"

"That's the cargo hold."

"Is there anything in there?"

Jamie replied, "See for yourself."

Jamie lifted the hatch to expose the lower deck. A blast of hot air rose from the lower deck and nearly knocked Richard down.

He couldn't see anything; the open hatch only held darkness.

"Here." said Jamie as he handed Richard a lantern.

Richard took the lantern and climbed down the ladder into the lower deck. He was baffled by what he saw. Chains and shackles hung from the ceiling of the deck. The ceiling was shallow, even for Richard. His head was only four inches shy of touching it. A grown man would have to stoop to walk through the deck. The cargo was stacked in the aft of the hull, bolts, and bales of woolen goods. More goods were stored at the far bow of the ship as well, goods that would be delivered to Madagascar during the first leg of their voyage.

Richard climbed out of the hull and asked, "What are the shackles for?"

Jamie replied, "Slaves."

Richard's eyes widened as he replied, "We will be hauling slaves? From where?"

"Madagascar. We sail to Madagascar to drop off the wool and pick up a load of slaves. Then we make for Charlestown to sell the slaves and pick up a load of goods from the colonies; tobacco, rum, sugar, and cotton."

Richard asked, "How many slaves will we haul?"

"We'll pick up around five hundred, but many won't make it to Charlestown. We'll be lucky if two hundred survive the trip."

Richard was shocked when he asked, "Five hundred men? Down here?"

"And women," Jamie replied matter-of-factly.

John broke up the conversation by asking, "Where do I find Mr. McGuire?"

"Oh yeah, follow me."

Jamie led them out of the mid-deck to the ship's main deck. They followed him to the quarterdeck located at the stern of the ship. The quarterdeck was a raised platform at the rear of the ship. The captain's quarters were located inside the stern castle underneath the quarterdeck. At the front or bow of the ship was another raised platform called the bow castle. Underneath the bow castle were the officer's quarters, where the first and second officers and the ship's doctor slept.

Jamie climbed to the quarterdeck and found Mr. McGuire standing next to another man about ten years junior to John. They seemed to be discussing the condition of the *Destiny's* sails. Jamie stood by, waiting to be recognized. McGuire finally paused and asked, "Yes?"

"Mr. McGuire, sir, this is the new helmsman, Mr. Ashworth, and his son Richard who will be a new ship's boy."

McGuire looked them over before asking John, "How much time have you served at the helm?"

"Nigh on nine years, sir."

"What ships?"

John replied, "I started out on the *Lady Anne* when I was younger, then transferred to the *Ocean Seeker* until a year ago. Then, my wife fell sick, so I stayed home to care for her until she passed."

"So you weren't on the *Seeker* when she went down?"

"No, sir."

McGuire paused before saying, "Mr. Ashworth, this is our other helmsman, Mr. Crane."

The two men exchanged nods.

McGuire continued, "I was just informing Mr. Crane about our lady, here. He, too, is new to our vessel. *Destiny* can be a hand full to handle in open water. Have you ever sailed a square-rigged ship, Mr. Ashworth?"

"Yes, sir! The *Seeker* was square rigged, only she wasn't as large as this fair lady."

"Aye! said McGuire. "She's good in the open water, although a bit cumbersome near the coast. You'll get the hang of her, though."

John replied, "I look forward to it, Mr. McGuire."

McGuire told Jamie, "You best be showing this young lad his duties, Jamie."

"Aye, Mr. McGuire!"

Jamie led Richard to the bow castle, where he introduced him to the ship's doctor, Mr. Greer.

"Mr. Greer, meet Richard Ashworth, the new ship's boy."

"Glad to meet you Mr. Ashworth."

"Likewise, Mr. Greer."

Jamie instructed, "You will help the doctor from time to time with whatever he might need. You'll also be emptying the privy buckets throughout the ship, daily. It's unpleasant, but you'll get used to it."

Jamie then took Richard to meet the ship's cook, Louis Hardy. Hardy was an older gent with two fingers missing from his left hand. Although he had served as cook for many years, his knife skills were lacking somewhat. Thus, the missing fingers. He had been at sea nearly all his life. He started as a ship's boy like Jamie and Richard but was unable to pick up on the finer points of sailing, like navigation, reading charts, and reading the winds. He couldn't read at all. So, he was destined to work as a cook as long as he could keep enough fingers and manage not to upset the captain too much.

Throughout the day, more sailors were brought aboard the *Destiny*. But, it turned out, most of them were brought aboard unwillingly. Some of them were dropped off by the Pressers unconscious with a knot on their noggin. Others walked aboard of their own free will.

As the sun began to fade in the western sky, all conscious men were assembled on deck to receive instructions from the captain. Mr. Faulkner called for the crew's attention as the captain stepped atop the quarterdeck.

Captain Horatio Billings was part owner of the *Destiny*. He held thirty percent ownership in the expedition of the five-hundred-ton ship. He provided the vessel while his partners, James Roark and Henry Bellamy, provided cash for supplies and trade goods. Billings was not a tall man, only 5' 10" tall. His skin was well-baked from years at sea, and the lines on his face almost told the stories of his travels. He wore a black patch over his right eye, the hazard of too many years as a navigator using the sextant. The retina had been burned from his right eye from too much time looking at the sun to calculate the latitudes.

Billings stepped forward to the quarterdeck rail and began to speak in a loud, clear voice. "All hands, listen. I am Captain Horatio Billings. You will address me as Captain or Captain Billings. You men have signed on to sail with me on this most capable ship as we travel the Atlantic Ocean over the next year or so. In just a few minutes we will set sail southward toward Africa where we will sail around the Cape of Good Hope turning east then nor-east to Madagascar. I consider myself a fair man, but I will not tolerate shirking of duties. You men will work hard and you will work long and you will be paid £33 at the end of our journey when we sail back here by this time next year, God willing. Now, everyman to his station! If you do not know your station, my officers will point them out. Mr. Faulkner!"

"Aye, Captain!"

"Cast off!"

"Aye, Captain!

CHAPTER 2

The winds of March blew strongly across the decks of the *Destiny* as she sailed southward toward France. The waves of the Atlantic splashed against the ship's hull, rocking her up and down like a carousel. Richard walked across the deck with his legs slightly spread, trying to keep his balance as the boat rocked back and forth, up and down. The wind was much colder than Richard had thought it might be. He was thankful for the warm wool coat he wore. He was also grateful for the scarf he wore across his face to fight against the stench coming from the buckets in his hands. The wooden buckets with rope handles held animal waste from the previous night. One of Richard's duties was daily filling and emptying buckets over the ship's side. Pigs, chickens, and goats were kept aboard the ship to help supply the sailors with fresh meat, eggs, and milk.

Richard approached the ship's starboard rail to pour his buckets over the side. Then, standing at the helm on the quarter deck, John noticed his son and called out to him.

"Richard!"

Richard paused to look up at his father.

"Spit!"

Puzzled, Richard looked at his papa, confused.

"Spit over the side!"

Richard nodded his head, then spit over the ship's starboard rail. His saliva instantly pelted him in the face. Richard wiped his face on his sleeve and then looked back at his papa. Then, Richard realized what Papa had been trying to tell him. Richard nodded his head, picked up the pails, and carried them to the port rail of the ship. He dumped the contents into the water and was glad none blew back into his face.

Richard looked back at Papa and smiled, knowing he had just been saved from an awful accident. Papa nodded to Richard and watched as Richard carried the buckets back below the decks.

Richard made several more trips to the port rail, dumping bucket after bucket over the side. Some of the contents were animal waste; some were food scraps from the galley where Louis Hardy was preparing meals for the crew. Richard was thankful that the crew had a privy in the ship's bow that didn't have to be emptied. It was located on the mid-level deck just above the water line. Vents had been placed at the ship's bow, allowing the sea's waves to naturally flush out the waste as the vessel rocked through the waters. Eventually, Richard made his way to the Captain's quarters. He rapped on the door and listened.

"Enter!"

Richard slowly opened the hatch and peeked inside.

"Excuse me, sir! I'm here to empty your bucket."

"Come in, boy!"

Richard carefully stepped inside, not knowing what to expect. Inside, he found a small room with a bed in the corner, a table in the middle, and shelves to one side of the room that held various charts and instruments Richard didn't recognize.

"What's your name, boy?"

"Richard, sir. Richard Ashworth."

"Hmm, are you son to the new helmsman?"

"Yes, sir."

The captain didn't seem nearly as scary as Richard had imagined him to be while he made his speech from the quarterdeck the day before. Richard saw the captain standing over the table, looking over papers on the tabletop. He asked the captain, "May I ask, are those maps?"

"No. These are charts. Maps are for landlubbers. Seamen use charts."

"What are those lines?" asked Richard.

"These are latitudes, and these running in the other direction are longitudes. So I can plot our line of travel using these and that instrument on the shelf. It's called a sextant."

"Can you show me how to use it?"

Captain Billings asked, "Can you read?"

"Yes, sir. I can do my sums too."

"Well then, we'll see how well you do as a ship's boy. If you do a good job, maybe we can promote you to junior officer and start training you how to use the sextant."

Richard's face lit up as he replied, "Thank-you, sir! I'll do my best!"

Billings pointed to the bucket on the floor in the corner of the room. Richard looked and noticed the bucket and realized it was time for him to return to his duties. So he snatched up the bucket and exited the captain's quarters with a slight bounce in his step.

Richard emptied the bucket over the port rail and returned it to the captain's quarters. Jamie saw Richard coming out of the captain's quarters and stopped him. "Do you know how to milk a goat?"

Richard replied, "No. I've never seen it done."

"Come with me. I'll show you how."

Jamie led Richard below the bow castle to a compartment where the animals were penned on the mid-deck. There were at least ten small pigs, about 75 pounds each, 20-25 chickens, and three goats. Jamie took a pail hanging from a hook on one of the beams; he placed the bucket beneath one of the goats and began milking.

Richard watched as Jamie squeezed the milk from each of the goat's two teats. Fifteen minutes later, the goat was empty.

"Here, you try the next one."

Richard sat on a stool next to the second goat and tugged at the teats, but nothing happened. Jamie instructed, "You've got to fill the teat from the bag before you squeeze. Lift your hand up, then roll your fingers through the teat to pull the milk out."

Richard tried again. This time, milk sprayed into the pail.

Richard looked up at Jamie and smiled with accomplishment.

"There you go! Keep at it!"

Richard milked the goat dry, then turned to the final goat and milked her, too. Then, Jamie and Richard carried the milk up the ladder and handed it to Mr. Hardy. Hardy took the milk and offered each of the boys a cup. They all dipped their cups into the bucket and drank the warm milk. Richard couldn't remember the last time he had enjoyed fresh milk. Milk was scarce in Wapping. For that matter, fresh food of any kind was scarce. Richard asked Mr. Hardy, "Do you think it would be alright if I took some to Papa?"

Hardy replied, "I think that would be alright. Just keep it to yourself, or else every hand on the ship will be expecting a cup."

"Thanks, Mr. Hardy!"

Richard escaped the galley and quickly walked to the quarter-deck, where John stood at the helm. John smiled at Richard as he saw him approaching.

"Here, Papa!"

"What is this?" asked John.

Richard quietly replied, "Fresh milk. I just milked a goat. I asked Mr. Hardy if I could bring you a cup."

John took the cup and sipped from it while holding onto the wheel with his other hand.

"Mmm," he said. "I haven't had fresh milk since I was a boy. Thank you, Richard."

John finished the milk and handed the cup back to Richard.

"How are you settling in?"

"I like it, Papa! I talked to the captain this morn. He said when I get older, they might train me to be a junior officer!"

John puffed out his chest and said, "Well now! Wouldn't that be a fine thing? Maybe someday I'll be steering your ship."

John set the cup on the top of the quarter-deck rail and said, "Here, son! Take hold of the helm and get a feel for her."

Richard stepped forward and stood in front of his papa. He took the wheel underneath the grip of Papa.

"Now, I'm going to let go. Be ready! She'll take you for a toss if you're not ready."

Richard gripped the wheel tightly and spread his legs apart to protect his balance. John carefully let loose the wheel and allowed Richard to control the ship. Unfortunately, the wheel jerked to the right and nearly ripped itself from Richard's grip. However, John was ready and snatched the wheel back into place.

John giggled and said, "Like I said, she'll toss you over."

Richard nervously smiled at Papa's jest.

"I better be getting back, Papa. I'll see you later."

"Alright, son."

Richard snatched the cup from the quarter-deck rail and scrambled back to the galley. As he trotted back to the galley, a voice called from behind.

"Hey, Richard!"

It was Mr. Faulkner.

Richard walked quickly back in Mr. Faulkner's direction.

"Yes, Mr. Faulkner?"

"What have you got there, lad?"

Richard replied, "It was a cup of milk. I took it up to my papa. Would you like some?"

Faulkner replied, "So, you've been stealing eh?"

"No, Mr. Faulkner!"

"And you're a liar too I see."

"No, Mr. Faulkner!"

The crew heard the commotion and gathered nearby to investigate. John, too, noticed it from the quarterdeck.

John called down to Faulkner, "Mr. Faulkner! Is there a problem?"

Faulkner turned and looked to John as he said, "Stay out of this, Ashworth! It is none of your concern!"

John anxiously strained his ear to hear what was being said.

He only knew it couldn't be good. The frightened look on Richard's face told all. Jamie and Hardy heard the men outside the galley and stepped onto the deck to see what was happening. The captain heard the commotion from his cabin and stepped out to discover the reason for the murmurs and groans from the crew.

"Mr. Faulkner! What is going on here?"

Faulkner replied, "Captain, I caught this boy stealing."

"What did he steal?"

"He took a cup of milk from the galley and gave it to his papa."

Billings looked at Richard and asked, "Is this true? Did you take a cup of milk from the galley?"

Hardy shook with fear that he might be implicated in the crime. He and Jamie looked wide-eyed at each other as the captain and the quartermaster continued interrogating Richard.

"Well, Richard? Is it true? Did you take a cup of milk from the galley?"

Richard replied, "Yes, Captain. First, I took a cup for myself, then I brought out a cup and gave it to Papa."

"Did Hardy give you the milk?" asked the captain.

"No, Captain. I took it while Mr. Hardy's back was turned."

The captain shook his head and stated, "I'm disappointed in you, Richard. I had high expectations for you. You realize that stealing is a serious offense aboard my ship?"

"I didn't know I was doing anything wrong, Captain. It won't happen again."

The captain replied, "I'm glad to hear it, lad. But, you will have to be punished. I can't have my men doing or taking whatever they please."

Billings then called out to the crowd, "Boatswain! Twelve lashes save one!"

Henry Gant, the ship's boatswain, stepped forward with whip already in hand. As boatswain, Gant was responsible for the ship's upkeep: the mast, rigging, sails, anchor, and so forth. He was also responsible for carrying out any corporal punishment on the ship.

Gant commanded, "Remove your coat and shirt, lad."

Richard slowly removed his coat, then pulled his shirt off his back and over his head but left it hanging from his arms, draped in front of his chest."

Gant said, "All the way off!"

Richard replied, "If you please, Mr. Gant, I'd like it to remain on my arms to protect me from the cold wind."

"Alright, then."

Gant nodded to two crew members standing by, who each took one of Richard's arms and tied him to the main mast rigging. Once secured, Richard braced himself for what was to come. Gant swung the whip backward, then forward to slash against Richard's back. **"Crack!"**

The crew called out, "*One!*"

Richard winced as the leather slapped across his bare back. He gritted his teeth and tried with all his might not to cry out. John dropped his head as he stood at the helm. He couldn't bear to watch his child as he received such brutal punishment.

"**Crack!**"

"*Two!*"

Richard gasped with each strike.

"**Crack!**"

"*Three!*"

"**Crack!**"

"*Four!*"

Richard began whimpering as tears rolled down his cheeks.

"**Crack!**"

"*Five!*"

"**Crack!**"

"*Six!*"

As he looked away from the child's brutal beating, tears ran down John's cheeks.

"**Crack!**"

"*Seven!*"

"**Crack!**"

"*Eight!*"

"**Crack!**"

"*Nine!*"

Gant never let up. His strikes seemed to Richard to increase with intensity as they continued.

"**Crack!**"

"*Ten!*"

"**Crack!**"

"*Eleven!*"

The captain called out, "Mr. Greer, if you please."

The doctor walked forward with Jamie, and the two untied Richard from the rigging. Each took an arm and escorted him to the doctor's quarters. They lay him face down on a table with his shirt hanging in front of him. Greer took a jar of salve from a shelf in his room and carefully coated the slashes on Richard's back.

"Why don't you lie here for a while before you get dressed?"

Richard rose and said, "No. I have to get back to work. I don't want to shirk my duties."

Greer faced him as Richard pulled his shirt back over his head. Greer noticed something odd about Richard's chest. The two met each other's glare, but neither said a word. Greer turned away to put away his things. Then, as Richard began to walk out the door, Greer said, "If you need anything, please don't hesitate to ask."

Richard nodded as he closed the door behind him.

CHAPTER 3

A month into the voyage, *Destiny* and her crew found themselves somewhere off the coast of Spain, sailing into rough winds. A storm approached them from the west, pushing the ship into dangerous waters. Rocky cliffs and outcroppings spread away from shore, providing dangerous obstacles for *Destiny* to evade.

Faulkner ordered Gant to call all hands. Gant took out his Boatswain's whistle and blew loudly, then announced, "All hands on deck!"

The crew scrambled from their hammocks and climbed to the main deck to prepare for the storm.

Faulkner ordered, "Batten down the hatches! Mr. McGuire, come about 10° starboard. Let's see if we can outrun this storm."

McGuire repeated the order, "Mr. Crane, ten degrees starboard!"

Crane replied, "Aye, Mr. McGuire! Ten degrees starboard!"

Captain Billings stepped from his cabin and climbed to the quarterdeck.

"Mr. Faulkner, what are your orders?"

"Sir, we're moving out 10° starboard to move away from those rocky cliffs. The storm's coming nor-west at us. We'll try to out run her if you please."

"Very good!"

The crew scrambled about on the main deck, securing anything that wasn't tied down. The ship rocked forcefully through the water, being pushed about by twenty-foot waves. The winds beat the sails like a scolded child, whipping them back and forth against the rigging. Small holes began to appear, which quickly turned into full-blown rips. The ship's wheel twisted in Mr. Crane's hands as he struggled to steady her. The strength of the sea against the rudder was too much for him alone. John ran to the quarterdeck to give aid and grabbed the wheel to help Crane hold her steady as the winds and the waves grew with each minute.

Waves sloshed over the ship's deck, knocking men off their feet as they attempted to keep *Destiny* afloat. Richard slid on his backside from starboard to port, nearly falling over the port rail. He righted himself in time as another wave tossed him from the port side. A hand grabbed him by the back of his shirt and pulled him upright onto his feet. It was Mr. Gant.

"Keep your feet, boy!

Suddenly, Richard heard a loud "**Crack!**" and looked up to see the main sail had broken loose from its rigging. It was coming right at him and Mr. Gant. Richard forcefully pushed Gant out of the way as the two fell to the deck and out of harm's way. The cross-tree of the main mast had broken loose and brought with it the sail, ripping it apart.

The captain saw what happened and ordered, "Mr. Faulkner, get that sail restored! We have little hope to out run the storm without it!"

Faulkner called out, "Gant! What's wrong with that rigging?"

Gant arose from the deck to examine the damage. As he rummaged through the rope, wood, and sail pile, he discovered the problem.

"The rigging broke, Mr. Faulkner!"

"Replace that rigging and let's get back underway! We've got to try to out run this storm!"

Gant replied, "Aye, aye!"

Gant barked orders at the men, sending two men to retrieve more rope from the deck below. Two other men worked at cutting loose the old rigging from the sail and cross-tree. When the new rope arrived, Gant took one end and handed it to Richard.

"Alright, boy! This is where you show me what you're made of. Take the end of this rope and climb that rigging. You see that ring at the top of the mast?"

"Aye!"

"Thread that rope through the ring just as you see it done on the other masts. Then, bring the rope back down with you."

Richard gazed at the top of the main mast. It must have been one hundred feet high. Richard gulped as he looked upward. He had never climbed anything so high before, but he had much to prove to the men on this ship, especially the captain.

"Aye, Mr. Gant!"

Richard took one end of the rope and tied it around his waist. He ascended into the tangled rigging that ran upward on the mast. He climbed quickly, using his bare feet to help hoist him upward against the knotting of the rigging. Richard's legs and arms slowly began to weaken as he climbed. His muscles ached with each tug he made against the rigging and gravity. The wind seemed to pick up the higher Richard climbed; he thought he might be blown away from the ship. Thirty feet in the air, Richard's foot slipped from a wet piece of rope as he was climbing. He managed to keep his handhold and pulled himself back up. Richard panted; his chest heaved as his adrenaline rushed through his body. He suddenly began to lose focus in his eyes and thought he might faint. Somehow, he managed to overcome the feeling and continued to climb.

At eighty feet, Richard's strength began to fail. His arms and legs began to shake and tremble. He paused for a moment to rest his limbs. Gant called to him from below, but it was no use. Richard couldn't hear anything except the roaring wind and the rain pelting against the remaining sails.

Suddenly, the ship rocked sideways as another large wave hit the craft. Richard's footing failed, and he found himself hanging from the rigging by only the grip of his left hand. Richard strained with all his might as he reached up with his right hand, snatched hold of the rigging, and pulled himself back up onto the rigging. He took a deep breath and then finished the climb to the top of the mast.

Richard swung his left leg around the mast to hold himself in place while standing on the rigging. Then, he untied the rope from around his waist and threaded it through the eyelet at the top of the mast. Richard gripped the rope's end with his left hand while loosely holding onto the rope's end, yet to be fed through the eyelet. Finally, he let go of the mast with his feet and dangled from the top while holding onto the rope. Richard slowly allowed the rope to slip through his right hand and found himself being let down, traveling closer and closer to the deck. With each foot he traveled, he found more confidence and quickly stood beside Gant on the deck. The men stood around him, congratulating him on a job well done, slapping him on the back, or tossing his hair. John watched from the quarterdeck with pride to see his son accomplish what many men could never have accomplished.

Gant then called out, "Hoist the main sail!"

The crew secured the sail to the cross-tree and worked together to lift it back into place. The rushing wind caught the sail, and the ship surged forward, gaining speed as it moved. Even though the sail had several rips, it still caught enough wind to move the ship quickly through the sea.

Rain pelted down on the crew as they struggled to keep *Destiny* ahead of the worst part of the storm. Black clouds circled to the northeast as the ship traveled southward. Thunder rumbled behind the crew, and lightning lit up the sky behind them.

The crew fought off the storm for nearly an hour, with the ship rising and falling on towering waves. Finally, the rain let up.

Although the rain eventually left, *Destiny* rolled through angry waves, lifting her and dropping her back down.

By nightfall, the crew was utterly spent. Richard could barely keep his eyes open. Henry Gant finally spoke to the men and made assignments. He sent half the crew below decks to rest. They would come back on deck to relieve the others at midnight, which gave them four hours to sleep.

Richard was among those sent down to make their beds. He climbed down the ladder leading to the mid-deck and rolled into his hammock. But, before Richard managed to settle himself in, he fell asleep.

Midnight came quickly, too quickly for the men who took the first shift in their hammocks. Richard rolled out of his hammock, climbed the ladder to the main deck, then searched out Gant for his orders.

"Mr. Gant, what would you have me do?"

Gant replied, "Young lad, you did well yester-evening. I have a special chore for you today. Those sails need mending. Have you ever used a needle and thread?"

"Aye, Mr. Gant. My mother taught me when I was younger. I can make a stitch."

"Good! Can you do it while hanging from the rigging?"

Richard looked up the main mast from which he had hung only hours ago. He didn't relish climbing the one hundred feet to the top and suspending himself while brandishing a needle and thread. However, he realized what was expected of him, and if he ever wanted to get in the captain's good graces again, he was willing to do just about anything.

"I'll give it a go, Mr. Gant."

"Good, lad!"

Then Gant turned to another man named David Rodgers and said, "You too, Rodgers. Help the boy hold the sail while he stitches her."

"Aye, Mr. Gant."

Rodgers and Richard began climbing the rigging. They started at the top to mend the sail at the highest point. Then, Gant designated other twosomes to climb the rigging of the other masts to repair the other sails. Rodgers led the way, having more experience in mending sails. He chose a small tear to show Richard how to mend the sheet correctly.

Rodgers took a needle from his shirt and threaded it, then made a whip stitch to close the hole in the sail. Richard asked, "Why a whip stitch? Why not a zig-zag?"

"Whip stitch is the only one that will hold against a strong wind. You know how to make a whip stitch?"

"Aye," said Richard.

He took out his needle and began working on a small hole nearby. Next, they worked together on the larger holes, one holding the edges of the sheet together while the other stitched it shut.

Occasionally, they could stand on the cross-tree while sewing the sail back together. Other times, they had to hang from the rigging to reach the holes that needed repair. The men worked steadily throughout the night. The sails were all repaired by the time the sun rose over the cliffs of Spain.

The rest of the crew went above decks to begin work for the day. Richard joined Jamie as the two tended to their daily chores. First, they milked the goats and fed the livestock, then delivered the milk to Louis Hardy. He then left Jamie to empty the captain's privy bucket.

Richard knocked on the door leading to Captain Billings' cabin and waited. After a long pause, he finally heard, "Enter!"

Richard entered the quarters and walked directly to the corner where the pail waited. Richard had not even looked at the captain since his unfortunate incident with the captain and Mr. Faulkner. Richard was so ashamed of the punishment he had received at their command. Especially since he hadn't been guilty of thievery, only of loyalty to Jamie and Hardy, who would have undoubtedly received punishment alongside Richard if he had exposed their part in the incident. Jamie and Hardy never thanked Richard, at least not verbally. They did, however, acknowledge him with a look of gratefulness; it was enough.

Richard emptied the captain's bucket and returned to place it in its proper place when Captain Billings said, "Richard?"

"Aye, Captain?"

"Mr. Gant speaks very highly of you. He told me how you were responsible for the quick repair of the rigging during yesterday's storm. I'm glad to see you've settled into your work here and I feel we've been able to put the mistakes of the past behind us."

"Aye, sir?"

"Aye, Richard. I think it's time we start training you in additional duties suitable to a lad of your...ambition and education. From now on, I want you to meet me here after the noon bell. I will begin showing you how to read charts, use the sextant, and any other duties associated with sailing."

Richard replied, "Thank you, sir!"

"Very well, then. Back to your duties."

"Aye, Captain!" he said with a smile, then excused himself from the captain's quarters.

CHAPTER 4

L ater that day, the noon bell rang, and Richard quickly reached the captain's quarters. He knocked and waited until he heard the familiar, "Enter!"

Richard opened the door, entered the cabin, and stood by waiting for instructions. The captain was studying his charts. Billings glanced up and saw Richard standing before him.

"Ah! Richard! Ready for our lessons are we?"

"Aye, Captain!"

"Well then, lad, have a seat here with me at the table and first we'll see what you already know."

Richard sat on a stool at the table next to the captain's chair. Billings proceeded to test Richard on his writing and reading abilities. Billings was pleased to see Richard was accomplished at both. Then, the captain tested Richard on his math skills. He soon learned that although Richard could add, subtract, multiply, and divide, he lacked geometry knowledge. First, the captain instructed Richard to use a compass to draw circles. Then, he showed Richard how to draw angles with a protractor. Finally, billings taught him about circumference and degrees relating to angles within a circle. Richard picked it all up very quickly, which pleased Captain Billings exceedingly.

After two hours of schooling Richard, Billings announced, "Alright, my boy! You've done well! We will pick this up on the morrow at the same time. For now, you must gather your gear and move into new quarters."

Richard confusingly asked, "Sir?"

"Richard, you are my new fourth mate. You will be working with the ship's doctor and carpenter from now on, thus you will move into the mate's cabin along with the others."

"Aye, Captain!"

Richard left the captain's quarters and climbed down to the crew's deck. He had very few personal items: his coat, an extra change of clothing, and his shoes. The mates typically wore a uniform, but the uniform would have to wait until one could be tailored to fit him. Richard would be expected to look and act like an officer and a gentleman now. He donned his shoes and gathered his clothes together before ascending back up the ladder.

As Richard reached the main deck, John saw him come from below decks. Richard saw his papa watching him as John stood at the helm on the quarterdeck. John smiled at his child as Richard walked across the deck and entered the officer's quarters.

Richard entered the mate's cabin and found three of the bunks made. However, a fourth bed remained unmade on the top of one of the bunks. Richard tossed his gear on the mattress, then left to find Mr. Greer. Suddenly, the door opened, and two young men entered the cabin. The oldest was about twenty, while the other was only sixteen.

"Richard is it?"

"Yes," replied Richard.

"I'm Samuel McKenzie, first mate. I work under Mr. Faulkner."

"Nice to meet you, Mr. McKenzie."

Then Samuel said, "This is David Reynolds, the second mate. He works under Mr. McGuire."

Reynolds held out his hand and replied, "Nice to meet you Richard!"

Of course, they all knew each other after spending five weeks at sea together. However, the mates had little to do with the cabin boys, so they had never formally introduced themselves.

Samuel continued, "Timothy Sawyer is the third mate. He works with Mr. Gant. You can have the bunk above his."

"Thanks!" said Richard. "I guess I need to go and find Mr. Greer. Captain Billings said I would be working with him as fourth mate."

Richard walked to Greer's cabin and knocked.

"Come in!"

Richard peeked in as he said, "Pardon, Mr. Greer, but I've been assigned as your mate, sir."

Greer was a tall, muscular man, not at all what Richard would have expected a doctor to look like. He had broad shoulders and strong muscular arms. His long, thin hair was pulled back and tied with a black ribbon behind his head. He wore long mutton chop sideburns on the side of his face.

"Yes, of course, Richard. Come in. I don't have any doctoring to do today, but I need to inspect the hull and see if she has any leaks. Grab that hammer, will ya?"

Richard picked up the hammer and then followed Greer out of the cabin. They made their way below decks, starting on the lowermost deck. Greer carried a lantern as they walked through the lower deck. He inspected the hull of the ship, looking for leaks. Whenever he found a trickle of water coming into the ship, he pulled out a piece of oakum to stuff into the crack where the water was leaking through. The oakum had been made from grass rope that had been unraveled. It was stuffed into cracks or holes in the ship's hull and hammered into place using a caulking iron. The caulking iron looked like a chisel, but the blade was somewhat blunter than a wood chisel.

Greer hammered the oakum into place, then searched for the next leak. When he found another leak, he said, "Here, Richard. You try this one."

Richard took the oakum from Greer's strong hand and fed it into a space between two boards on the ship's hull. He then took one of the small irons and the heavy hammer and hammered the oakum into the crack to seal it. The hammer weighed about ten pounds, a significant amount for a twelve-year-old. Richard swung the hammer clumsily at the iron and struck it several times. Once or twice, he missed his mark and hit his hand holding the iron rather than the iron.

"You'll get the hang of it," Greer remarked. "You need to build up some strength in that boney little body of yours."

Richard smiled through the aching pain in his hands.
"How often do you do this, Mr. Greer?"

"Oh, I check the hull every few days. We can't let it get away from us. We wouldn't want *Destiny* to go down now would we?"
"No, sir."

"Having you as my mate, will allow me to do other duties. I'll have you check the hulls many times alone. If you come across something you don't know how to fix, come fetch me. It isn't glamorous work, but it's important."

"Aye, sir."

Once they finished checking the lowermost deck, they climbed up the ladder to the mid-deck.

Richard asked, "How did you become a ship's doctor?"

"I'm not a doctor, not really. I'm a carpenter by trade. Very few ships can find a real doctor who is willing to travel the seas to practice their trade. The ones who are real doctors are usually running from something or someone. Others, like myself, are expected to patch up sailors when needed just like we patch up holes on the ship."

Richard asked, "So, how did you learn to be a doctor?"

"I have my books, medical books that I've picked up through the years. Whenever I'm in port, I'll look up the local physician and ask him about ailments that I have encountered while at sea. Can you read, Richard?"

"Aye, sir!"

"Good! I'll let you borrow my books whenever you want. It would be good for you to learn as much from them as you can. You never know when I might not be around to help the men. It would then befall upon you to fix their ailments."

Suddenly, Richard felt an ominous amount of anxiety just thinking of having to serve as a ship's doctor alone.

"I pray that never happen, Mr. Greer."

"Aye, me too! But one never knows."

Richard got used to a daily routine, inspecting the ship for needed repairs in the morning, two hours of training with Captain Billings at noon, then studying Greer's medical books for the rest of the day and sometimes in the evening. Of course, there were some days when he was pulled away to work on an unexpected duty assigned by one of the officers, but for the most part, every day was routine.

Almost daily, one of the crew would show up at the infirmary with an ailment. With seventy-five men aboard, it was bound to happen. Most of the time, it was dysentery, nausea, or a headache. On other days, a simple sunburn might need attention. However, there were more extreme cases as well.

One day, while Richard was studying, Bob Wilkes showed up after catching his hand in the ship's rigging. He lost one of the fingers on his right hand. Richard had to sew up the wound without any painkillers or anesthesia. Two other men were brought in to hold Bob down while Richard sewed up the end of Bob's finger. After stitching up the finger, Richard dusted the wound with sulfur powder and wrapped it in cotton bandages. Mr. Greer was impressed by Richard's work.

"It won't be long, lad, before they won't be needing me here," he said with a smile.

Richard smiled in return, then went back to reading.

Two months into their cruise, the crew of the *Destiny* found themselves at the southern tip of Africa. The Cape of Good Hope provided a path for *Destiny* to travel east toward Madagascar. As they crossed the Cape, *Destiny* passed by False Bay, where all kinds of sea creatures could be seen at that time of year.

Richard left his cabin when he heard a group of men admiring the wildlife they had spotted on and off the coast of Africa. He went to the port rail and searched the waters. He finally saw a large creature emerge from the water and dive back in.

"What is it?" he asked one of the crew.

"That be a humpback whale, laddie."

As Richard watched the waters, more sea life became visible. The same seaman announced to Richard, "You see that? That's an Orca. You don't want to tussle with one of them. They be killers."

Richard watched in amazement as the black-and-white creature swam through the sea. Then, Richard looked at the shore and spotted even more animals lying about on the beach and rocks. Seals lay about barking at each other, sometimes chasing one another. Then Richard witnessed some funny little birds waddling around on the beach, sometimes climbing the rocks and diving back into the sea.

"What kind of birds are those?"

The seaman replied, "They're called penguins."

Richard asked, "Are they dangerous?"

"Naw, but they be funny little creatures, eh?"

Richard smiled as he watched the coastline—so many species of birds, sea creatures, and wildlife that he had never heard of before. Then, as the ship rounded the bend along the coast, something else caught Richard's eye.

"Are those monkey's?"

The old seaman answered, "The natives called them Chacma. They are akin to monkeys, but they are baboons. This area is filled with them."

Richard said, "I'd sure like to get a closer look at them. Will we ever go ashore here?"

"Nay, lad. And you don't want to get too close to them anyway. They be angry little monks. Sharp teeth too. You want to keep your distance from them."

Later in the evening, the sun lowered its light below the horizon, and darkness fell over the coast of Africa. The crew left the port rail and returned to their regular duties.

CHAPTER 5

Six weeks later, Destiny docked at Port St. Felix on the south-west coast of Madagascar. Richard was both excited and nervous about finally arriving at the African island. He was excited to be on dry land again and anxious to be in a foreign land, not knowing what to expect.

Immediately, the crew was ordered to begin unloading *Destiny's* cargo. The captain and first and second officers stood either on the quarterdeck or the bow deck. They gave instructions to the mates, who then oversaw the work the crew carried out. Richard was left with the task of seeing the lowermost deck was cleared of cargo and made ready for new cargo to be loaded. He felt somewhat awkward ordering men two and three times his age. Richard tried to sound confident but not overbearing as he gave his instructions. He even complimented the crew whenever he could to encourage them to do a good job.

"That a way, men! Good job! We'll show the crew on the mid-deck who is the better crew! Smith! Pick up that line before someone falls over it! Brown and Langley, you men hoist that bale out of here. Let's get another line in here and hook up the next bale. Come on, men!"

The men felt kindly to Richard. Most of them were used to taking orders from a younger superior, and they found Richard to be a pleasant sort of fellow.

"Alright, men! Hook up that last bale and let's clear the deck. Riley, you and Brown start sweeping the deck. Make sure there aren't any nails protruding in the hull. Check all the chains and shackles, too!"

As the last bale of wool cleared the lower deck, Richard inspected the deck and hull for anything that might have been overlooked. He also inspected the hull for leaks; he didn't want to spend much time below decks while three or four hundred slaves populated the area. Finally, satisfied everything was sound, Richard followed the last of his crew to the main deck. Then, he called out to the captain, who stood on the quarterdeck, "All clear on the lowermost deck, Captain!"

"Very good Mr. Ashworth!"

Richard then set his crew offloading the woolen bales from the ship to the docks below, where they were loaded onto wagons to be transported to the auction house for sale. The wool and cotton were divided into lots and sold to the highest bidder. Crates of firearms were also brought to Port St. Felix by *Destiny* to be sold.

Once *Destiny* was entirely unloaded, Captain Billings walked off the gangplank to explore St. Felix. Mr. Faulkner walked with the captain, leaving Mr. McGuire responsible for *Destiny*. Most of the crew were permitted to go for four hours. Each was instructed that if they failed to arrive at the designated time, they would be subjected to the punishment of death for desertion. Most men had no money to spend, so there wasn't much to do other than walk around the village and see the sites.

Richard and John left *Destiny* together to see what they could see. Along the way, they stopped at Seafarer's Tailor Shop. Captain Billings had given Richard a little money to buy a proper officer's uniform. Richard witnessed all sorts of uniforms displayed in the shop window as they entered. A bell rang as the door was opened, and a frail-looking gentleman walked out of the back room.

"May I help you, gentlemen?"

Richard handed the man a letter from Captain Billings and a £5 note. The letter instructed the tailor on what kind of uniform Richard would need.

"Come right in. My name is Samuel Tate. Who might you be, young man?"

"Richard, sir. Richard Ashworth, and this is my father, John Ashworth."

Tate then instructed, "Well, young Richard, let's get you measured for a new uniform why don't we."

Tate had Richard stand on a platform near the back of the shop and measured the young man up and down and from this side to that side. He even measured the circumference of his head. When Tate was satisfied he had all the measurements he needed, he then rummaged through a stack of pants, shirts, coats, stockings, and undergarments to find what he thought would be the correct sizes. Tate led Richard to a changing screen where he could try on his new uniform. Richard shyly tried on the clothing, turning his back to the tailor. As he dressed, John began to ask questions.

"How long have you been working here, Mr. Tate?"

"Oh, I've been here at St. Felix for nigh on twenty years."

"What brought you to St. Felix?"

"Well, I was a sailor much like you two gentlemen, but I wasn't cut out for that sort of work. When our ship came into St. Felix, I had the occasion to meet the owner of this shop who needed an apprentice. So I stayed here, and eventually I took over the shop after the original owner died."

When Richard finished dressing, Tate checked the fit of the uniform. "Well let's see. We'll need to take it in in a few places, but the length we'll leave alone. You'll grow into it."

Tate pinned the uniform jacket and pants in a few places, then had Richard remove them.

"You gentlemen can come back in a couple of hours and I'll have it all ready for you."

John and Richard left the shop and made their way through the streets of St. Felix. There were many shops to explore: mercantile, hardware, clothing, haberdasheries, pubs, and inns. St. Felix was lively, especially when a ship pulled into port. The sailors of the various vessels saw fit to paint the town red, so to speak, with the gold and silver in their pockets. Men cooped up on a ship for months tended to go wild whenever they reached shore.

John and Richard went to the auction house to see what might be going on with the load of wool and fabrics that *Destiny* had brought into port. Richard had never been to an auction house and was intrigued by how things were sold there. *Destiny's* goods were divided into many sizes and sold to the highest bidder. A man stood atop a platform next to the lots and called out bids from the crowd as they were announced. Cheers and jeers came from the crowd as the items were sold. It was as if everyone were attending a gaming event and were cheering for their favorite contestants.

Occasionally, a fight might break out as drunken participants disagreed about selling the merchandise. Then, the participants would often come to blows. Men armed with clubs would then toss the miscreants back onto the street to calm the crowd so the auction might continue.

Captain Billings walked into the auction house just as the crowd was being brought back to order. He saw Richard and John standing over to the side and approached them.

"Richard, have you been to the tailor's yet?"

"Aye, Captain. Mr. Tate said my uniform would be ready in a couple of hours."

"Fine! I look forward to seeing you in your uniform. It's time you start looking like an officer."

"Aye! Thank you, Captain."

Billings stood by a while longer, watching as his goods were sold to the highest bidders. Once satisfied with the proceedings, he excused himself and walked away. He had other matters to attend to. A new cargo needed to be loaded onto the ship, and he needed to complete a transaction allowing his crew to begin loading the cargo.

After watching the auction, Richard and John returned to the tailor's shop to retrieve Richard's new uniform. As they entered, they were greeted immediately by Mr. Tate.

"Come in, gentlemen! I have your uniform all ready for you Master Ashworth."

Richard took the finished uniform into a dressing closet and donned his new clothing. When he walked out, John and Tate smiled at Richard, who was wearing his new uniform.

John commented, "My don't you look like a real officer now?"

Tate replied, "Indeed he does."

Tate handed Richard a new pair of black leather shoes with a buckle. Richard put on the shoes and walked around the floor in them.

Tate asked, "How do they fit?"

"Much better than my old shoes. My old ones were getting a little small."

Tate suggested, "Maybe we should go with a size larger, you are a growing boy you know."

Richard replied, "Let's try one larger then."

Tate handed Richard a larger pair and waited while Richard tried on the shoes.

Richard walked around again and then commented, "Yes, I think these will be better."

"Fine!" said Tate. "Now for the hat."

Tate handed Richard a three-cornered hat.

Richard had never worn a hat before, only his knitted skull cap. The hat fit perfectly. Richard looked into a tall, looking glass to see himself displaying the new uniform. He smiled, then looked back at John and said, "Is that *really* me?"

"Yes, darlin', that be you alright. It makes me proud to see it too. Now, come along, it's time we got back to the ship. They'll be needing us."

Richard approached Tate, handed him the £5 note, and said, "Thank you, Mr. Tate."

"You are most welcome, Master Ashworth."

Richard and John walked back to the ship with an extra spring in their steps. Richard noticed the glances people gave him as they saw him on the street. They admired the young officer in his new uniform. Many of them tipped their hats to him and remarked, "Good day to you, sir!"

As the Ashworths approached *Destiny*, they found Second Officer McGuire standing at the top of the gangplank. As they walked up the gangplank, McGuire asked, "Well, now, who have we here?"

Richard replied, "Fourth Mate, Richard Ashworth reporting for duty, sir!"

McGuire said, "Mr. Ashworth, you look very smart in your new uniform. However, there is much work to do, so change back into some work clothes and let's get to it."

"Aye, Mr. McGuire!"

Richard quickly walked to his cabin and pulled his sea chest from under Timothy Sawyer's bunk. He opened the trunk, changed into his work clothes, and placed his new uniform, shoes, and hat into the chest. Then, he pushed the chest back under the bunk and proceeded to the main deck to receive his orders.

Richard saw a procession of people approaching the ship as he walked onto the deck. They were being led by several of the *Destiny's* crew. Dark-skinned men and women, linked together in single file, were led down the streets of St. Felix to the port. The string of people approaching the ship looked a mile long.

Mr. McGuire instructed Richard, "Mr. Ashworth, I'll need you to oversee the cargo as it is brought aboard. Make sure they are all secured below decks; men to the bow, women to the stern."

"Aye, Mr. McGuire!"

As the line of slaves was led onto *Destiny*, McGuire tallied the number of men and women. Richard supervised several of the crew below decks as the slaves were sent below. All the slaves were barely dressed, some wearing only a loin cloth. Most of the women were unclothed above the waste. The slaves seemed relatively young, most likely between fifteen and twenty years old. Richard wondered how these people could have allowed themselves to be captured and led to this situation. He had sympathy for them all but knew there was nothing he could do to help them other than see that they were treated as well as he could manage.

Once the tally was completed, McGuire had the count manifested as ninety-eight female slaves and three hundred seventy-six male slaves. Richard ensured the crew had secured them below decks, then went above deck to report to Mr. McGuire.

Food supplies were then loaded and stored on the mid-deck. Richard made sure those were appropriately stowed as well. Once everything was packed and secured, Captain Billings ordered Mr. Faulkner to sail from the port.

Mr. Faulkner then ordered, "All hands, prepare to sail! Loose the bow line! Loose the stern line! Mr. McGuire, take her out to sea if you please!"

McGuire told John Ashworth, "Mr. Ashworth, two points off the starboard, steady as she goes. Mr. Gant, lower the sheets; we'll be on our way!"

Destiny slowly and steadily floated out of port, heading south and west toward the Cape of Good Hope. Once outside Port St. Felix, McGuire ordered, "Mr. Gant lower the main sail, full spee d.!"

CHAPTER 6

Richard awoke from his bunk early when he heard a commotion on the main deck. He quickly dressed and stepped out of his cabin to find many of the slaves had been brought above deck. The slaves were being exercised to help keep them from wasting away. If they starved or could not move, they would be worthless when they reached the auction in Charlestown.

The slaves were fed daily, but the portions were meager. Then, a month into their voyage, Richard began to notice several of the slaves were showing signs of illness. Many suffered from nose bleeds, their fingernails were brittle, and their gums hurt.

Richard consulted his medical books to find a diagnosis and treatment for whatever might be ailing the slaves. Mr. Greer walked in and found Richard hard at work studying the books.

Mr. Greer asked, "Are you looking for anything in particular?"

"Yes, Mr. Greer. I'm wondering what might be the cause of the slaves ailments."

"Let me guess. Sore gums, skin peeling, broken finger nails, bloody noses?"

"Yes, sir! Do you know what it is?"

"Scurvy, my boy!"

"Scurvy? What causes it?"

"Not enough vitamin C in the diet. We get vitamin C from fresh fruits and vegetables."

Richard asked, "Why aren't the slaves being fed any then?"

"The cost is too high. Besides, there's barely enough fresh vegetables and fruit for the crew. The Captain isn't likely to spare any for a lot of slaves."

Richard was a little appalled by Greer's answer. He hated to see anyone suffer, no matter who they might be. So, he brought it to Captain Billings' attention during their afternoon session.

When Richard entered the Captain's quarters, he found Billings busy looking over his charts. Billings glanced up and saw Richard as he entered.

"Oh, Mr. Ashworth. Is it that time already?"

"Aye, Captain."

Billings responded, "Well then, have a seat and we will begin."

Richard asked, "If you please, sir."

"What is it, lad?"

"Captain Billings, I have noticed of late that many of the slaves are sickly."

"Really?"

"Yes, sir! I asked Mr. Greer about them and he says they are suffering from scurvy."

Captain Billings replied, "Yes, of coarse. It is quite common among those who find themselves at sea for a long period of time. There is little to do about it, however."

Richard asked, "Why not feed them fresh fruits and vegetables? Mr. Greer says that's what causes scurvy. That is, the lack of fruits and vegetable, sir."

"Well, Mr. Ashworth, we simply don't have enough for the crew or the cargo."

Richard asked, "Can we not find some on an island, perhaps along the way to Charlestown?"

Billings replied, "Well, that would delay out journey you see. We need to get to Charlestown before we lose too many of our slaves.

The quicker we arrive in Charlestown, the fewer slaves we will lose along the way."

"I'm sorry, Captain. I don't mean to sound impudent, but may I ask, sir? Do you make more money with healthy slaves than those who are near death?"

Captain Billings paused before answering, "Well, yes of course."

Richard continued, "And would we make more money if you sell four hundred healthy slaves rather than one hundred sickly slaves?"

Billings again paused, then replied, "Yes we would."

"Then Captain, would it not behove us to see that we deliver as many healthy slaves to Charlestown as possible even it it delays our journey by say a week or two?"

"Well of course but it just isn't done that way, my boy!"

Richard asked, "Isn't done by whom?"

"Well, anyone! This is the way we have always transported slaves on any ship I have been aboard as a seaman or an officer."

Richard then asked, "Might you be setting a precedence if you were to sail back into England having made more money than any other merchant ship in the fleet?'

The Captain was silent as he muddled the thought.

"Captain, how many slaves did you deliver to Charlestown last voyage?"

The Captain referred to his log and read, "One hundred and thirty-six."

"How many did you start with?"

Billings rechecked his log and stated, "Four hundred and six."

"Captain, how much did your slaves bring you at auction last voyage?"

Again, the Captain checked his log, "£3,400!"

"And in what kind of condition were they?"

"Well, most of them were not very well off. I admit we could have gotten more had they been healthier."

Richard asked, "How much more?"

Captain Billings slowly replied, "Well, a healthy, strong, male can bring as much as £40."

Richard then found a piece of parchment and wrote down some figures to do the numbers. "Captain, if you had received full price for your last slaves you could have received, £5,440 and, if you had delivered four hundred and six slaves at that price instead of the one hundred and thirty-six, you would have received, £16,240."

Billings stood before Richard with his mouth agape. He thought for a long time before saying anything. Then, finally, Billings replied, "My boy, you are quite intelligent! How did you become so smart?"

Richard replied, "I went to school when I was younger. The headmaster told me I had an analytical mind. He had never seen anyone better with solving problems he said."

"Well, I'd have to agree. So what shall we do, then?"

"Well, Captain, I believe we should put to port at the nearest island or port that would supply us with fresh fruits."

Billings thought momentarily, then said, "That would be Campos." He studied his chart and pointed Campos out to Richard. "The problem is, fruit cost money, of which we are running low."

"Yes, sir. But we have the slaves. We could trade a few healthy slaves to get food for the rest."

"I am betwattled, Richard! I believe you've solved all our problems. Come, let's speak to Mr. Greer about our plan. We need ten of our finest slaves to get ready for port at Campos!"

Captain Billings led the way as they exited his quarters and walked to the quarterdeck. There, they found Mr. McGuire and John Ashworth standing at the helm.

Captain Billings announced, "Mr. McGuire, set a coarse for Campos!"

"Campos, sir?"

"Aye!" said the Captain. "We'll lay up there for a day or two to replenish our supplies."

"Aye, Captain!"

The Captain and Richard then walked across the deck to the bow deck to find Mr. Greer. They found Greer in his cabin reading one of his medical books. As the Captain entered Greer's cabin, Greer stood to welcome him. "Captain Billings! To what do I . . ."

"Never mind, Greer. I have a task for you and Mr. Ashworth here. We're about to lay up at Campos in a few days. I'm pulling ten of our best slaves out of the hold. I want you and Mr. Ashworth to see that they are well fed and in prime condition. I plan to trade them for fresh fruits and vegetables to help the crew and the rest of our cargo to stay as healthy as possible. I don't want anymore slaves to die because of hunger on this voyage. We lost far too many on our last."

"Aye, Captain!" answered Greer. "We will make sure of it, sir!"

The Captain turned to leave and said, "Richard?" as he stepped through Greer's doorway.

Richard followed the captain as he walked out onto the deck.

"Mr. Ashworth, I want you in charge of selecting the slaves we will trade out on Campos. Take four of the crew to help you get them up on deck."

"Aye, Captain!"

Richard selected four men standing around the deck, trying to look busy while the captain was atop.

"Hatcher, Smythe, Haddock, and Bryce! You four grab a lantern and come with me!"

The men did as Richard commanded and then followed Richard down the hatch to the lowermost deck, where the slaves were kept. The stench was nearly unbearable. Richard took a lantern from Smythe and proceeded through the deck, searching for men he thought were still in somewhat good health. He found one right away: a tall man, very muscular. His eyes were vigilant, and he showed no fear.

Richard commanded, "Take this one!"

Hatcher asked, "Take him where, sir?"

"Just prepare him to be taken up top. We're looking for ten strong men, not yet overcome with scurvy."

"Aye, Mr. Ashworth."

They led the slave past all the others while the remaining slaves began to murmur in some unknown tongue. Finally, the slave was left with Bryce near the ladder that led upward. Bryce nervously stood by, waiting for the other crew to return.

"How 'bout this one, Mr. Ashworth?" said Haddock.

"Yes, he'll do." replied Richard.

More murmuring occurred as the new slave was chosen. The crew searched through the deck endlessly, looking for suitable specimens. Finally, they had chosen ten. Richard led the crew and the slaves back up the ladder to the main deck, where they temporarily fastened their chains to the main mast.

Richard ordered, "Bryce, get these slaves some fresh water and let them drink."

"Aye, Mr. Ashworth!"

Richard turned to the others and said, "You three, come with me."

They followed as Richard led them to Mr. Hardy's cabin. As they entered, Mr. Hardy asked, "Mr. Ashworth, what can I do for you, sir?"

"Hardy, we are in need of fresh fruits or vegetable for some of the slaves the captain has deemed to be special. He wants them kept healthy until we reach Campos."

Hardy said, "Well, I'm stewing some turnips tonight for the crew, but if you need something now, There are six oranges there on the table."

Richard glanced over at the table and saw six over-ripened oranges. He took a knife, sliced the oranges in half, and then handed them to Hatcher and Smythe.

"Take these and pass them out to the slaves on the main deck."

The men did as instructed. Richard only sliced five of the oranges. It would not be easy to divide the last orange ten ways. Richard followed Hatcher and Smythe onto the deck and watched as the slaves received the oranges. Each slave took half of the fruit and began eating ravenously. Juices from the half-oranges ran down their chins. Each man quickly chewed the pulp, savoring every bite. They even consumed the peal. Once the oranges were utterly consumed, each man licked the juices from their hands and arms.

Later in the evening, Richard and his crew returned to check on the slaves. Haddock and Bryce helped Richard spoon out helpings of oat mush to each of the chained men. Again, the slaves quickly ate the sloppy soup. Richard then had the men carry large buckets of the mush below to feed the rest of the slaves. The crew members shuffled between the lines of men and women waiting for any morsel of food they could get. The sailors spooned out the mush into the cupped hands of the slaves. They slurped, gobbled, and licked until their hands were utterly void of every crumb.

Richard climbed down the ladder to check on the progress of his men. He saw a woman slumping over against the ship's hull as he walked through the masses. When Richard walked over to check on her, he found blood leaking from her nose. Her skin was flaking off her bones. She was dead.

Richard called for two more men to come down into the hull to retrieve the lifeless body and carry it onto the deck. Richard climbed out onto the deck behind the men carrying the woman. As he reached the top step, he heard the slaves chained to the mast begin to murmur again. They spoke to one another in a language only they knew. They reached out to Richard as he walked by them, seemingly asking him for answers. Richard glanced at the men with a look of concern but continued to accompany his men to the port side of the ship, where they swung the woman's lifeless body over the side and into the depths of the sea.

CHAPTER 7

As the days droned by, Richard found himself more and more curious about the men who were chained on the deck of the *Destiny*. Whenever he had a spare moment, he tried to communicate with them, using simple words like food, water, stand, sit, and anything else to help them acclimate to their predicament. One of the men seemed particularly receptive to Richard's efforts to communicate. It was the tall, muscular man that Richard had first chosen to come up top. After a while, Richard discovered that his name was Batimkoo.

Richard could tell that Batimkoo was a leader among his people. The other men with whom he was tethered seemed to look to him for answers, except for one. One man who was slightly smaller than Batimkoo would often argue with Batimkoo. They appeared to debate everything, but Batimkoo always had the last word in every matter.

After two weeks of sailing west, *Destiny* found a port on the coast of Campos early one morning. Campos was a sizable Portuguese village on the eastern coast of South America in what would eventually become Brazil. Although Campos was known for its fishermen, it also contained several large plantations farther from the beach. Sugar cane and tobacco were their main crops, but groves of mango, orange, lemon, and lime trees could be found nearby.

Destiny could not dock on the shore because the water was too shallow. So, instead, she anchored off the coast while several of the crew were sent to shore on two row boats called dories. Richard was on one of those boats along with Mr. Faulkner, *Destiny's* first officer. Captain Billings had sent Richard along because of his relationship with the slaves and because he knew Richard had a mind for business and negotiations. In addition, Faulkner was fluent in Portuguese, so between the two of them, they shouldn't have any trouble striking a deal for what was needed.

The slaves were divided into two groups of five for each boat. Batimkoo rode in the boat with Richard, Smythe, and Haddock. Brown and Bryce rowed the boat that Mr. Faulkner commanded, carrying the other five slaves.

The boats rowed side by side toward the coast of Campos, the sailors straining against the oars they pulled. The black men began questioning what was going to happen to them. They all started speaking at the same time, searching for answers. Richard thought there might be a rebellion of some sort being planned. Richard stood in the boat and called out, but only loud enough to be heard, "Batimkoo! Batimkoo!"

Batimkoo turned to look at Richard to see why he was calling his name. When Richard had Batimkoo's attention, he raised his forefinger to his lips, indicating the need for silence. Batimkoo repeatedly said something to his men until they all were silent. Faulkner noticed what Richard had done from the other boat and was impressed by the young officer's ability to control a potentially harmful situation.

It took ten minutes to reach the shore. The crew and the slaves disembarked and tied the boats on the beach. A group of men approached them and began speaking in Portuguese to them. Faulkner conversed with them, telling them they were looking to trade for food rations for their voyage. One of them directed Faulkner to a nearby plantation owned by a man named Juan Santos de Miguel.

Miguel was a descendant of men who had settled in Campos in the late 1400s. He owned most of the land around Campos and most boats that sailed from its coast, whether fishing vessels or trade ships.

Faulkner instructed Richard to stand by with the slaves and two of the crew while he took Brown and Bryce. Mr. Faulkner carried a pistol in his belt but knew it would be of little help if they were taken captive. He hoped this would be a joint meeting between business people. Brown and Bryce were also armed, but Faulkner instructed them to keep their hands away from their weapons.

It took them two hours to reach their destination on foot. The man who led them, Pedro Mateos, acted as a tour guide, pointing out famous sites or structures along the way. Faulkner conversed with Mateos as he was led through the stone streets of Campos. Brown and Bryce followed along, not understanding anything that was being said.

At mid-morning, Richard found a shady spot near the boats to sit and wait. He invited Smythe, Haddock, and the slaves to join him. They all relaxed under the giant leaves of Palm trees that towered above them at the beach's edge.

Four hours later, Bryce and Brown ran back to the beach while looking over their shoulders. Bryce ran to Richard and said, "Mr. Ashworth! We've got trouble, sir!"

"What is it, Bryce?"

"Mr. Faulkner has been taken prisoner! They're holding him for ransom!"

Richard asked, "What do they want?"

"They want the slaves, but they are not willing to trades food for them. Only Mr. Faulkner."

Richard thought for a while before speaking.

"Bryce? How long will it take for you to get back to where they are holding Mr. Faulkner?"

"If I run, sir, about an hour."

Richard instructed, "Don't run. Take your time. We need time to prepare down here. Tell them they can have the slaves but they must deliver Mr. Faulkner to us on the beach. We will make the exchange here."

"What if they refuse, sir?"

"Tell them, no deal! If they want the slaves, they must come here to get them. If Mr. Faulkner isn't brought along and in good condition, it's no deal. Tell them I'll instruct our ship to fire its canons on their town."

"But, Mr. Ashworth, Destiny has no canons!"

"Aye, Mr. Bryce! But they don't know it, do they?"

Bryce nodded his approval and began the long walk back to where Faulkner was being held captive. Richard turned to Smythe and Haddock, saying, "I need you two to row back to the ship. Take the slaves back with you, quickly! When you get on board, tell Captain Billings what happened. Ask him to send back ten armed men with both of you. The ten men who come back with you need to black their faces and arms. We'll have a surprise waiting for those kidnappers when they come to claim their ransom."

Smythe replied, "Aye, Mr. Ashworth! That we will!"

Smythe and Haddock loaded the slaves into the boats and rowed back to *Destiny*. Once back on board the ship, they sought out Captain Billings and told him what had happened.

Billings instructed McGuire to select ten good fighting men. "Arm them to the teeth, Mr. McGuire and then have them black out the color of their skin. I think I know what young Mr. Ashworth has in mind."

"Aye, Captain!"

McGuire armed the men with knives, sabers, and pistols. Then, each man rubbed charcoal on their faces, backs, and arms to hide the pale color of their skins. Finally, twelve men climbed down to the rowboats and returned to the beach where Richard awaited them. They found Richard and Brown waiting as they jogged through the sandy beach. Richard smiled as he saw the white-eyed men running toward him.

Richard ordered, "Mr. Brown, head back to the village and watch to see when Bryce and Mr. Faulkner come back. When you see them report back to me."

"Aye, Mr. Ashworth!"

Brown ran to the edge of the village to keep a watch out. Then Richard commanded the rest, "You men line up here before me. We want these people to think you are the slaves they are trading for Mr. Faulkner's release. Stand your cutlasses in the sand behind you so they can't be seen. The men did as Richard ordered.

Half an hour passed when Brown came running back to Richard. "They're coming Mr. Ashworth!"

"Alright!" said Richard. "You slaves put your hands behind you and take hold of this chain. That way they will think you are all chained together. When I give the order, drop the chain and pick up your blades."

The men all rumbled their approval of the plan.

As Bryce approached with Faulkner and six other men, Richard stood with Brown, Smythe, and Haddock in front of the chained crewmen and waited.

One of the men approaching spoke English with a strong Portuguese accent. He said, "Here is your man, unharmed. Give us our slaves."

Richard asked, "Are you aright, Mr. Faulkner?"

"Aye, Mr. Ashworth. I'm good as rain."

Richard told Faulkner's captive, "Alright, cut him loose, and you shall have your slaves."

The man nodded to his compatriots, and one of them took out a knife and cut away Mr. Faulkner's bonds. Once Richard saw his superior was free, he yelled to his men, "Now!"

The men dropped their chains and grabbed their cutlasses, then charged at the six men who had held their officer captive. Richard's crew quickly surrounded the six and held them at bay, each with at least one blade pointed at their gut.

Richard turned to the spokesman and said, "Now, sir, you and your men will lay down your arms."

The man dropped his pistol and a knife from his belt and commanded his men to do likewise.

Richard then ordered, "Alright, men. Tie them up and gag them. Mr. Faulkner, what say you we help ourselves to the food stores while we're here?"

"Aye, Mr. Ashworth! I think we shall!"

Fourteen men ran toward the village while two others stood guard over the prisoners. Richard and Faulkner led the way as they sprinted toward a large building where food was stored for the town. They broke down the door and went inside to find mounds of oranges, lemons, mangos, and yams. They found a pile of burlap sacks and began filling them with food. Each man carried two sacks back to the rowboats and loaded them. Four men rowed the boats back to *Destiny* while ten stayed behind to carry more food to the beach. They worked throughout the night transporting food back to *Destiny*, and when the sun began to rise, their hulls were full. Captain Billings ordered the ship back out to sea as they continued the voyage to Charlestown.

Billings ordered Mr. Hardy, "Double rations for all the crew and slaves. Make sure everyone has fruit or vegetables this morning for breakfast."

"Aye, Captain!"

Billings then said to Richard, "See that everyone is fed, then meet me in my cabin, lad."

"Aye, sir!"

Richard, Louis Hardy, and several of the crew met to prepare food for the slaves. They passed out the usual oat mush but then gave everyone fruit. The smell of fresh-cut oranges, mangos, and lemons filled the ship's hull, almost hiding the stench that typically lingered beneath the decks.

Batimkoo and the rest of the ten were returned to the lower deck with the other slaves. Richard was sorry to see him go down into the darkness again. Richard was beginning to develop a slight friendship with the big man. However, he knew there was little he could do for Batimkoo. Richard resigned to the thought that he could only try to keep him alive until he could think of something else.

Once the slaves had finished eating, Richard returned to the Captain's quarters. First, he knocked, then heard, "Enter!"

Richard stepped inside and found the captain standing at his table, once again staring at his charts spread out on the table.

"Come in, Richard! Did you eat, lad?"

"No, sir. Not yet."

"Well, come in and sit. There will be plenty of time to eat later."

Richard sat at the table, and Billings sat on the adjacent side.

"Richard, I can't tell you how pleased I am with how you handled yourself last night. You made decisions and commanded the crew in the absence of Mr. Faulkner like a true officer."

Richard was a little embarrassed as he replied, "Thank you, Captain."

"No, I mean it, lad. Most men would have pissed themselves when confronted with the danger and obstacles you endured last night. You were able to make decisions quickly and soundly, and the men followed you without question. That, my boy, is the mark of a true leader. I'm proud to have you as one of my officers."

Richard replied, "Thank you, sir."

Just then, Louis Hardy knocked on the door. The captain exclaimed, "Enter!"

Hardy brought in a tray of food for the captain and set it on the table in front of Billings.

"Hardy, bring in another tray for Mr. Ashworth. He and I will be dining together this day."

"Aye, Captain."

Chapter 8

Weeks rolled by as *Destiny* glided through the seas, heading northwesterly. The weather had been favorable for the journey, with little rain. But, of course, little rain also meant that fresh water was running low. So Captain Billings found it necessary to find an island nearby that could supply them with fresh water—a chain of islands just southeast of Puerto Rico. The largest of the islands and the farthest north was known as San Pueblo, translated as Saint Town.

Billings had the ship anchor on the eastern shore of San Pueblo and then ordered six men to carry water barrels by rowboat to the beach off the coast. Three large barrels were placed in each rowboat before the crew rowed toward the island. Timothy Sawyer, the third mate, was sent with the crew to supervise.

Once they reached the beach, Sawyer led the crew into the forest only fifty yards from the water's edge. Each man rolled one of the empty barrels through the sand and into the forest, following Mr. Sawyer. Timothy led the way, swinging a machete to clear a path for the barrels to roll. Birds would fly into the air in great flocks whenever the humans came too close. Monkeys squealed and ran through the treetops, scattering from the approaching strangers. Occasionally, Sawyer stopped in his path to listen, hoping to hear something to tell him which way to travel. Finally, he looked above the treetops that towered over them and saw a mountain in the distance to his west. He thought, "Surely there must be a water source somewhere around that mountain."

Timothy trekked onward, searching for the much-needed water to help *Destiny* survive her voyage. Finally, after two hours of searching, Timothy heard a waterfall in the distance. He followed the sound of the water falling from a high cliff. Sawyer hacked his way toward the source of the sound until, finally, he found a large pool of fresh water lying at the bottom of the mountain.

The men all cheered, relieved that they had found fresh water. They all left their barrels temporarily and ran to the pool to bathe themselves in its cool, clear waters. They splashed around like children playing in a summer's rain. Squirrel monkeys gathered in the treetops around the pool to watch the crazy humans as they celebrated in the clear waters of the pond.

After some time, Timothy instructed the men to fill their barrels with water so they could begin the trek back to the beach. The men worked together, filling each of the barrels with the cool, fresh water of the stream that filled the pool. The barrels were much heavier now that they were filled and more cumbersome to roll through the jungle. However, the path had been made and was easier to follow from there, having moved the barrels through the first time.

Again, Timothy Sawyer led the way as the crew rolled their casks through the jungle. The wetness of the men changed from cool water to sweat as they pushed their barrels through the forest. Each man panted as he strained to push the barrels through the fallen debris on the jungle floor. Then, just as they reached the beach's edge, something pricked Sawyer's right leg and caused him to cry out. He looked down to see a snake about three feet long crawling away into the forest.

"Did you see that?" Timothy asked the man following him.

Jim Crawly replied, "Aye, Mr. Sawyer! I saw rit!"

Sawyer asked, "What kind was it?"

"I don't know, sir. It was colored a green and black and tan, and had an awful looking head on it. Sorta bumpy looking."

Sawyer urged the men, "We must hurry back to the ship!"

The men strenuously rolled their barrels through the sand, finally reaching the rowboats. Once they loaded the barrels into the boats, they pushed the boats back into the ocean. By then, Sawyer was beginning to feel the effects of the snake's venom. He became feverish and light-headed. He could no longer command the party of men. They instead followed the lead of one Gerald Springer, the most senior of sailors.

Springer urged the men to pull on their oars hard and fast. "Come on, lads! We've got to get Mr. Sawyer back to the ship and quickly!"

Each boat had only two oars and one man on each. Nevertheless, they pulled with all their might toward *Destiny* as she rested in the waters of the Atlantic. After fifteen minutes of hard rowing, they finally reached the side of the giant ocean vessel. Springer called out to the ship, "Hurry! Get Mr. Greer! A snake has bitten Mr. Sawyer and he is in poor condition!"

A rope was let down from the ship's deck to the rowboats. Mr. Sawyer was tied with the rope and lifted to the main deck where Mr. Greer and Richard were waiting. While the crew loaded the water barrels from the rowboats, Richard and Greer helped Timothy into the infirmary to be examined.

Timothy was unconscious when they finally loaded him onto a table to be examined. Richard found the bite on Timothy's right leg. The area around the bite was red and inflamed. Suddenly, Timothy's body began to convulse. He shook like an earthquake had struck his body. Foam started erupting from his mouth and nose. His eyes rolled into the back of his head. Then, suddenly, it all stopped. Greer checked to see if Sawyer was breathing. His breathing had stopped. He was dead.

Greer said to Richard, "You best go inform the captain, Richard. One of his officers is dead."

While Greer cleaned Sawyer's body and prepared him for burial, Richard went on deck to find the captain. When Richard made it to the deck, the crew was still hoisting the rowboats back onto the ship. He looked around to see where Billings was. Richard finally spotted him on the quarterdeck. As he walked to meet the captain, Richard was stopped by Mr. Faulkner.

"How is Mr. Sawyer?"

"He's dead, sir!"

Several men standing close by gasped and asked, "*What?*"

Richard asked the men accompanying Timothy onto the island, "Did any of you see what bit him?"

Jim Crawly stepped forward and said, "Aye, Mr. Ashworth. I was right behind him when it happened. It was a snake. But I have never seen such a snake before."

Richard asked, "What did it look like?"

"It was about a yard long, it was colored all green, with black and tan markings all over it. And, it had a most peculiar head. It was like the snake had horns."

Faulkner said, "Sounds like a Fer de Lance."

Richard asked, "Fer de Lance, sir?"

"Aye! It is common on some of the Caribbean islands. It's one of the most deadly of snakes in these parts."

Richard replied, "Thank you, Mr. Faulkner. I must report to the captain, now."

Richard climbed to the quarterdeck to meet with Captain Billings, who stood beside Mr. McGuire and John Ashworth at the helm.

"Captain Billings, I'm sorry to report that Mr. Sawyer has succumbed to his wounds."

"What wounds did he acquire, Mr. Ashworth?"

"He was bitten by a poisonous snake, sir. Mr. Faulkner said it must have been a Fer de Lance from the description Mr. Crawly gave, sir."

The Captain furrowed his brow as he muttered, "Yes, I've heard of the Fer de Lance. A most deadly viper indeed. Thank you Mr. Ashworth. Mr. McGuire?"

"Aye, Captain!"

"We'll have a memorial for Mr. Sawyer at dusk if you please."

"Aye, Captain! I'll see to it."

Then the captain turned to Richard and said, "Go and help Mr. Greer prepare Mr. Sawyer's body for burial, Mr. Ashworth."

"Aye, Captain!"

Richard left the quarterdeck and returned to the infirmary to help Mr. Greer. Greer had already finished washing the body after stripping off all his clothing. Richard then helped Mr. Greer wrap the body in burlap, tied it up, and weighed it down with stones, also wrapped inside the burlap that encased Timothy's body.

At dusk, four of the crew were given the duty of retrieving Sawyer's body from the infirmary. They placed the body on a plank, carried Timothy onto the deck, and rested the plank on the starboard side atop the rail. All the men gathered around to pay their respects to the young officer who had led them for a short while on the *Destiny*. Timothy had only begun serving as the third officer on this voyage. He, like Richard, had started as a ship's boy on another vessel the year prior. Timothy's family in Bristol would certainly be heartbroken at the news of his loss. The Sawyers relied upon his service as a source of income, but he was also a loving son they would forever miss.

Captain Billings stood before the crew and loudly spoke as he honored the young officer, Timothy Sawyer. Timothy was a kind young man who was well-liked by the crew. Just eighteen years old, Timothy was on his way to a successful career as a merchant ship officer.

Then, men bowed their heads as they listened to the words spoken in honor of young Mr. Sawyer. Many a sniffle could be heard as the words rang true in their ears. Richard's eyes watered as he listened to Captain Billings honor the young officer to whom Richard had quickly grown close.

Finally, Billings ended with the words, "We therefore commit his body to the deep, … in sure and certain hope of the resurrection of the body, when the sea shall give up her dead."

One end of the plank was lifted, and Sawyer's body slid into the ocean's waters below. The burlap-wrapped body quickly penetrated the water's surface and plunged beneath the waves, traveling downward until finally resting on the ocean floor.

Richard returned to his cabin. It had been a long, stressful day, and he was ready for bed. When he walked into his cabin, he noticed Timothy's bed. Richard felt a sinking feeling in his belly. He would never see the young officer again. Richard climbed into the upper bunk and quickly fell asleep.

CHAPTER 9

The *Destiny* was still about a month away from Charlestown. The crew worked hard, keeping her in front of the wind. However, they didn't seem to mind as much now that their bellies were full. Everyone seemed in high spirits as they worked together. Many of the men sang a chantey as they worked among the rigging and sails to make repairs needed to keep *Destiny* afloat and on course. Boatswain Henry Gant sang the lead as the crew sang the refrain:

Haul on the bowline, homeward we are goin' (Haul on the bowline, the bowline Haul!)
Haul on the bowline... before she start a–rollin' (Haul on the bowline, the bowline Haul!)
Haul on the bowline... the captain is a-growlin, (Haul on the bowline, the bowline Haul!)
Haul on the bowline... so early in the morning (Haul on the bowline, the bowline Haul!)
Haul on the bowline... to Bristol, we are going (Haul on the bowline, the bowline Haul!)

Haul on the bowline,
..Kitty is my darlin' (Haul on the bowline, the bowline Haul!)
Haul on the bowline...Kitty comes from Liverpool, (Haul on the bowline, the bowline Haul!)

Haul on the bowline…It's far cry to payday (Haul on the bow-line, the bowline Haul!)

Richard sang along with the crew as he continued his chores. He saw to it that the slaves were fed and exercised above decks and then helped Mr. Greer with any medical care that the crew needed.

After noon, Richard proceeded to Captain Billings' quarters for his daily lessons. He knocked on the door.

"Enter!"

As Richard stepped inside, Billings acknowledged him. "Ah, Mr. Ashworth. Just the lad I was wanting to see."

"Me, sir?"

"Aye, Richard. You and I have much to discuss. I find myself once again short a junior officer. The tragic loss of Mr. Sawyer has found me in quite a pickle. I want to promote you to third officer and set you under Mr. Gant."

Richard was a little displeased by this. He immensely enjoyed working with Mr. Greer in the infirmary.

"Please, sir! Does this mean I won't be helping Mr. Greer any longer?"

The Captain asked, "Would that displease you?"

Richard replied, "Captain Billings, sir, I quite enjoy working with the doctor and learning about illnesses from his medical books."

Billings replied, "That's excellent, Mr. Ashworth. But, you need to learn everything about sailing too. By working with Mr. Gant for a while you'll learn how this old girl works, how to keep her afloat, and what to do should she fail."

"Aye, Captain. May I still work with Mr. Greer when I'm not needed on deck? I can do both, sir."

Billings thought for a moment before replying. "It is a strange request, lad. As long as you understand you have first duty to work with Mr. Gant and learn his trade. I'll speak to Mr. Gant and as long as he is in agreement, we will try it for a while."

Richard's face lit up with joy at the Captain's words. "Thank you, sir!"

Richard and the Captain entered into the day's lessons: Captain Billings showed Richard how to chart a course from their present location to Charlestown, then from Charlestown to Bristol. Then, they went onto the quarterdeck and practiced using the sextant. Next, Richard lined up the sextant with the sun and the horizon to determine *Destiny's* location on the seas. As Richard made his measurements, Billings measured alongside to check Richard's calculations.

Richard carefully twisted the adjustment knobs on the sextant to line up the sun's image with the horizon. Once he finished his adjustments, he turned the sextant in his hands to read the measurements on the dial. Billings compared Richard's sextant with his own, then said, "Excellent, Mr. Ashworth! Your measurements are only a tenth of a degree off from my own. You will be an excellent navigator."

"Thank you, Captain!"

Once he had finished his lessons with Captain Billings, Richard reported to Mr. Gant for duties. Gant taught Richard about the riggings of a ship, the sails, the rudder, and the steerage of the helm. They inspected each mechanical part of the ship daily. Richard would oversee the repairs of any part of the ship as needed. Once his duties had been met with Mr. Gant, Richard was allowed to meet with Mr. Greer. The two would inspect the ship's hull and make any repairs needed, and then Richard attended to the infirmary to care for any sailor in need. If no one was ailing, then Richard used his time to study the medical books in Mr. Greer's library.

Richard also found time to look after the slaves. He saw that they were fed and kept healthy, and he made sure that they were exercised as much as possible. Richard and Batimkoo developed a friendship during their time together. Batimkoo learned English very quickly, and Richard learned *Swahili.* Richard walked along next to Batimkoo whenever he was exercised, and they traded words, each learning the other's language.

Richard pointed to the sky and said, "Sky!"

Batimkoo replied, "Sky. *Anga!*"

Richard repeated, "*Anga.*"

Richard pointed to the sun and said, "Sun!"

Batimkoo answered, "Sun. *Fremu.*"

Richard repeated, "*Fremu.*"

This went on and on daily whenever they found themselves together on deck.

"Ocean."

"Ocean. *Bahari.*"

"Ship."

"Ship. *Meli.*"

Richard eventually saw that Batimkoo was teaching his fellow slaves the English language he was learning. The crew of the *Destiny* all seemed to join in with educating the slaves as they walked the ship's decks.

Mr. Faulkner observed that the crew also educated the slaves as they walked the decks during their exercise period. He decided to mention this to the Captain. He went to Billings' cabin and knocked.

"Enter!"

Faulkner opened the door and entered, then waited to be acknowledged by the Captain.

"What is it Mr. Faulkner?"

"Captain, sir. Have you noticed what has been happening with the crew and the slaves?"

"What do you mean, Faulkner?"

"Sir, the men have been teaching the slaves our language as they walk the decks."

Puzzled, Captain Billings asked, "Have you asked why?"

"Aye, Captain! The men say that young Mr. Ashworth has been teaching one of the slaves, the one called Batimkoo. They say it has been easier managing the slaves since this has begun."

Captain Billings said, "Mr. Faulkner, please ask Mr. Ashworth to report to me immediately."

"Aye, Captain!"

Faulkner went back on deck and searched for Richard. He found Richard standing next to Mr. Gant at the base of the main mast. Faulkner approached the two and said, "Mr. Ashworth, the captain would like a word with you in his quarters."

"Aye, Mr. Faulkner!"

Richard reported directly to Captain Billings' quarters and knocked on the door.

"Enter!"

Richard opened the door and stood before the captain. "You wished to see me, sir?"

"Aye, Richard. I understand you have been teaching the Africans to speak English."

"Aye, Captain. Actually, I just started teaching the one named Batimkoo, but then he started teaching some of his compatriots. Then, some of the crew joined in while the slaves were exercising on deck."

"To what purpose did you think it necessary to teach these creatures to speak our language, Richard."

Richard replied, "Well, sir, it makes it easier to get them to do what we need them to do. Maybe, they will be worth more to the buyers if they already know how to speak English."

Billings thought for a moment before saying. "You may be correct, Mr. Ashworth. However, I fear that you may be developing friendships with these individuals and that could be costly. These people are like stray dogs. You can't keep them like pets. They will turn around and bite you if they have the opportunity. You'll get too close to them and one day they will leave. Mr. Ashworth, these people have a long hard life ahead of them. There is nothing you can do to change that other than don't get attached. Do you understand?"

"Aye, Captain."

Richard returned to the deck and continued to stand by with Mr. Gant as Gant gave orders to the men working on the rigging of the ship's sails. Richard's mind wandered as he stood next to Gant. He wondered what would become of the men and women who sailed below decks of the *Destiny*. He felt sorry for them, knowing that their lives would be forever changed because of the greed of men. Richard had never known anyone from Africa before. However, he had heard of people from Ireland who had been pressed into slavery because of their religious beliefs. They were called *indentured servants*, but they were slaves nonetheless.

Later that day and after the evening meal, Richard stood at the port rail watching pelicans glide along the top of the sea. They reminded him of mythological creatures he had read about in books his mother had borrowed for him before she died. The great birds stretched out their wings and hovered over the waters in search of their prey. Then, suddenly, one dove into the water, disappearing momentarily from sight before emerging once again with a fish wriggling in its bill. The bird quickly pointed his beak to the sky, letting the fish slide down his throat. Richard thought about how free the birds were. No one kept them in cages. No one told them what they could and could not eat or where they could or could not go. Richard wished Batimkoo and his fellow slaves could be free like the pelicans.

Richard knew freeing four hundred or so slaves would be impossible. However, he might be able to devise a plan to free one. Richard had developed a friendship with Batimkoo and didn't want to see the proud African sent into a life of hard labor, degradation, and humiliation. Batimkoo had once been a fierce warrior and leader among his people. Now, he was relegated to a humble servant.

Richard decided to speak with the captain to see if something might be done to help his friend. He knew it wouldn't be likely, seeing how Batimkoo was not considered a man but only a piece of cargo; however, Richard needed to explore at least the idea to see if there might be a resolution.

John Ashworth was manning the helm this evening, so Richard stepped onto the quarterdeck to join his papa. The sky was clear, and the stars shined brightly. Then, suddenly, Richard saw a star falling through the sky.

"Look, Papa!"

"Aye!" said John. "You better be quick and make a wish!"

Richard closed his eyes and made his wish as the star faded into the dark skies. John asked, "What did you wish for?"

"I can't tell you Papa! It won't come true!"

"Aye, of course. Well, I hope all your wishes come true."

Chapter 10

Land appeared on the port bow early one morning. Henry Sikes sat in the crow's nest and called out, "Land Ho! Off the port bow!"

The crew scrambled to catch a glimpse of what was sure to be the east coast of Florida. Unfortunately, it was still too far off to see from the ship's deck. However, the mere idea that *Destiny* would soon land lifted everyone's spirits. They were still at least two days from the port of Charlestown, but having the recently discovered continent of the Americas in site was uplifting.

The coast of Florida was unsettled. Although *Destiny* soon was within viewing distance of the shore, it was only shoreline, no civilization. There would be no civilization until they reached the northernmost point of Florida, where St. Augustine and Fernando Beach lay. From there, they would follow the coast of Georgia until they found their way to the Carolina coast, where Charlestown lay.

Richard continued his daily duties as third officer. He worked under the tutelage of Henry Gant, checking the rigging, sails, and steerage of the ship daily. Afterward, he spent time in the infirmary with Mr. Greer, caring for injured or sick crew members. Richard and Mr. Greer then checked below decks for any repairs the ship might have needed.

New lessons began as Mr. Faulkner showed Richard how to use firearms and blades. Richard learned how to load and shoot muskets and pistols. He was also instructed in swordplay using wooden broomsticks cut to the proper length. Richard was excited at the training he received as he and Mr. Faulkner exchanged *lunge, parry, and riposte.* Over and over, Richard practiced the moves, day after day, until finally, broomsticks were exchanged for swords. The sound of blade against blade rang out as Faulkner and Richard danced around the deck, sparring. Faulkner would lunge while Richard parried. Back and forth, they moved against each other. Richard found the swordplay exhilarating.

Richard's afternoon lessons with Captain Billings became shorter and shorter. Richard had become quite skilled at charting courses, using the sextant, and reading the winds. However, Richard did spend time with the captain daily for discussion periods. They might discuss Captain Billings' past as a seaman and the adventures he encountered. Other times, they talked about battles at sea that Billings had taken part in while serving in His Majesty's Navy. Today was quite different, however. Richard decided to breach the subject of Batimkoo.

"Captain! May I ask, would it be possible for me to purchase one of the slaves with the money I earn working on *Destiny*?"

Billings was shocked by Richard's question. Then, disappointedly, the captain asked, "Mr. Ashworth, did I not warn you not to get attached to slaves?"

"Aye, Captain. But I feel a close connection to the one called, Batimkoo. Is there anyway that I might be able to afford him with the money I earn?"

Captain Billings silently thought for a long time as they sat together at his table. What Richard was asking was unprecedented upon any of Billings' ships. No one had ever asked to purchase one of the slaves before.

"Mr. Ashworth, let me ponder your request. I will have an answer for you by the time we reach Charlestown."

"Thank you, Captain.

For the next two days, Richard earnestly and faithfully performed his duties to the best of his abilities. However, he never brought up the subject of Batimkoo to the captain again. Richard was afraid if he kept asking the captain about purchasing the slave, the captain might find it too annoying and decide not to allow Richard to buy Batimkoo simply because he was tired of hearing the subject.

Finally, *Destiny* arrived at the port in Charlestown. John Ashworth steered the ship into a slip next to the shore where she could be tied. Mid–May provided a most desirable day of sunshine and mild temperatures in Charlestown. Unfortunately, most daylight had already faded when *Destiny* was tied up at the docks. It was too late to unload the cargo but not too late for the crew to take leave to find their way into some tavern or house of ill repute.

Richard, Captain Billings, Mr. Faulkner, and the other two junior officers stayed onboard to protect their cargo. Each man was armed in case someone tried to board the ship with the intent to rob her. Richard took watch at the port bow facing the docks. He watched as men and women strolled down the boardwalks along the front of the buildings facing the sea. Taverns, shops, and the like lined the streets of Charlestown. Music and singing could be heard from several of the pubs. Laughter and sometimes screams of joy could be heard coming from the upper rooms of the buildings facing *Destiny*.

At midnight, Richard rotated to watch the starboard bow. He watched the Atlantic's waters in case someone approached *Destiny* by boat. All seemed calm as Richard stared over the rail toward the horizon. Suddenly, around two o'clock, Richard heard water lapping beneath his watch. The moon was at half-phase, which made it difficult to see beyond the darkness. Then, grappling hooks flew over the starboard rail and caught the rail as the ropes were pulled downward. Richard searched over the side and witnessed a small vessel carrying several men; he could not tell how many. Richard called out, "Boat off the starboard rail! We've been breached!"

David Reynolds, who had taken Richard's previous position on the port, was first to arrive at Richard's aid. Samuel McKenzie followed from the ship's stern. Faulkner and Billings came soon after. Eight men climbed over the rail with swords in hand. Richard drew his pistol and fired at the first man to climb onto the deck. A bullet entered the man's neck and severed his artery. He lay on the deck, grabbing his throat, trying to stop the bleeding. Finally, Richard dropped his pistol and drew his sword just as Samuel fired a shot at another intruder, hitting the man squarely in the chest. The man fell immediately dead.

One of the attackers swung his blade at Richard and knocked Richard's sword from his hand, causing Richard to fall backward onto the deck. The man lost his balance and collapsed next to Richard. Richard regained his footing but could not reach his sword because it slid away past the man. Richard spotted a belaying pin sticking up from the starboard rail. He quickly snatched it from its perch and swung it down into the attacker's head, crushing his skull. Richard stepped over the man's body and retrieved his sword.

The battle continued with each officer firing their weapons first, then drawing their blades for close combat. Invaders attacked while crew members defended their vessel. Richard noticed another grappling hook had caught itself on the starboard rail. He quickly chopped at the rope, which was severed with two swings. More hooks were thrown, and Richard continued to cut the lines before more attackers could climb aboard.

Richard peered over the side to see if more grapplers would be thrown and saw a musket pointed at his face. He quickly reacted and dodged as a musket ball flew past his left ear. Richard sat on the deck against the rail, eyes wide open, realizing how close he had come to losing his life. As Richard caught his breath, he glanced over and saw a lantern burning while hanging from the main mast. He scrambled to his feet and took the lantern from its hook. Richard ran back to the rail and plunged the lamp downward into the small boat where eight more men were waiting. An explosion of flames erupted as the small vessel was engulfed in burning oil, setting each man on fire. Some of the men quickly dove into the sea to extinguish the flames that ate their skin away from their bones. Others were stunned by the fire that quickly burned their hides, causing them to scream, swat at the flames, and spin uncontrollably in the small boat.

Once Captain Billings and his crew finished off the would-be attackers who had boarded their ship, they reloaded their firearms and fired them into the sea, killing the remaining miscreants who had tried to raid their cargo. Billings checked his crew and found Faulkner with a minor cut to his left cheek. David Reynolds had incurred a heavy gash to his upper left arm and was bleeding badly. All others were unscathed.

Captain Billings ordered, "Mr. Ashworth, please take Mr. Reynolds to the infirmary and see to his wounds. Mr. Faulkner, you should go along and have him look at your cheek as well."

Richard replied, "Aye, Captain!"

He led the two wounded men to Mr. Greer's quarters and attended to the injuries. Richard washed Mr. Faulkner's cheek with whiskey to kill any infection and washed away the blood. Once he discovered it only to be a flesh wound, he released Mr. Faulkner so he could go back and report to the captain.

David's injuries were much worse. A blade had sliced his arm open, a gash nearly six inches long and two inches deep. Richard cleaned the wound as best he could with the whiskey, then used a needle and thread to sew the gash shut and stop the bleeding. David winced in pain each time Richard pushed the needle through Reynold's flesh. Thirty minutes later, Richard finished his sewing. "David, I'll help you back to your bunk so you can rest a while. You're going to be very sore for a few days. We need to watch and make sure you don't run a fever, so lie still until you've had time to heal."

Once Richard got Reynolds settled into his cot, he reported back on deck to the captain. As Billings saw Richard moving toward him, he smiled and said, "Mr. Ashworth, I commend you on a job well done. You showed yourself once again to be more than capable to handle yourself during tense situations."

"Thank you, sir!"

Then the Captain ordered, "Alright, gentlemen, check your weapons and report back to your post. We still have three hours until sunrise. Keep a sharp eye out for anymore intruders."

"*Aye, Captain!*" they all replied in unison.

Richard moved to his next position at the starboard stern, reloaded his pistol, and then scanned the seas for anyone who dared approach the *Destiny*.

As the sun began to rise above the eastern horizon, it burned bright orange against a clear blue sky. Richard wiped his eyes, trying to stay awake, as crew members slowly returned aboard their vessel. By twos and threes, the men came meandering back onboard, many still intoxicated from a long night of rumming.

Billings instructed a few of the more sober men to stay on deck and relieve the men who had stayed onboard to watch for trespassers. John Ashworth was one of those individuals who returned to the ship only slightly tipsy. He was assigned duty at the gangplank, along with Mr. McGuire, to check in the sailors as they boarded to make their assignments.

Richard was instructed to retreat to his quarters for sleep. However, it would be a short rest. At eight o'clock, Captain Billings would expect all hands on deck to start the movement of the cargo from the ship.

CHAPTER 11

R ichard was startled awake as the ship's bell began to ring. "All hands! All hands!" was the call from the main deck. Richard quickly gathered himself, his coat, and his hat and scrambled to the main deck. He recognized the voice calling above the bell as Henry Gant's. Richard took his place by Gant's side and waited for orders.

Captain Billings stepped forward to speak once all the crew had been assembled. "Gentlemen, it is time to unload the cargo from below decks. Young Mr. Ashworth, if you please, take four men below and begin extricating the cargo to bring them on deck."

Richard called out, "Smythe, Crawley, Brown, and Haddock, if you please."

The four men climbed down to the lower deck to begin removing the shackles that held the slaves in position below. Richard followed to show them which ones he wanted brought out first.

Richard started with the slaves lying closest to the hatch and began clearing a path so that the chosen could easily walk to the hatch. Twenty men were chosen first. They were sent to the main deck, where they were handed off to more of the crew waiting on deck. These twenty slaves were then escorted by four armed men off the ship and onto the docks.

Richard couldn't help but wonder if Captain Billings had decided whether or not he would allow Richard to purchase his friend's freedom. He and the captain had not spoken of it since the day Richard presented the idea to Billings. Richard's stomach churned with anxiety as he continued selecting which slaves to send above decks. He consciously avoided making eye contact with Batimkoo.

The first twenty slaves were moved to the center of Charlestown to a place designated for auctioning off goods known as the *Marketplace*. Once offloaded from Destiny, they were held in a holding pen. When the first group reached the holding area, they moved the first twenty slaves into the pen and left two guards behind them while the other two retreated to the ship.

As they quickly walked to the ship, they met the next group making their way to the pens. This group happened to be all women slaves. When this group reached the holding pens, they were placed in a separate enclosure from the men.

The unloading of slaves from the ship continued for over an hour until the last group was ready to be taken to the pens. Batimkoo was among them. Richard followed the group as they walked across the decks of *Destiny*, prepared to walk the gangplank down to the dock. Richard stood next to Captain Billings, watching the last of the slaves as they made their way off the ship. Finally, after a long moment, Billings asked, "What is it, Mr. Ashworth?"

"Excuse me, Captain. I was wondering if you have thought about what we had discussed a few days ago? I mean about Batimkoo."

Billings looked down into Richard's eyes, then pulled him off to the side, away from unwanted ears. "Richard, are you sure about this? What will you do with a slave?"

"I will train him to be a sailor, sir! He will be one of the crew. Please, sir!"

Captain Billings struggled with his decision. He felt obliged to the young officer who had done so much to make their voyage successful, but what would the crew think? What would other captains on other vessels feel about a black sailor in his crew? There were black sailors on other vessels, but typically, they were on privateers or even pirate ships, not bonafide merchant ships. Finally, Billings gave in to Richard's request.

"Alright, lad. £25 will be deducted from your wages when we reach port back in England."

"Oh thank you, Captain!"

Richard happily stepped away from the captain and stood next to Batimkoo, who was waiting his turn to walk the gangplank to the dock.

"Batimkoo, you can stay here."

Puzzled, the large black man furrowed his brow to search for understanding. "Stay?"

"Yes! I have purchased your freedom. You can stay with me and work here on the ship. You will become a sailor."

Batimkoo was still confused, "I do not understand. I will not go with my people?"

"No! Your people will endure great hardship. They will work in the fields and be whipped or beaten whenever their masters please. You will not be treated badly anymore. You will be free."

Batimkoo asked, "Free? Why will I be free, but not my brothers and sisters?"

Richard replied, "I wish I could free them all, but I only have enough money to free one. I chose you."

Batimkoo said, "I am thankful to you, but I will not be free."

"Why not?"

"I am *Deni la maisha*. Life debt. I now owe you. I am responsible for your life since you have freed me."

"No, Batimkoo. You don't owe me anything."

"Please! Do not call me Batimkoo. I am no longer Batimkoo, I am Deni la maisha."

Richard somehow felt that he had offended Batimkoo by trying to make him free and happy.

"Deni la maisha is a long name. May I call you something else?"

The large black man stood proudly before Richard and said, "Since you have freed me, you may call me whatever you like."

Richard replied, "I once read a book about a king in northern Africa in a placed called Egypt. The people there called their king, Pharaoh. So I would like to call you Pharaoh."

Batimkoo smirked, a slight smile on his lips, although his eyes did not indicate glee. "As you wish!"

Three hundred, ninety-four slaves made it to market in Charlestown aboard the *Destiny*. One free black man remained aboard. When Captain Billings arrived at the Marketplace, he was greeted by the auctioneer, Clovis Gentry, a small man with a tenor voice. Gentry's red hair was sprinkled with wisps of white, and he wore mutton chops that extended halfway down his jawbone.

"Good day, Captain!"

"Good day, sir!"

Gentry began, "You have some of the healthiest slaves ever brought to our market, Captain. If you please, sir we will sell your slaves in lots of ten."

Captain Billings said, "That is agreeable. Shall we begin?"

Ten naked men stood on a platform before hundreds of buyers and onlookers. Both men and women from all over the Carolinas and Georgia attended the event. Four large oak trees spread over the Marketplace, providing a canopy of protection against the morning sun.

The bidding began as Gentry announced, "We will start at £10."

Someone from the crowd yelled out, "I bid, ten shillings!"

Gentry replied, "Surely you jest, sir!. These slaves are the finest lot ever brought into the Carolinas. There isn't an unhealthy one among them."

Suddenly, one of the slaves spoke to the crowd in English, "What do you want with us? Why have to brought us to this strange land? You must return us to our home!"

Many of the slaves began to cry out, "Take us home! Take us home!"

The crowd of people was astounded to hear the blacks speaking in English. They were dumbfounded, but the chants of the slaves continued. Then, finally, one of the caretakers who worked for Gentry walked up to the man who had spoken out and thrust the butt of his musket into the gut of the slave. The black man doubled over in pain while his compatriots quieted themselves.

Finally, a serious bidder announced, "£8!"

Gentry replied, "That's fine! Now we're talking. Just remember gentlemen, you're bidding the cost of one slave, your final tally will be times ten for the lot. Now, I have £8, who will give nine?"

A voice from the left side of the crowd said, "£9!"

The crowd finally felt the excitement generally associated with an auction, and bids quickly rang out.

"£10. . .£12. . . £15. . . £17. . . £21."

Things slowed down at £21, and Gentry tried to coax more bids from the crowd, "I have £21; who will give twenty-two?"

The bids had stopped. Gentry had determined that £21 would be the final bid. "£21 going once! Going twice! Sold! Your name please, sir?"

"Richard Bellamy!"

"Thank you, Mr. Bellamy!"

Throughout the morning, the slave men were brought out in lots of ten to be sold. Because of the quality of the slaves *Destiny* had brought to the Carolina auction, none of the men sold for less than £20, and the highest bidding got £26.

Eighty-nine naked slave women were finally brought out by lots of ten. They ranged in age from twelve years old to no more than twenty. At the end of the morning, all eighty-nine were sold for an average of £18. Gentry's accountant added up the total and then deducted Gentry a ten percent fee. The total given to Captain Billings for three hundred ninety-four slaves was £8,668. Billings had never earned so much on his journeys across the sea. His partners would be delighted.

Richard and Pharaoh stood at the top of the gangplank as the captain and crew returned from the Marketplace. Richard greeted the captain by asking, "How did it go, Captain?"

"Quite well, my boy! Quite well! *Destiny* has never had a more successful voyage and I have you to thank, Mr. Ashworth."

"Me, Captain?"

"Aye, Mr. Ashworth! It was you who encouraged me to provide a healthy diet for the crew and slaves. You who rescued Mr. Faulkner from imprisonment in Argentina. And, you who taught them to speak our language. Once the crowd heard the slaves speaking English the bids began and climbed like never before. Buyers were pleased that they wouldn't be burdened with trying to work slaves who didn't understand our language. We couldn't have done it without you, Mr. Ashworth!"

Richard had mixed feelings about how successful the sale went. He was pleased that the Captain and his partners would be happy with the money made upon this voyage, but at what expense? Nearly four hundred Africans had lost their freedom and were torn away from their families, never to see their homes again. It disturbed Richard that he had played a part in this scandal. Would the Africans not have been better off dying at sea than living in servitude for the rest of their lives?

Captain Billings purchased supplies and more cargo before leaving Charlestown. The main items loaded onto the ship were tobacco, cotton, and sugar. *Destiny* had never before carried so much cargo back to England from her journey to Charlestown. There had never been as much money to spend on products as there was now.

Destiny embarked on the last leg of her journey back home to England the following day. Richard found a hammock on the crew deck where Pharaoh could sleep. He was on the same deck as the rest of the crew but in an area away from the others.

Richard approached Mr. Crawley shortly after *Destiny* got underway and asked, "Mr. Crawley, I am wondering if you have a spare set of clothing you might be willing to give me?"

Richard thought Crawley, being close to the same size as Pharaoh in stature, might have something Pharaoh could wear to make him more comfortable while on board a ship during windy and sometimes rainy conditions.

Crawley replied, "Aye, I have extra clothes. Why?"

"Pharaoh has nothing to wear. Since you are close to the same size, I thought maybe you have something that might fit him."

"Pharaoh? Who's Pharaoh?"

Richard pointed back to the tall black man standing in the distance.

"I thought he was called, Batimkoo."

Richard replied, "He was, but I have changed his name. He likes Pharaoh."

"Why wasn't he sold with the other slaves?"

Richard answered, "Captain Billings allowed me to buy his freedom."

Crawley asked, "Why would you do a foolish thing like that? Seems like a waste of money to me."

"Not at all. He is my friend. He is going to be trained as a sailor. He is now one of the crew. Now, do you have any clothes that might fit him?"

Crawley answered, "Aye, I have some old clothes but they're full of holes."

"May I have them?"

"Well, since you're so rich that you can buy a slave, how 'bout you pay me for the clothes?"

Richard stuttered before replying, "Well, I don't have any money right now, but how about a trade?"

"What kind of trade?"

Richard thought momentarily, then replied, "How about I give you a portion of my rations every day until we reach England? I'll give you half of my fruit."

Crawley scratched his chin as he thought, then said, "I'll take three-quarters of any fruit and half your meat."

Richard wasn't pleased with the thought of giving up so much of his daily rations, but he didn't have much choice.

"Fine! It's a deal!"

Crawley rummaged through his knapsack and dug out a ripped pair of trousers and a torn knitted red and white striped shirt. He handed them to Richard and said, "Nice doing business with you, Mr. Ashworth."

Richard held up the pants and shirt to examine the damage, then replied, "Thank you, Mr. Crawley!" and then walked away.

CHAPTER 12

The ship had its wind on the trip back to England. They made good time with little in the way of severe weather to slow their momentum. Richard continued with his training as a ship's officer, working with Henry Gant in the morning, meeting with the captain in the afternoon, and studying with Mr. Greer and his medical books whenever time would allow. He also spent as much time with Pharaoh as possible, teaching him the ins and outs of sailing a ship, rigging sails, repairing leaks in the hull, and everything else a good sailor should know.

Pharaoh was a quick learner and enjoyed his time on the ship's deck. The fresh sea air agreed with him. During the lull of duties, Richard and Pharaoh would stand together at the bow next to each other in silence, enjoying the breeze on their faces. The wind whistling past their ears was deafening, a constant roar that was almost hypnotic.

Most crew members were unhappy having a slave work alongside them on their ship. They looked at him with disdain and belittled him at every turn. Pharaoh ignored their comments of contempt for the most part. He understood how they felt. He knew, in their eyes, he was not a man. However, things changed for him a month into their voyage back to England.

Arnold Brown, a seasoned sailor, was standing on the end of the yardarm of the mainmast, stitching a hole in the sail, when a gust of wind pushed the sail into him and knocked him from the yardarm. Brown fell fifteen feet, hitting his head on the port rail and falling into the sea. Mr. Hardy saw the accident and called out, "Man overboard!"

Hardy quickly moved to the belaying pin securing the main sail and loosed it to release the sail. Richard did the same on the port side. Pharaoh, without hesitation, dove into the sea after Brown. He swam out to where he had seen his fellow sailor enter the water, then dove under to find Brown.

All the other sailors scampered about, dropping sails to bring *Destiny* to a near halt. Mr. McGuire stood by the helm and ordered, "Drop the dory!"

Two sailors moved to the port side and began raising the small boat that sat just above the deck and on the ship's rail. They began lowering the dory toward the water when Richard called out, "Wait!"

Richard ran to them and climbed into the dory as they lowered it into the water. But, first, Richard scrambled to place the oars into their oarlocks. Then, Richard began rowing back to where Pharaoh and Brown had entered the water as the dory landed in the ocean.

McGuire then ordered, "Drop anchor!"

The anchor was unlikely to hit the bottom and stop the ship from moving forward, but McGuire thought it might help to slow her progress and momentum.

Pharaoh found Brown hovering in the water just below the surface and wrapped an arm around his chest to pull him up out of the water. Pharaoh saw a welp on Brown's head and a large cut that was bleeding. He held onto Brown and began swimming toward Richard, who was rowing with all his might.

Suddenly, Pharaoh caught a glimpse of something in the water to his left. A large fin rose out of the water about forty yards out. Pharaoh knew very little about sea creatures but knew what the fin meant. So he began swimming faster toward the dory and calling out to Richard, "Shark! Shark!"

Richard searched the waters to spot the fish moving toward Pharaoh and Brown. Unfortunately, Richard was fifty yards from the stranded swimmers and would not make it in time to help them fight off the eight-foot menace with razor-sharp teeth.

Pharaoh reached for his sailor's knife in its sheath around his waist. He brandished it in his right hand while holding Brown in his left, kicking his feet all the while so he could stay above water. He knew fighting off the demon while holding onto the unconscious Brown would be difficult, but he would keep him above the water as long as possible. The shark swam straight toward the two men floating on the surface. The smell of blood dripping from Brown's head led the shark to its prey. Suddenly, the fin plunged below the surface and disappeared. Pharaoh gasped, realizing the shark would be coming at him from below. He released Brown and dove under the water, searching for the shark. Pharaoh twisted below the surface, searching for the grey monster. He looked in the direction he had seen it coming but didn't see it. He spun to look behind him and still couldn't spot it. Pharaoh continued turning as he searched when suddenly it appeared just above him. The shark rapidly swam toward Brown.

Pharaoh lunged upward toward the shark and struck it with his knife. The knife slightly pierced the fish's belly but caused minor damage. However, it did deter the shark momentarily. It swam away only a few yards before circling back toward Brown again. The smell of Brown's blood was just too tempting for the aquatic beast.

Pharaoh placed himself between Brown and the shark and readied his knife once again. He allowed himself to float to the surface, raised his head, and took a quick breath before dipping his face back under the water. Suddenly, the shark was on him again. Pharaoh raised his knife out of the water, then swung his arm downward with all his might, striking the shark squarely in the head between the animal's eyes. Pharaoh twisted the knife with both hands to ensure it did as much damage as possible. The shark froze. Blood flowed from its head, releasing a trail similar to a stream of smoke from a fire.

Pharaoh raised his head above the surface and reached over to move Brown once again above the water. Richard moved closer and closer to them, eventually reaching the two sailors. As he reached them, Richard retracted his oars back into the boat and reached over to grab Brown and reel him into the boat. Pharaoh pushed upward against Brown's body to make it easier for Richard to retrieve the unconscious sailor. Then, Pharaoh climbed into the boat as well.

Richard then placed the oars back into the oarlocks and rowed back to *Destiny*. Richard rowed for only a short while before he was utterly spent. His young, wiry arms were not built for such strenuous duty. Pharaoh took over for him, and even though he, too, was quite tired, he was a full-grown man and more robust than most men. Finally, after nearly an hour of rowing, the little dory reached the port side of the larger vessel. Pharaoh tossed the bowline and then the stern line to men standing on the ship's deck. They threaded the lines through pulleys and raised the dory out of the sea.

Two of the crew carried Arnold Brown to Mr. Greer's quarters to have his injuries attended. The rest of the crew congratulated Richard and Pharaoh for jobs well done. Everyone wanted to shake Pharaoh's hand or pat him on the back. The crew no longer scorned him; he was one of them. Richard was delighted to see the men accept Pharaoh as a part of the crew.

Forty days at sea found *Destiny* docking on the banks of Bristol. Like the rest of the crew, Richard was excited to see his home after being at sea for nearly a year. The sailors unloaded the cargo from the lower decks as quickly as possible. Everyone was looking forward to spending time on shore. Some had a family to reunite with, while others wanted to catch up with old friends and spend their money as quickly as possible, which meant they would most likely be back to make *Destiny's* next voyage.

After the men unloaded the ship, they all lined up side by side for their wages to be dispersed. Mr. Faulkner and Mr. McGuire sat at a table together in front of the men on the main deck. As McGuire read out each sailor's name, the man would step forward to receive his pay.

"John Ashworth!"

Richard's father stepped forward and stood before the table while Faulkner counted out £33 in silver and handed it to him.

John said, "Thank you, Mr. Faulkner. Will you be needing me on the next voyage?"

Faulkner looked up and replied, "Mr. Ashworth, you're a good man and a fine helmsman. Captain Billings has requested you join us in one week if you please."

"Please offer my gratitude and regards to the captain. I would be delighted to join *Destiny* on her next voyage."

McGuire called out the next name, "Arnold Brown!"

Brown gingerly stepped forward, still ailing from his injuries from nearly a month ago. Faulkner counted out his £33. Brown asked, "What about me, Mr. Faulkner? Will you be needing me again?"

Faulkner replied, "Come back in a week, Mr. Brown and let Mr. Greer have a look at you. If he thinks you're sound enough, we'll bring you along. We need men in tip top condition understand?"

"Aye, Mr. Faulkner! I'll be ready, sir!"

Brown walked to the gangplank and exited the ship, somewhat downtrodden.

Man after man was called forward to receive his wages, leaving the ship immediately.

"Carrington! Dodson! Drake! Eddings! Gates! Grimes!"

The names continued until all seventy of the regular crew were paid and had left—all except Pharaoh.

After everyone else had been paid, Mr. Faulkner called out, "Pharaoh!"

The tall black man was taken aback by his name being called. He stepped forward to the table, and Mr. Faulkner spoke to him. "Captain Billings has determined that you should be paid as one of the crew. However, since you only recently began as a sailor upon our fine ship, you will only receive partial pay."

Faulkner counted out £12 and handed it to Pharaoh. Pharaoh looked at Faulkner and then at Richard as if saying, "*What should I do with this?*" Richard nodded to Pharaoh, letting him know it was okay to take the silver coins. Pharaoh took the money and dropped it into his trouser pocket, just as he had seen the other men do. Richard smiled at the big man as Pharaoh came and stood next to John Ashworth.

Faulkner then called out the officers' names, Mr. Greer, Henry Gant, Samuel McKenzie, and David Reynolds, so they could be paid. Finally, he called forth. . . "Richard Ashworth!"

Richard was a little shocked to hear his name called. He hadn't expected to receive any pay because of his deal with the captain.

As Richard's name was called, Captain Billings stepped onto the deck. Richard slowly stepped up to the table and looked at the Captain. Billings could tell that Richard was confused by his name having been called. Mr. Faulkner handed Richard £42 in silver coins. Richard was dumbfounded.

"Captain! We had a deal! I am to forfeit my pay in order that Pharaoh would be free."

Billings replied, "Yes, my boy. However, after much contemplation I have decided to reconsider our deal. Mr. Ashworth, you are a most exceptional young man and are developing into a first rate officer. *Destiny* has just finished her most successful voyage and it is no doubt because of you. You've made me realize how much more money is to be made by making sure our cargo arrives to market in excellent condition. By spending a little more on proper food, we have made more money than we could have hoped for. I want you to come back next week and I will be promoting you to first officer. Mr. Faulkner will be leaving us. He has taken a commission on another vessel, so Mr. McGuire will be first mate, Mr. McKenzie will be promoted to second mate, and you will be taking Mr. McKenzie's position. I have no doubt that you will make first mate in no time at all."

Richard's face lit up, and he replied, "Thank you, Captain! I won't let you down!"

CHAPTER 13

John, Richard, and Pharaoh descended the gangplank onto the docks at the edge of Bristol, England. Walking on solid ground was relatively unfamiliar for the three, having spent most of the past twelve months at sea. They walked along the cobbled streets together, noticing little had changed in the past year. Water Fort was just as dirty and run down as when they left a year ago.

However, everything was new to Pharaoh. He had never seen such tall buildings before. He had only ever lived in a hut with no doors or windows. These structures had large wooden doors with heavy iron hardware and glass windows. The stench of human waste filled the air as they walked through town. From time to time, dead bodies could be seen piled up next to the street, waiting for someone to collect them for burial.

They came upon a shop familiar to Richard. Although Richard knew Brighten's Clothing Shop existed, he had never shopped there; he could never afford it.

"Papa, I'd like to go into Brighten's."

John looked at Richard curiously. "Are you sure?"

"Yes, Papa! I have always wanted to go in there. Beside, Pharaoh needs new clothing."

John shrugged and followed Richard into the shop. As they entered the store, Mr. Brighten met them with a suspicious look. However, when Richard was dressed in his officer's uniform,

Brighten relaxed, knowing these weren't the usual rabble that wandered the streets looking for a handout.

Phineas Brighten was a gentleman of about forty years. His red hair was thinning, and he wore a sparsely grown beard. He was heavy in stature, having found it too difficult to push himself away from the table when he should have.

"How may I help you, uh gentlemen?"

Richard said, "We have just arrived from a year long voyage at sea and my companions and I would like to buy some new clothes to replace our old rags."

Brighten asked, "What sort of clothing did you have in mind?"

"They just want to replace their work clothing; however, I need something a little nicer. Maybe something suitable for a gentle-man?"

Brighten replied, "I see! Well you gentlemen may want to look at the clothing against that wall. There are trousers and shirts suitable for men working at sea. Young man, I think I have just what you want over here if you would follow me, please."

John and Pharaoh examined trousers on a table along the wall while Brighten led Richard to a rack holding jackets, waist-coats, shirts, and trousers suitable for everyday wear in the city. Richard found a gray wool suit that he favored over all others. He tried on the suit to check its fit and was pleased to see it fit reasonably well; maybe a little large, but it would allow for his growth during the following year. Richard was shown a tie and shirt that would go well with the outfit, so he told Mr. Brighten he was ready to purchase them.

John found a new pair of work trousers and a work shirt, then helped Pharaoh find the same. Finding clothes to fit the large man wasn't easy. Most of the clothing was designed to fit an average-sized man. However, they found a pair of trousers suitable enough to wear on a ship. They would be warm and rugged enough to stand against wear and tear.

John and Pharaoh brought their items to the counter to finish the transaction. Richard told Mr. Brighten, "Please put them all on the same ticket."

Brighten said, "It all comes to £6."

John said, "No, that won't be necessary. I'll pay for my own."

Richard replied, "No, Papa! I will pay! It would be my honor to furnish you and Pharaoh with new clothing. Besides, you will need your money for other things."

John then said, "Thank you, Richard."

Pharaoh also replied, "Thank you."

Mr. Brighten wrapped the clothing in brown paper and tied it with twine. Then, the three left the store and proceeded down the street toward home. Along the way, John stopped at a cart in the marketplace and purchased a loaf of bread, a pound of cheese, and ten pounds of potatoes. Richard bought some figs, apples, and a gallon of cider.

They left the marketplace and proceeded to the Ashworth apartment. John's village flat was on the third level of a five-story dwelling house. It was a tiny place with a stove for cooking and heating, a table with four chairs, a small wardrobe, and two beds, all in the same room. A curtain hung from the ceiling beside each bed to provide Richard and his parents privacy.

As they entered the room, Pharaoh was impressed with how much room there was. His hut back in Africa was nowhere near this large. It was a little dusty from being empty for almost a year but neat and tidy. Richard took Pharaoh over to the bed that had once been his and said, "You can sleep here. Papa and I will share the other bed."

Pharaoh walked over to the bed. It was pretty small, considering his size. Pharaoh placed his hand on the mattress and pushed downward; the bed bounced underneath his touch. He sat on the bed, and it sank nearly to the floor. Pharaoh quickly bounced up and stood with a concerned look on his face.

"I will sleep on the floor. This is too soft for me and too small."

Richard smiled and replied, "Maybe we should put up a hammock for you to sleep in. You're used to that after all. I'll find one for you tomorrow."

Richard suddenly woke from a deep sleep as he heard a commotion outside the window of their flat. Down below on the street, several men with clubs snatched men they found wandering the streets late at night. The press gangs abducted men to serve on the local merchant vessels. Richard woke his papa, "Papa! The press gangs are back!"

John quickly dressed and told Richard, "Quick! Put on your uniform! Wake Pharaoh and have him hide!"

Richard scrambled to Pharaoh's hammock and awoke him, "Pressers are coming! Find a place to hide! They will try to steal you away to another ship!"

Pharaoh leaped from his hammock and found a dark corner to hide in. His dark complexion made him nearly invisible in the caliginous room. Richard quickly dressed in his uniform, but someone began banging on the door before he could finish.

"Open up! We know you're in there!"

John chose not to open the door. He stood next to Richard and waited. He knew they would break through, but he had no intention of offering himself to the mob on the other side of the door. *Boom! Boom! Boom!* The door collapsed into the flat as six ruffians tripped into the darkened room. John tried to reason with the mob, saying, "Wait! We are seamen serving on the *Destiny*! My son here is the first officer!"

One of the men grabbed Richard by the back of his collar and announced, "Not anymore!"

John received a blow to the back of his head, which knocked him unconscious. Pharaoh watched from the dark corner as his companions were forced to go with the pressers. Two men dragged John, one holding each of his arms. Two others took Richard and escorted him out the broken door. The last two men quickly searched for anything of value but found nothing to their liking, so they followed the others into the night.

Pharaoh exited his dark corner and followed from a distance, careful not to allow himself to be seen. He crouched behind carts or wagons, hid in corners of buildings, and lay flat on the ground, anything to conceal himself from everyone. The pressers carried John and escorted Richard back to the docks, where they took them aboard a ship called the *Wind Chaser*, a square-rigged merchant ship not quite as large as *Destiny*.

Pharaoh watched as the pressers left the ship, counting and dividing the money paid by the ship's officer on duty. He waited until the gang of thieves disappeared into the darkness, then scrambled through the docks, searching for *Destiny*. One hundred yards to the north, Pharaoh found her moored where they had left her. He spied the area to ensure no one was watching, then ran to the gangplank, where he found Mr. McGuire standing on the deck.

"Mr McGuire, sir!"

"Pharaoh? What are you doing out here at night? Don't you know the pressers are about? You might have been captured!"

"Yes, Mr. McGuire! I have come to tell you Richard and John Ashworth have been taken by the pressers. They have been taken to another ship by force."

Standing next to him, McGuire turned to David Reynolds and ordered, "Wake the captain, Mr. Reynolds! Tell him what has happened."

"Aye, Mr. McGuire!"

David ran to the captain's quarters and awoke him to tell him how Richard and his father had been captured.

McGuire took out his whistle and began to blow. He blew several times before announcing, "All hands! All hands on deck ready for battle!"

About forty of the seventy-five-man crew stayed onboard the ship while it was docked in Bristol Bay. Others were home with their families or had found someone he could share a bed with on land.

The crew climbed onto the deck, armed and ready for what might lie ahead. Captain Billings was escorted from his quarters by Mr. Reynolds. Billings quickly approached Mr. McGuire and asked, "What is our situation, Mr. McGuire?"

"Sir, Mr. Ashworth and first officer Ashworth have been captured by pressers and taken to another ship against their will."

"Do we know which ship?

"Not by name, Sir. Pharaoh witnessed the kidnapping and knows which ship she be, sir."

Captain Billings looked at the dark man standing nearby and said, "Very well, Mr. Pharaoh, will you arm yourself please and show us the way?"

Pharaoh replied, "Aye, Captain Billings!"

Pharaoh took a sword from one of the men standing by who offered it to him. As they began to walk the gangplank, Captain

Billings turned and ordered, "Mr. Reynolds, the ship is yours. Keep ten men and guard her with your lives."

"Aye, Captain!"

Billings led the way with Pharaoh by his side as they walked southward down the docks. The sun was not yet peaking above the horizon; however, its light was evident because the night was no longer pitch black. As they approached the *Wind Chaser*, Pharaoh raised a finger and pointed in her direction, "That is the ship where Richard and Mr. John were taken."

Captain Billings led the crew to the ship's gangplank, where he began speaking to the officer in charge, "I am Captain Horatio Billings of the *Destiny*. May I come aboard and have a word?"

The man looked over the crowd of armed men following the captain and replied, "Aye, Captain Billings! You may come aboard but your men will need to stay behind."

Billings walked up the gangplank and greeted the officer, "May I have your name, please?"

"I am first mate, Lawrence Young. What is your business here, Captain?"

"Two of my men were brought aboard your ship only a short while ago. I have come to retrieve them. One of them is my first officer Richard Ashworth. The other man is my helmsman and his father, John Ashworth."

Young was a man of slight stature, aged and well-worn. Billings quickly determined that the man was little to be concerned about should it come to a fight to retrieve his men.

Young replied, "I know of no such men having been brought aboard our ship. You must be mistaken, sir."

"One of my men witnessed the pressers bringing them aboard not one hour ago. You will quickly present them to me."

As Young started to deny the charge again, Captain Billings pulled a small pistol from his waistband and pointed it into the officer's gut. The captain spoke quietly so that only Young could hear his words, "Now, sir, you will bring my men forward immediately or I will be forced to open up your gullet and see what you had for dinner last night."

Young began to quiver with fear as he felt the gun barrel pushing against his belly.

"Have my men brought forward and make no fuss of it. All I need do is wink to my first mate there, and you and your ship will be under attack. Do it now."

Young nodded, then slowly turned to one of his crew and ordered, "The last two men brought aboard, have them brought up on deck. They belong to the *Destiny*."

The man turned and went below deck to find the two new men brought aboard. After five minutes, he returned with men carrying John Ashworth and escorting young Richard.

Billings saw that John could not walk alone and asked, "Young Mr. Ashworth, what is wrong with your father?"

"The pressers, sir! They hit him in back of the head with a club for no reason."

"Did they, now?"

Billings turned back to Young and asked, "Did you not notice this young man to be wearing an officer's uniform? Did you think you could steal another ship's crew?"

Young said nothing.

Billings ordered, "Mr. McGuire, please escort Mr. Ashworth and first mate Ashworth back to *Destiny*."

"Aye, Captain!"

Two of Destiny's crew walked up to help John as they walked him back to their ship. Richard followed behind. Young protested by saying, "I paid twenty-one shillings for those men. I expect to be repaid."

Billings replied, "Consider it a lesson learned. No one steals my officers or my crew. Let everyone know, if they try again, they will lose more than twenty-one shillings."

Billings stepped away from Young and whipped the back of Young's head with the pistol before joining his men below. The crew of the *Destiny* cheered the captain as they escorted him back to the ship.

CHAPTER 14

A TIME FOR CHANGE

Bristol, England – 1705: Fifteen-year-old Richard stood at the helm of the merchant ship *Destiny* with a strong wind at his back. He had served *Destiny* and Captain Billings faithfully for three years. Richard was four inches taller, and his body had filled out to meet his five-foot-ten-inch frame. Richard was on his fourth voyage on the square-rigged ship, serving as second mate. Mr. McGuire found a Captain's position on another merchant ship. Samuel McKenzie was now Destiny's first mate. David Reynolds found a first mate position on another vessel. Richard was the youngest to reach the rank of second mate on any merchant vessel sailing out of England.

Destiny was four months into her journey, having sailed around the Cape and nearing the coast of Madagascar. They would soon pull into port and unload their cargo before loading their new shipment of slaves to be delivered to Charlestown.

Pharaoh still served on the ship and was now a competent seaman. He worked directly alongside four other Africans whom Richard had rescued from slavery. Richard needed very little money since he practically lived on the ship. He spent most of his wages on buying the freedom of men fated to live as slaves in the colonies. He had purchased two on each of his last two voyages.

On his second trip to Charlestown, Richard selected two men similar to Pharaoh to add to his crew. *Muuaji Simba*, whose name means Lion Killer, was nearly as tall as Pharaoh. He was leaner than Pharaoh and a little quicker on his feet. Richard changed his name to Caesar.

Mtu Waoga was not as tall as the other two men. However, he was of average height but very strong. He kept his head shaved, making him an easy target for his taller companions, who constantly rubbed his head as if they were making a wish. Richard changed Mtu Waoga's name to Attila.

Richard's last trip to Charlestown brought him in contact with two other men, one quite different from the others. His name was *Mwama wa Mfalme*, whose name meant Son of the King. Richard renamed him Nero. Nero was very intelligent, and although he presented himself with a regal persona, he was in no way above working hard. However, he was also keen to work smart rather than hard. When an obstacle presented itself, Nero stood back to analyze the situation before running in headstrong like the others.

Shujaa Shujaa was the fifth to join Richard's band of African sailors. His name meant Brave Warrior. Richard renamed him Alexander after Alexander the Great. Alexander was afraid of no one and nothing. He wore a contemplative stern look on his face always. Alexander was not as keen about serving on a merchant's vessel as his companions. He cared very little about learning the white man's language. However, serving on a ship was better than the alternative.

Richard stood next to his father, who was manning the helm. Richard took out his spyglass and checked the horizon. The coast of Africa was off the port side of the ship. While he scanned the seas ahead, swinging his glass to the port, starboard, and aft, John checked to see if anyone was within earshot of them. Satisfied they were alone, he said, "I have noticed how much you have grown lately."

Richard looked at his papa and nodded without commenting. "You have to be more careful now."

"I will, Papa."

John commented, "I have noticed you are letting your hair grow out. You have your mama's hair."

Richard's hair was pulled up and tied in the back, but the long, red, curly locks were now prominent. Most men wore wigs to get the look that Richard now wore naturally.

Richard smiled as he said, "Aye, Papa. Better to have Mama's beautiful hair than your little outcroppings."

John snickered.

The two of them stood silently for a while. John then noticed Pharaoh showing the recruits how to secure the sail rigging properly.

"Pharaoh has become quite the sailor," John said.

"Aye, he is smart." replied Richard.

John asked, "Tell me, how many slaves do you intend to rescue?"

Richard looked at his papa and answered, "As many as I can. Someday, maybe I will have a whole crew of Africans."

"What about me? Can I not serve on your crew?"

Richard smiled and replied, "Aye, Papa. We will paint your face black and you will fit right in."

They both smiled at one another, then chuckled.

Destiny pulled into Port St. Felix four days later to unload their cargo. As the crew offloaded the goods brought from England, Richard accompanied Captain Billings to negotiate terms on the sale of the shipment. Typically, the first mate's job was accompanying the captain in such transactions. However, Billings had grown entirely reliant on Richard for his advice on such matters. Richard seemed to have a right mind for negotiating. He was quick-witted, clever, and could see a deal from every angle. Mr. McKenzie was in control of *Destiny* while Richard left the ship with the captain.

They went to the marketplace and met with a man named Rivera. Oscar Alejandro Rivera was a Spanish exile who was making a living through trading. Rivera followed Captain Billings and Richard to the docks where *Destiny* had offloaded her goods. He found one thousand bolts of cloth, two hundred bales of wool, and two tons of sugar there. Rivera was delighted to see the goods that Billings had brought this time, much more than his usual load.

Rivera said, "It is wonderful that you have brought so much to trade, however, I'm afraid you have arrived a little too late. Most of our Africans have already been purchased by a Spanish ship here last week. I only have three hundred slaves to trade you."

Billings replied, "Well these goods are worth so much more than three hundred slaves."

"Si Señor Capitan. Never worry, I will pay the rest in gold. You will not leave here empty handed. I will give you the slaves and pay you £100 in gold."

Billings looked at Richard with a questioning look. Richard entered the conversation for the first time. "Excuse me, Señor Rivera, I believe you have over estimated the value of your Africans. We would need all the slaves and £500 in gold."

Rivera furrowed his brow, looking at young Richard. "Who is this?" he asked Billings.

Billings replied, "This is Mr. Ashworth. He is my negotiator. All deals are now made through him."

Rivera looked back at Richard and replied, "There is no way I will pay £500 and give you three hundred slaves for what you have brought me."

Rivera thought for a minute, looking into Richard's eyes. Richard's expression was stoic. He did not indicate he was worried; he simply waited patiently for a counteroffer.

Finally, Rivera offered, "I will pay you £200 gold, no more."

Richard stared into Rivera's eyes and noticed a slight sense of doubt. "Captain, maybe we should keep going east. We could go to the orient and fill our ship with tea. It would take a little longer but there would be fewer mouths to feed."

"Yes, I see what you mean. They do have good tea in China!"

Rivera began to panic, "I will give you £300 in gold, twenty barrels of salted meat, and all the fruits and vegetables you can carry!"

Richard feigned a look of agony as he pursed his lips and slightly shook his head.

"£350!"

Richard looked at Billings, who then nodded his head in approval.

"Alright, Señor Rivera. You have a deal."

"Ah, bueno! Bueno! We will begin loading right away!"

Captain Billings shook Rivera's hand to seal the deal, then Rivera shook Richard's hand and said, "Señor Richard, you are a very good negotiator. I want you to come and work with me. I will pay you whatever you want."

Richard looked at the Captain, then back at Rivera, and replied, "No, thank you, Señor Rivera. My duties are with the *Destiny.*"

As Richard and Captain Billings walked away, the captain asked, "Are you sure you want to pass up an opportunity like that?"

"Aye, Captain! I love my life at sea and I love the *Destiny*. Even if I were offered a captainship on another vessel I would not take it."

Billings replied, "Glad to hear it, my boy. Glad to hear it indeed."

Shortly after returning to the ship, Rivera's men began loading three hundred Africans onto *Destiny*. Richard stopped at the gangplank and watched as each slave walked aboard. Over and over, Richard would say the word, "*Usiogope! Usiogope!*" Which meant, "Don't be afraid!"

Richard's clan of five, along with some of the white seamen, took the Africans below to the lowermost deck, where they were shackled. The new Africans repeatedly asked Richard's men, "*Utafanya nini na sisi?*" (What will you do with us?)

Pharaoh and the others tried to comfort them by saying, "*usijali utatunzwa vyema!*" (Don't worry, you will be well cared for.)

One man asked in his native tongue, "Who is the white man who speaks our language?"

Pharaoh replied, "He is our savior. He cares for us."

Then the man asked, "Where are they taking us?"

"Far far away to a place called Charlestown. Many of you will be sold to farmers to work for them."

"Why are you not working on these farms?"

Pharaoh replied, "Richard saved me. He saved all of us from becoming slaves to the white men. He purchased my freedom."

The African then said, "But you are not free! You work for him on this boat!"

"I am a sailor. I get paid just like the white men who work on the boat. I am not a slave. What is your name?"

The African replied, "I am *mtu wa tembo*. (elephant man)"

"Why do they call you that?"

"Because my nose and ears are so big!" he replied with a smile.

Pharaoh smiled in return and said, "I have to go now. I will come back later and we can talk some more."

Richard saw Pharaoh come back on deck from the lower deck while Richard stood on the quarterdeck. Richard was proud of his friend, who had taken well to his duties as a sailor. He knew Pharaoh must have missed his family back home in Africa, but Pharaoh never mentioned them.

It took most of the afternoon to finish loading the three hundred slaves and all the food and supplies they would need for their journey to the Americas. At five o'clock, the captain walked out of his quarters to check on the progress and asked Mr. McKenzie, "Are we ready, Mr. McKenzie?"

"Aye, Captain! That we are."

Then Billings asked Richard, "Ready at the helm, Mr. Ashworth?"

"Aye, Captain! Ready at the helm."

"Alright, Mr. Ashworth, take us out bearing west by southwest."

"Aye, Captain!"

Richard announced to the crew, "Let go the bow line!"

A call came back, "Letting go the bow line!"

Richard then called, "Let go the stern line!"

"Letting go the stern!"

Destiny slowly moved away from the docks, floating out to open waters. Then, as she drifted a little from the docks, Richard called out, "Mr. Gant, please lower the foresail!"

"Aye, Mr. Ashworth!" was his answer.

As the foresail was unfurled and tied in place, the ship began to pick up a little speed while catching a bit of a wind from the north. Mr. Crane held the wheel at the helm, steering past reefs and rock formations throughout the bay off Madagascar. John Ashworth stood alongside Crane in case he was needed to help.

Crane had made the journey more than ten years and was quite intimate with the waters around the Cape of Good Hope. John was not quite as familiar, although he, too, had made the trip each of the last four years.

Once *Destiny* passed the coral reefs in the narrow inlet between Madagascar and Africa, Richard commanded, "Full speed, Mr. Gant! Let loose the mainsail, please!"

Gant replied, "Aye, Mr. Ashworth! Gant shouted to men standing on the yardarm of the main mast, "Drop the sheet!"

Several men untied the thongs, which kept the mainsail tied up, allowing the sail to drop toward the deck where other sailors were waiting to stretch the sail by tying the rigging down on the lowest yard of the mainmast. Instantly, the ship lunged forward under the force of the wind, pushing *Destiny* across the waters seemingly without effort.

Chapter 15

Thirty-six days after leaving Madagascar, the ship ran into a storm like none the crew had ever seen. Hurricane-force winds whipped the sails into shreds, and thirty-foot waves bashed the boat's hull, tossing her from side to side and flooding her hull. All hands were summoned above decks to save the ship and her cargo. With no sails to speak of, *Destiny* was at the mercy of the waves and Almighty God. John and Richard stood at the helm, trying desperately to keep her on course. Henry Gant barked orders to the crew as they attempted to fashion together any makeshift sail they could.

The Ashworths worked together at the helm, trying to steer the ship into the waves to keep her from being turned over by the monstrous waves. Several men working on deck were constantly tossed off their feet as wave after wave spilled over the ship's rails.

Strong winds from the southwest moved the ship off course, sending her northwesterly. Another wave dashed over the port rail, sending five crew overboard. There was nothing anyone could do to save them; they were at the mercy of the sea.

As John and Richard pulled against the helm, trying to direct the ship back against the waves, they heard something "*snap*." The ship's steering wheel turned freely in its grasp. They were no longer in control of the rudder or of the ship. Richard knew what must have happened. The rope connecting the rudder to the helm must have snapped in two. There would be no controlling the ship now—all they could do was hold on for dear life and pray for God's mercy.

Destiny was taking on more and more water. Captain Billings called for men to prepare to abandon ship. Several men began preparing the two dories to be set in the water. They would never hold all the men who were still on the ship. They would be lucky to get twenty men in each one of the little boats. Nevertheless, they prepared to abandon ship. Richard asked the captain, "What of the Africans below decks, sir?"

"There's no time, Mr. Ashworth. They are now in the hands of God Almighty!"

Richard was unwilling to accept that fate on their behalf. He called for his "Kings of Africa" to help,

"Pharaoh! Get the others and meet me below! We have to rescue those who are below decks!"

Pharaoh nodded and called for the others, "Caesar, Attila, Alexander, Nero!"

They all looked in his direction as he beckoned them to move toward him. They followed Richard below and began quickly unchaining the slaves shackled in the ship's lowest part. They waded through three feet of water to reach the stranded Africans. They worked quickly, unlocking the chains that held the captives below the ship's decks. The water rose higher and higher as they continued to work. They were running out of time. There would never be enough time to free all three hundred slaves, but they would continue unlocking the shackles for as long as possible.

Six men freed only seventy slaves before a large crack appeared in the ship's hull. Timber began snapping against the weight of the storm's winds and the crashing waves. Richard knew there was no more they could do for the captives without losing their own lives. He called for his men to abandon ship.

"Pharaoh! Nero! All of you, get out of here now! We can't save anymore!"

Richard's African kings abandoned the remainder of the slaves still held under decks and moved everyone up out of the ship's hull. Many were swimming underwater, trying to reach the hatch leading to the next deck. They climbed into the second deck and then onto the main deck, where waves still crashed. The dories were already filled with crew, even overfilled, as Richard climbed out of the ship's hull. Richard searched for his father, calling, "Papa! Papa!"

John had made it into the first dory, waved, and said to Richard, "Richard! Over here!"

It was too late for Richard. The dories were too far away from the sinking *Destiny*. Richard looked around to see who was still on the ship. He saw Captain Billings and First Mate Samuel McKenzie standing at the helm on the quarterdeck. Neither seemed to be concerned that their ship was sinking fast.

Suddenly, a large crack appeared on the deck, and *Destiny* split into two halves. The two parts began to sink away from each other. Richard searched for something they could use to save themselves from the depths of the seas. He soon saw it, the masts. He called out to his men, "Cut loose the mast! All three! We will use them to float us! His men quickly began hacking at the ropes that held the masts into their places on the ship's deck. Some used axes, others used sabers, but they hacked away until each mast was free from the sinking ship. When they freed the masts from the ship's deck, they cut away the yard arms. All three masts began floating away from the quickly sinking ship. Seventy five Africans and Richard found a place for themselves, gripping one of the masts as the sea continued to roll and toss them about.

Richard called out to his people and said, "Tie yourselves to the masts so you don't lose strength and go under."

Those with swords or knives began cutting rope into manageable lengths so that the enslaved people could once again be shackled together, this time so that their lives could be saved. Richard looked around to see where the dories were. He saw them to the west of his location and witnessed men holding onto his papa to keep him from diving into the sea after him. The ship's crew knew there was no way to rescue those in the water. There was no room in the tiny boats for anyone else. Richard looked back at *Destiny* and saw the last of her fall beneath the water's surface, taking Captain Billings and Samuel with her. Tears filled Richard's eyes as he realized his beloved captain was no longer there. He had become so close to the captain. Billings had taught him so much about sailing, navigation, and life in general. He couldn't believe he would never see the good captain again.

Most of all, he realized his father was drifting away from him. Even if Richard somehow managed not to be killed in this storm of the raging sea, he might not ever see his papa again.

The dories continued to move westward through the sea under the power of those who pulled their oars through the waters. Richard and his crew of Africans had no such ability to move through the sea in any particular direction or rate of speed. They were at the mercy of the sea's currents. They would float to wherever the seas took them. If they were lucky, another ship might come along and find them in a few days, or they might find themselves drifting near an island at some point.

Lost items began to float from below the decks of *Destiny* over time. Mostly food items such as oranges, mangos, and papayas. A sea chest floated to the top eventually and floated nearby. Richard recognized it as Captain Billings' chest. With great struggle,

Richard moved the water with his free hand, trying to coax the trunk to move toward him. Frustrated with his lack of success, Richard let go of the mast and swam out to retrieve the chest. He grabbed the chest by one of its leather handles and swam back to his place on the mast, where he tied the chest next to him.

The rains and wind were still pelting the castaways as they floated along together, holding onto the masts. Some of them managed to connect the masts so that they wouldn't drift apart. Others found planks floating in the water and attached them to the masts, creating a makeshift deck for some to lie upon and rest.

The dories were long lost when Richard succumbed to the riggers of holding on for dear life. His clothes were ripped, and he had a gash on his forehead from what he did not remember. His eyes began to droop and finally closed as he fell into a deep sleep.

Richard suddenly woke to screaming, yelling, and thrashing of water. Someone was tugging his shoulders, trying to lift him from the water. He looked up dazedly to see Pharaoh lifting him out of the sea and onto the makeshift raft. Just as he came out of the water, something brushed up against his leg. Richard looked down at the water and saw a fin swimming by him, sticking up out of the water about two feet long. "*Shark*! he realized.

Richard curled his legs up to wrap himself into a ball on the raft. Others were struggling to exit the water and find safety on the raft. One poor man didn't make it in time. He was helping one of the women to take her place on the raft, lifting her from underneath the water. Before he could find his spot on the raft, the shark took a bite out of his right leg and pulled him under the water. The man screamed as his body was plunged under the water. He screamed in anguish as the fish took him underwater, shaking him from side to side like a dog shakes a varmint to kill it. A cloud of blood filled the space where the man had once been. Women and men murmured and cried as they realized the man would not return.

Pharaoh looked at Richard with wide eyes, and Richard thought it was because of the gruesome spectacle of the shark attack. However, when Richard realized Pharaoh was looking at Richard's chest, he knew it was something else. Richard's linen shirt was ripped to shreds and exposed his body to his African friend. Pharaoh looked around to see if anyone else had seen what he had seen. Everyone focused on the waters, searching for more finned monsters. Pharaoh removed his shirt, pulled it over Richard's head to hide his exposed body, and quietly said, "You are not a boy. You are a woman."

Embarrassed, Richard replied, "Yes, and my name isn't Richard, it is Raven."

"Why have you hid yourself for all these years?"

Raven replied, "I had to. After my mother died, it was the only way I could go with Papa to sea. No one would hire a young girl to work on a ship. He had me dress as a boy and said I should tell everyone my name is Richard."

"Does anyone else know about this?"

"No, only you and Papa."

What will we do now?"

Raven replied, "First thing we do is find land. After that, it all depends on where we end up. We have no way to steer this raft so it will be up to God as to where we land."

Pharaoh asked, "Will you tell the others?"

"I see no reason to hide it any longer. Besides, those wraps I had to wear to hide my body were extremely uncomfortable. Thank you for your shirt, by the way. I know African women are used to going without a shirt or anything to cover their breasts, but I don't think I could walk around half naked."

"You are welcome. Raven?"

"Yes, my mother called me Raven. It was one of her favorite birds and they are very talkative. My mother said it was much the same with me. I never knew when to shut my mouth." she said with a smile.

Pharaoh commented, "Ravens are black and you are not black. Even your hair is not black, but red. You are a red raven. I think I would like to call you that. Red Raven."

Raven smiled at her friend as though she agreed. She rather liked the name Red Raven.

CHAPTER 16

Seven days after *Destiny* sank, Raven and her new crew still floated in the sea, clinging to their make-shift raft. Raven's lips were chapped from the blaze of the sun's rays combined with the brisk sea air. Her skin exposed to the sunlight was blistered, red, and sore.

Her companions were no better. Many had drifted away from the raft, unable to hold their grip. The sea's waves eventually took them away and buried them below the surface for eternity. Others fell prey to sharks looking for trails of blood running from the castaways.

Raven scanned the horizon to the east with dreary eyes, hoping to glimpse land in the distance. She rotated her head and looked north. She blinked, then raised her head and blinked again. Her stomach turned, and her heart flipped. Was she imagining things, or was she *actually* seeing land in the distance? She looked around to find Pharaoh; he was hanging onto a plank attached to the main mast, half asleep.

"Pharaoh!" she called. "Pharaoh!"

Pharaoh raised his head and looked toward her. Raven pointed north and asked, "Do you see it? Is it land?"

Pharaoh looked to where Raven was pointing and saw a slight bump on the horizon. The sky was grayish blue, but there was a slight change in hue where the sky met the sea. Pharaoh realized Raven was right. The land was within their grasp. Pharaoh called to the people who were still hanging onto the raft. "Land! There is land! We must move the raft in that direction! Everyone help me!"

Everyone moved to the south side of the raft and dropped their bodies into the water while still holding onto the raft. They all began kicking the water to move the raft toward the little island before them.

Raven feared that the commotion might draw the attention of more sharks, but they had little choice. She kicked along with everyone else while checking behind her for any menacing creatures that might be moving into their area of the sea.

They kicked for what seemed an hour. Everyone's legs and backs were burning and aching, and they could hardly catch their breath. Little progress had been made. It seemed that the tides were working against them. However, they dare not give up. The island was, at the moment, their only chance for survival. So, they continued to kick.

Suddenly, a fin appeared in the distance from behind the raft. It raised from the water, moving east to west, then dipped underwater. A man called out to the others when he spotted the demon slowly hunting for them.

Unfortunately, one of the men had suffered an injury to his right calf muscle, and the injury presented a target to the shark, like a dinner bell ringing in the distance. The fish picked up on the scent of dried blood and damaged flesh as it swam directly for the man. Some people who swam next to the injured man saw the beast approaching them. They abandoned their grip on the raft and swam away from the man, who panicked as he saw the shark heading straight for him. He couldn't move, and he couldn't let go of the raft. He could only manage a scream as the shark bit into his leg and dragged him away from the raft. The shark and the man temporarily disappeared underwater as men and women began screaming as they feared they would be next to fall prey to the giant fish.

Suddenly, the man rose out of the water, gasped for air, and screamed, "Help me! Help me!"

Alexander swam toward the man and took him by his outstretched hand to pull him back to the raft. The man continued to scream for help as Alexander moved him back to the raft. Nero helped Alexander raise the man onto the raft. He wasn't nearly as heavy as they had thought he should be. They realized why when they pulled him up out of the water. The lower half of his body was missing. With wide eyes, the two Africans continued tugging the man to pull him onto the raft. Fear filled their eyes as they witnessed the mangled flesh, bare bones, and bloody pulp dangling above the water where the man's legs were once attached.

Seemingly, out of nowhere, the shark raised itself out of the water and snatched the half-man from Alexander and Nero's grasp. The man disappeared again below the sea's surface and was taken to the depths of the deep blue sea.

Everyone who saw what happened panicked. They either scrambled out of the water and onto the raft or kicked ferociously, attempting to reach the island at record speed. Their adrenaline kicked in, and they seemed even more determined to reach their destination.

They continued swimming and pushing the raft forward for another hour. There had been no more sign of the shark. They had hoped he was satisfied with the single morsel he found among them. The island was much closer now. However, it was still at least two miles away. Luckily, the tide was in their favor, pushing with them as they swam toward the tiny stretch of sand and trees. The sun was sinking fast, and they could feel the waves pushing them toward the slight bit of land. They relaxed and let the waves push them toward the island. Their muscles ached and burned, and their lungs were gasping for air. Each of them dragged themselves back onto the raft and lay sprawled on the planks, unable to move another inch. Their energy was utterly spent. After a week without fresh water and days without food, they had all but given up hope of finding a place of refuge.

Slowly, the raft inched its way to the shore of the tiny island. Two hours later, the raft landed on the beach. Many of the castaways had fallen asleep from exhaustion. Raven suddenly recognized that they were no longer moving along with the rhythm of the waves. Instead, the waves splashed over them as they lay on the raft. She raised her head and saw that they had come to rest on the sandy shore of the island they had hoped to reach.

"Wake up!" she called to her companions.
"Wake up! We made it!"

The others began to stir slowly, raising their heads and peeking around to see where they had landed. They began murmuring to each other in their African tongues. Some were excited to be no longer stranded on an unprotected raft. Others were upset that they were in the middle of nowhere. How would they survive here? How could they get back home?

Raven called her five kings together and instructed them, "We need to get that raft up on the beach so the tide doesn't carry it away. We might be able to build a seaworthy boat out of the materials."

Pharaoh and the others instructed the people to drag the raft away from the water. They all gathered to one side of the raft, lifted it out of the water, and began pulling it toward a group of palm trees at the edge of a forest. The three masts were very heavy, and trying to carry them all simultaneously was too cumbersome, so Raven suggested, "Cut the ropes and carry the masts one at a time."

The people did as Raven suggested. They cut the raft's ropes apart, then carried each mast onto the beach. Then, they took the planks used as decking for the raft and laid them alongside the masts. They also brought the items they had fished from the water while the *Destiny* sank. A sea chest was one of those items. Raven decided to open it and see what was inside that might be of use to them. She found a spyglass, a sextant, and several sea charts inside. The charts were soaking wet and beginning to disintegrate. Raven carefully removed the charts and laid each one out to dry.

Raven decided to divide the people into five groups, each led by one of the five kings. She instructed Pharaoh, "Call the people together and tell them to line up to be counted."

Pharaoh did as Raven requested, speaking in his native language. "Everyone! Everyone! Please come together and stand before Raven so you can be counted."

The people murmured to each other but did as they were told.

"Pharaoh, you and my other men will stand with me in front of the people, please."

Pharaoh, Attila, Alexander, Nero, and Caesar stood beside Raven.

Raven then walked along, counting the men and women who had survived the shipwreck. She counted sixty-eight men and five women. She then returned to her men and said, "Pharaoh, Caesar, and Attila, I want each of you to select thirteen men to work with you. Nero and Alexander, you will select twelve men each. Please take your men tomorrow morning and begin exploring the island. We need fresh water, food, shelter, and firewood for warmth and cooking. We will take shelter under the trees tonight and hope it doesn't rain. Select one of your men to guard the camp while the rest sleep. Set up a rotation to relieve each guard every two hours. At daybreak, we will begin our search of the island."

Raven's kings did as they were instructed. Each man chose one of their group to stand watch for the first two hours while everyone else slept. One man in Pharaoh's group was a disgruntled individual named Kuwa na Wasiwasi (Be Worried). He seemed never to be happy about anything he was told to do. When instructed to take the first watch, he asked Pharaoh, "Why do I have to watch first?"

Pharaoh replied, "Worry, why not? Are you better than any other man here?"

Worry asked, "Why do you take orders from a woman who pretends to be a man?"

"She is not just a woman. She is the woman who saved our lives. We would all be slaves in a white man's world if she had not saved us. Unlike the white man who steals us from our homes, she treats us well. You would be sitting at the bottom of the ocean if she had not saved you. She has taught us to speak and read her language and she has taught us how to be sailors. She has put clothes on our backs and food in our stomachs. She will do the same for you all. Now go, and do as you have been told. Someone will take your place in two hours, then you can sleep."

Pharaoh handed Worry a machete to use as a weapon should the need arise. Worry joined the other guards who had been selected for the first watch from the other clans.

Raven took the women with her to the center of the camp. They made their beds among the men who had spread themselves around the camp's perimeter. Raven had not talked to any of the women until now, so she took the opportunity to introduce herself and learn their names. "I am Raven Ashworth." She said in their language. "You may call me Raven or Red Raven."

She then listened as each woman introduced herself. The first was called Ua Nyekundu (Red Flower). Raven said, "How pretty! I would like to give you all a name in my language. I will call you, Rose. The rose is a beautiful red flower in my country."

Rose smiled at Raven and nodded her approval. Raven guessed Rose to be about sixteen years old. She was the tallest and one of the older women.

The next woman said she was Wimbo wa ndege (Bird Song). Raven thought her to be much younger, maybe twelve or thirteen. She was small and delicate. Raven said, "I will call you Birdie."

Next came Mwanamke wa maisha mapya (Woman of New Life). Raven had to ponder this name. New life to her reminded her of Spring when everything grew anew. Raven decided to call her April.

Then there was a woman about Rose's age. She said her name was Wimbo wa usiku (Night Song). Raven decided to name her Melody. It suited her well because Melody often hummed to herself while working on any task or even sitting idle.

The last young woman was about fourteen years old. She was a bit plumper than the others, and she never seemed to be happy. Raven asked her, "What is your name?"

The girl didn't want to tell her. She sat staring at Raven and the others but said nothing.

"Do you speak?"

The girl still said nothing.

Raven then said, "You are Moja tulivu (Quiet One). It is alright not to speak. Sometimes people speak too much. I would like to call you Whisper. That is what your name means in my language. Is that alright?"

The girl gave only a slight nod to Raven.
Raven then said, "Alright, we have had a strenuous day. Let's all go to sleep. Tomorrow we have much to do."

CHAPTER 17

Raven awoke to seagulls squawking overhead and waves crashing against the beach. A strong breeze blew in from the sea, chilling her to her bones. They had not yet been able to build a fire, and wearing wet clothing during the night wasn't helping.

When she rose, Raven saw Caesar standing beside the ocean, looking at the empty sea. Raven walked over to him and stood next to him.

"Are you searching for something?"

"No. I'm just wondering about how I came to be here. Three years ago I was hunting with my brother to get meat for our village. As we walked down a trail that we have walked many times before, we suddenly fell into a trap. We were caught into a net and we dangled from a tree. White men came and cut us down after a long time, but they did not free us. They took us captive and intended to make slaves of us."

Raven asked, "Where is your brother, now?"

"I do not know. He was sold to another ship and taken away before I was bought by Captain Billings. I hope he is well, but I will never know for sure."

"I'm sorry, Caesar. I wish I could have saved him too."

They stood silently for a long while before Attila ran toward them and said, "Raven! One of the women is missing!"

"Are you sure? Maybe she just went into the forest to relieve herself."

"No! The man called Worry is also missing. I think he has taken her."

Raven, Caesar, and Attila ran back to the camp. They found Pharaoh searching the beach for tracks left by Worry and the young girl, Birdie. Birdie's tracks were distinctive because her feet were so small. Raven followed Pharaoh along with Caesar and Attila, as Pharaoh followed the young girl's tracks while Nero and Alexander stayed behind to watch the rest of the people. Worry's tracks were visible, too. From time to time, only his tracks were visible.

Pharaoh pointed them out and said, "Look! He has picked her up and carried her. She is not with him willingly. He has taken her by force."

Raven asked, "Can you tell how long ago?"

"Two or three hours. We must hurry!"

Pharaoh led the band quickly through the forest. Now and then, Pharaoh would pause to examine the tracks more closely, then lead on, sometimes changing direction. After an hour, he suddenly stopped and raised a hand, signaling the others to freeze. He put his finger to his lips to tell them they needed to be quiet. Pharaoh peered through tree branches and saw something important. He turned to Caesar and signaled for him to move around to the right. He then motioned for Attila to circle to the left. When he was sure the other two were in position, Pharaoh slowly moved forward with his sword ready. He and Raven tip-toed into a clearing, where they found Worry and Birdie asleep under a large tree. Worry never heard them coming. Pharaoh walked up to the man and then placed the point of his blade at the man's throat under his chin. Worry slowly opened his eyes, then realized he had a sword at his throat.

He raised his hands in surrender as Attila and Caesar walked into the clearing. Birdie whimpered as she lay curled up next to Worry just inches away. She shivered in her sleep, either from fear or the chill of the night or both. Raven walked over to Birdie and carefully awoke her.

"Birdie? Birdie! Are you alright?"

Birdie awoke and found Raven stooping next to her. Uncontrollably, she began crying as Raven took Birdie into her arms to comfort her.

Pharaoh asked Raven, "What will we do with this one?"

Raven replied, "Tie his hands. We will take him back to camp. I'll decide what to do with him after I have spoken to Birdie."

Pharaoh did as Raven said. He tied Worry's hands behind his back and pushed him forward at the point of his sword toward the beach. Birdie was so distraught she could hardly walk, so Attila picked her up and carried her.

Two hours later, they arrived at camp to find everyone stirring, but nothing was being done. No one had taken the initiative to begin foraging for food or firewood, and Raven was upset by the sight. Everyone stood in silence as she and the others walked into camp.

"Pharaoh, have one of your men stand guard over Worry. Put him somewhere away from camp. There, under that tree."

Pharaoh selected one of his crew to stand guard over Worry. Samaki Mtu (Fisherman) was given a machete and instructed to guard the prisoner. Fisherman was no more than eighteen, thin and tall, but Pharaoh thought he could do a simple task like watching a bound man.

Raven gathered her five and instructed them to search the jungle for food, fresh water, and firewood.

Caesar asked, "What about Worry? Will he be punished?"

Raven replied, "He will be dealt with, but we need to take care of other things right now."

Each band of men was sent out in five different directions throughout the island. Raven stayed behind with the women, Fisherman, and Worry. Raven tried to comfort Birdie and get her to tell her what had happened to her. Through sobs and tears, Birdie told Raven, "The man took me while I was sleeping. He put his hand over my mouth so I could not scream. He dragged and carried me into the jungle very far away. He then took my body to be with his and did terrible things to me. He hurt me!"

Raven again tried to comfort the young girl, "Don't worry, he will not hurt you again. No one will hurt you. Not as long as I am around to protect you. Understand?"

Birdie looked into Raven's eyes and asked, "How can you make such a promise? You are only a woman like us."

Raven stood at the beach's edge, contemplating the morning's events. What would she do with the man Worry? She had never been in complete charge of this many people. The second mate was quite different from being captain of an entire crew. Everyone looked to her for answers, guidance, and discipline regarding Worry.

Worry sat beneath the tree, fidgeting with his ropes. The young guard, Fisherman, took little notice of the man to whom he was given charge. Somehow, Worry loosened his bindings enough that he was able to free himself. He made a plan.

"Ah!" he screamed. "Something has bitten me! Can you check my hands?"

Fisherman walked over and bent down to check Worry's hands. Worry swung both his hands from behind him and crushed the boy's ears into both sides of his head. Fisherman fell to the ground in pain, letting go of his machete. Worry quickly grabbed the machete and swung it down into the boy's neck, nearly decapitating him. Fisherman died immediately.

Raven heard the scream Worry made in faking injury to the boy. She turned to witness the slaying of Fisherman by the hand of Worry. She quickly took up her sword and ran to the tree where Fisherman's body lay. Worry faced Raven with the blade in his hand and announced, "I am a warrior, and you are only a girl. You are no match for me."

Raven smiled with the knowledge that she had been well trained in the art of hand–to–hand combat with sword or fist. Although Worry was much larger and stronger than she, he would be no match for her. Her saber had a much longer blade than the machete giving her an additional advantage.

Worry lunged at her with his machete, and she raked away his blade with her own. He then gathered himself and swung the machete wildly at her repeatedly, never coming close to striking her. Raven playfully pierced his left shoulder with the tip of her sword, causing him to bleed. Worry shook off the minor wound and lunged at her again. Raven swiped his blade away again like she might a bothersome mosquito. For some unknown reason, Worry decided to taunt Raven.

"After I kill you, I will take your body just as I did with the girl last night!"

Raven was done having fun with her opponent. Her anger boiled at the mention of how he had defiled the young girl. He would never harm another living being. Raven lunged at Worry driving her saber through his heart and out of his back. Worry fell into the sand, and the blade of her sword protruded six inches from his back.

Worry gurgled on his blood that had welled up into his chest, throat, and mouth. His eyes were frozen open in pain and shock at having been beaten by a young girl in a sword fight. Raven turned her back and left him to slowly die as she returned to Birdie and the other women.

Raven was not new to killing. She had killed her first man at the age of twelve on her first voyage on *Destiny*. There had been others too. She wasn't bloodthirsty by any means. However, she never shied away from a fight.

Raven returned to the women who had witnessed the sword fight between Worry and Raven. They all looked at Raven with a new sense of respect and loyalty. Raven had done what most men were either unable or unwilling to do for one of them. April commented in her native language as Raven stood before them, "The Red Raven has protected her young. We vow our allegiance to you, Raven."

The other women uttered their agreement to April's comment. Each of them stood and embraced Raven one at a time. Birdie was the last to hug Raven. Her embrace continued for a while before she let go.

Raven said, "I will give my life to protect all of you."

The five clans began filtering into camp about an hour before sundown. Caesar's group was the first to arrive. His men carried clusters of bananas, mangos, and coconuts. As Caesar approached Raven, he glanced over to the tree where Worry had been tied and saw two bodies lying lifeless in the sand. He looked at Raven and asked, "What happened?"

"Worry managed to free himself of his bonds. He attacked Fisherman and killed him. I did the same to Worry."

Caesar replied, "We must bury our friend, Fisherman quickly before his spirit gets lost and cannot find its way. We will burn the body of Worry so he can never find his way home."

Caesar took his men and started preparing a burial site for Fisherman in the sand near the jungle. Some dug a grave with their hands, while others gathered wood to create a great fire to burn Worry's body.

Pharaoh and his men returned soon after Caesar returned. They carried food as well. When he approached Raven, he said, "We have found fresh water. A spring feeds water into a pool about three miles from here. There is a clearing nearby where we can build huts."

Raven replied, "That sounds good. We'll return at first light tomorrow."

"What has happened here?"

"I will tell everything once the others have returned."

Moments later, Attila and Nero's groups arrived. They carried wood suitable for burning and bamboo that they intended to make spears out of for fishing. Not long after, Alexander arrived. They, too, brought food and firewood.

Everyone gathered around Raven as she prepared to inform them of her plans. She spoke to them in Swahili, saying, "People of the great ship, *Destiny*. We have found ourselves stranded on this island far from our homes. We have few supplies, weapons, or tools, but we have our lives and we have our determination to survive. If we work together we can accomplish whatever we want. Worry has already shown what happens when we think only of ourselves. He chose his needs and wants above everyone. If we don't work together as one, we will not survive. However, if we work together and look after one another, we will not only survive but thrive."

The people began low vocals of approval.

"The first thing we will do is deal with our dead. I will leave that up to you. I know little of your burial customs and don't want to interfere with them, so the ones I call my kings, Pharaoh, Caesar, Attila, Nero, and Alexander will see to it. They are your leaders. Treat them with respect and they will serve you well as they have served me."

The people grew a little louder with their comments of approval.

"Pharaoh has found a place suitable for our survival while here on this island. A place we can build temporary shelters, and we will have fresh water to drink and bathe in. We will travel there in the morning. Let me say this, this place will not be our new home. It is a place we must abide for a short time. We will build longboats that will allow us to travel across the seas, all the way to Africa if need be. It will take time, but we can do it. None of you will be slaves for any white man as long as I have a say in the matter."

The people began to cheer, and they raised their hands and voices in approval of the words of The Red Raven.

Chapter 18

The next morning, Raven woke her people just before day-light. Many of them had not had fresh water in several days. The coconuts and mangos they had the previous day helped replace some of their fluids, but they still needed water. They packed up what little gear they had and began the trek to the new location Pharaoh and his crew had found three miles away. Pharaoh and his crew led the way, cutting a trail with their machetes. The women followed, with all the other men bringing up the rear.

Black spider monkeys gathered in the trees to watch as the odd parade passed them. Some of the monkeys threw mango pits at the strange beings that walked below the jungle's canopy. They squealed and hooted as they ran from tree to tree.

Several times during the walk, Pharaoh or one of his men spotted a snake and killed it with their machete. They cut the head off, then handed the snake to someone near the middle of the caravan to carry. The snake would provide needed protein for the group.

Raven took notice of several species of trees growing along the path; Mahogany would be helpful in building their longboats, Penny Piece and Lois Doux provided an edible fruit, and Bitter Ash leaves could be crushed and rubbed onto their skin to act as an insect repellent, and Mahoe a tree whose bark could be made into rope. Most everything they might need to survive could be found here in the jungle; they just needed to know what to look for. Luckily, Raven had studied Mr. Greer's medical books intently while serving on the *Destiny*. Her studies provided her with knowledge of medicinal plants and various other types of plant life.

An hour and a half later, they arrived at the pool Pharaoh and his band had found the day before. The people instantly flocked to the pool, jumping in to cool themselves and quench their thirsts.

The pool was about a quarter of an acre in size. On the west side of the water was a tall cliff providing a waterfall that filled the pool from a spring somewhere above inside one of the small mountains on the island. On the south side of the pond was a small stream providing a spillway for water to overflow from the pool. The stream flowed to some unknown location on the island that had not yet been discovered.

Seventy-seven people splashed and played in the water like little children. The cool water was exhilarating.

Raven allowed everyone to have fun for a while, then brought them back to reality.

"There is much to do. We need shelter right away. Cut bamboo and palm fronds; enough to build six large shelters. Some of you find some Mahoe trees and gather bark to make rope to tie the bamboo together. We will need more than those few snakes to feed us so make spears for fishing. It will take much fish to feed all of us. Let's begin!"

Pharaoh and the other kings put their men to work, clearing bamboo and trees around the pool to construct shelters. All the people were well versed in building huts since they had done so many times back home in Africa. More than seventy strong men and women made the six structures quickly. They finished by dusk that night.

Raven proved to be a great leader. She could see things that needed to be accomplished before others thought there might be a need. She made plans for the future. The future did not include living on the island indefinitely. The future to Raven meant getting off this island and back onto a ship. She loved the sea and the freedom it provided. She could go anywhere and see anything by traveling across the ocean.

Since shelter was no longer a concern, Raven assigned her crew two primary tasks: building the longboats that would take them away from this island and training her people in hand-to-hand combat. Pharaoh and the other kings were already well-trained in using swords, knives, and guns. Since there were no guns to train their men, they would teach them how to fight and protect themselves using knives and swords.

Every day before work began on boat building, The men were taught the art of fencing. Since there weren't enough swords or machetes, they used bamboo sticks to teach their students. Raven taught the women how to fight, too. She didn't want anyone to rely on someone else to save them in dire circumstances. Everyone would be capable of protecting themselves. Not only were they taught the finer points of fencing and fisticuffs, but Raven also taught them all the dirty tricks they might need to win a fight. She believed there was nothing noble about losing your life in a battle that could be won by alternate means. Survival was all that counted.

After fighting class, everyone went about their regular duties. Twenty of the men were sent to the beach to fish. They made fishing spears out of bamboo rods. They split one end of the rod into four sections and sharpened the tips of each section with a knife. They then placed a rock into the base of the split and tied it into place with reed. This helped to spread the prongs apart on the spear so that more area could be covered as the spear was thrust underwater.

They waded into the ocean and waited, searching for fish to come within reach of their spears. The water was clear, with beautiful hues of aqua blue, making it easy to see any fish that might happen to swim near them. As fish were speared, they were tossed onto the beach, where someone else would place them into a basket made from reed found on the island.

The remaining men were sent into the jungle to search for suitable wood to build their boats. Mahogany was plentiful and would be ideal for what they would need. They searched for just the right shape and size, tall and straight, about three feet in diameter. They had no axes, so they would have to cut the trees down with their machetes. It was long, tedious work. Although the machetes were sharp, they didn't provide the weight a good ax would have given to make deep cuts into the tree's base. What usually would have taken less than an hour using an ax took nearly three hours with the machete. Wood chips and tree limbs procured from bucking off the branches were gathered and carried back to camp to use as firewood and starter.

Once a tree had been cut down, it was split in half using wooden carved wedges and stone mallets. Each half of the tree would be suitable for carving out a canoe. One end of the tree was shaped to present a point so the canoe could move quickly through the water. The other end was left squared so a rudder could be attached later. They removed the bark from the tree, then began carving out the half-tree's center to create the canoe's inner shell where they would sit while paddling. They used fire to burn the inside and cut away the burnt areas.

Once the trees had been cut down and the carving of the canoes had begun, twenty men were left to finish the canoes. The rest of the men started building weapons and boat paddles from materials on the island. Some spears were carved out, but they were most intent on making bows and arrows. All the men were skilled at making weapons; they had done so back in Africa as soon as they were old enough to hold a carving knife.

Three weeks had passed since they had washed up on the island. Raven was pleased with how the men and women of her crew worked well together. They would make a fine crew for a ship if they ever made it back onto one.

Once the canoes were shaped entirely to their liking, they were moved to the beach. While on the beach, they were fitted with outriggers so the waves wouldn't easily tip over the canoes.

Six canoes were finally ready to challenge the open sea. None of the crew had ever rowed in the open sea except Pharaoh who had rowed a dory while trying to save a fellow crewman on the *Destiny*. It would take practice for each canoe crew to get used to the movement of the canoe through the water and the cadence of their rowing. Raven and each of the five kings would take their place at the helm of each canoe. They would be responsible for calling out the cadence of the strokes with the paddles.

The crews spent days practicing their strokes and cadences as the boats moved quickly through the water. The men learned quickly and worked together well. They rowed mile after mile each day, developing their skills and stamina for the day they would finally leave the island.

One evening, as they returned to camp, Raven heard a tiny squeak just off the trail. She left the trail to investigate and found a small white-faced Capuchin clinging to his dead mother on the ground. Raven couldn't discern how the mother monkey had died but knew the little one wouldn't survive without help. Raven picked up the baby and cradled him against her chest, rubbing his little head. "Come with me, little one. I'll take care of you."

Raven and the monkey became inseparable. She carried him on her shoulder everywhere Raven went. She decided to name him Captain Billings because the white hairs of his face mimicked how the Captain had always brushed his beard outward from his face. At night, the captain would lie curled up against Raven's face as she slept. The crew was quite amused by Raven and her monkey. Many people began calling them the Raven and the monkey, only not to her face.

Day 73 after the sinking of Destiny

The sun had not yet risen, but her light was already evident in the gray sky over the ocean. A man called Mtoto wa Daktari (son of the healer) stood at the edge of the jungle searching for anyone or anything that might present danger to the crew. Raven continued the ritual of rotating guards throughout the night, not only for safety but also for the possibility of rescue. Guards were set up on each side of the island. Raven also set up an observation station at the top of the tiny mountain in the island's center. Five men, one from each clan, were stationed atop the hill. Their sole mission was to search for approaching ships. Raven had sent her spyglass with them to the mountaintop.

Daktari caught a glimpse of movement to the south. He thought he had seen a quick flash of light in the distance. He stared in the direction he thought he had seen the light, hoping to spot it again.

Mtazamaji wa Anga (Sky Looker) searched the horizon with the spyglass. He looked west, then turned to the south. A small light flashed in the lens of the spyglass. Sky froze in his position, pointing south. He waited. There it was, another flash of light. Sky waited, keeping his glass pointed in the same direction he had seen the light. Fifty feet in front of the light, Sky noticed what appeared to be a small boat. He waited and watched as the vessel moved closer to the island. After several minutes, he could finally see that it was a dory. In the dory were eight men and four barrels. He surmised they were coming to collect fresh water for their ship. Sky still couldn't see the ship but chose to signal the camp anyway.

Sky took out his conch shell and blew. The deep whistle of the conch could be heard for miles from atop the mountain. Daktari also blew his conch to acknowledge the sighting.

Raven awoke to the sound of the conch horns. She was suddenly adrenaline-filled as she exited her hut, Captain Billings clinging to her shoulder. Raven waited for another signal. One prolonged blast on the conch indicated a ship was in sight. Raven found Pharaoh and said, "Sound the return!"

Pharaoh took a conch, blasted three blasts, waited, and blew three more times. Everyone in the camp scattered from their huts and assembled at the center of the camp. Raven asked the crowd around her, "Did anyone hear the second horn? Where did it come from?"

Attila replied, "It came from the south beach."

Raven ordered, "Alright, everyone gather your weapons and scatter into the jungle around camp. We will wait for them here. They will come to fill their water barrels no doubt. When I blow the horn we will surround them. Don't kill them unless they try to kill you. Understood?"

The crowd murmured their understanding. Suddenly, Raven heard another succession of horn blasts, two quick blasts of the conch blown three times, indicating two dories, not one. Daktari heard the signal as well. He stared into the southern distance and saw the second dory a quarter of a mile behind the first. He continued to wait to see if another dory would be sent from the ship, which was still out of sight. Daktari decided to shimmy up the trunk of a coconut tree just inside the jungle at the beach's edge. He hid himself among the branches at the top of the tree and watched the small boats as they rowed to shore.

Thirty minutes later, the first boat arrived at the beach. The dory carried four large barrels, which the eight men unloaded onto the sand and began to roll into the jungle. The group leader was dressed in an officer's blue naval uniform with white trim and carried a sword and pistol on his belt. The rest of the men were dressed in typical merchant sailor attire.

As the officer approached the jungle, he noticed a clearly cut trail. He paused at the entrance, wondering about the path. He had been to this island before, and the path was never this clear. Then he noticed the footprints in the sand.

"Keep an eye out. Someone has been here recently."

The sailors rolled their barrels into the jungle, each man shifting his eyes from left to right. They tried to listen for signs that someone might be watching; however, the sound of the barrels rolling over the sand and dried fallen branches on the trail was too loud.

CHAPTER 19

Thirty minutes later, the second dory arrived on the beach led by a junior officer wearing a blue naval uniform. The boy was not more than sixteen and quite green as an officer of a merchant vessel. Daktari heard the young officer as he spoke to his men. Somehow, Daktari got the impression that the men under his command did not respect the boy. He heard one of them call the officer, Mr. Sidney.

Mr. Sidney spoke to his men as if they were new recruits who knew nothing about retrieving supplies from the island.

"Alright, Mr. Lindsey, tie up the dory on those rocks over there. Men, let's get those barrels unloaded, now. Alright, roll them this way, toward me. Right then, follow me."

Daktari saw several men shake their heads with each of the young officer's orders. One spoke loud enough for Daktari to hear him say, "What did we do to get lined up with this landlubber?"

Another one said, "Aye, I druther be keel hauled."

Young Mr. Sidney ignored the comments and continued leading the crew through the jungle. He either didn't care that they didn't respect him, or he was oblivious that they talked about him.

Once Sidney and his group vanished from Daktari's view, He let out from the top of his tree with a peacock's call, "*Ah-ah, ah-ah, ah-ah!*"

From deep in the jungle, his call was returned, "*Ah-ah, ah-ah, ah-ah!*"

Raven heard the calls informing her that the last of the sailors who would be coming onto the island had arrived. Just as the call was received, the first group entered the camp area at the spring. The small band of sailors was led by a man the others referred to as Mr. Gaines. He, unlike Mr. Sidney, was well respected by his men. Gaines didn't feel the need to hover over his men like a mother hen.

As they entered the clearing, Gaines was shocked to see six large bamboo huts spread out in the clearing. He cautioned his men, "Keep an eye out. Someone's been living here of late. They might still be around."

The men rolled their barrels into the pool and began filling them. Filling the barrels would take a while. First, they removed a cork stopper on one end of the barrel where a tap was typically placed. They submerged the barrel below the water to let it fill as much as possible. Then the men used gourd dippers to pour water into the small hole where the stopper had been removed until the water level was all the way to the top, then they replaced the plug.

Thirty minutes after they had begun filling their barrels, the second crew arrived to fill the second load. Raven waited until the second crew entered the water and began filling their barrels before she blew her conch.

Suddenly, the sailors found themselves surrounded by dark-skinned men holding primitive weapons. The sailors raised their hands to signal they were no threat. Raven stepped out from her hiding place in the jungle and walked closer to Gaines as she spoke, "Whose crew are you?"

Gaines replied, "We sail on the merchant vessel, *Scarlett Marie*."

"What does she carry? Is she a slaver?"

"She is. We're bound for Accra on the coast of Ghana."

Raven said, "So, what are you carrying to Accra?"

Gaines replied, "We picked up a load of textiles from London. We aim to trade them in Accra. What do you know of merchant ships?"

"I was second sate on *Destiny* until about three months ago. She got wrecked in a storm south of here. Captain Billings and our first mate went down with her. We lost about two hundred Africans to the deep. I don't know where the rest of our crew ended up."

Gaines asked, "You were second mate of *Destiny*? But you're a girl! What does a girl know about sailing a merchant ship?"

"Glad you noticed! I've been sailing on *Destiny* since I was twelve years old. I reckon I know just about everything about sailing there is to know."

Gaines scoffed.

Raven then asked, "How many crew you got on the little bitty ship of yours?"

"She's got fifty good strong sailors."

"Got any canon?"

Gaines chose not to answer any more of Raven's questions. Raven noticed he clammed up on her and replied, "Well, I reckon we'll see soon enough, won't we?"

Gaines sneered.

Raven spoke to her crew in Swahili and said, "Tie them up! One per tree!"

Raven then blew three long blasts on her conch, indicating to everyone within earshot that the men had been captured and all should return.

Daktari climbed down from his tree and waited for everyone to join him on the beach. One by one, he was joined by other lookouts from other beaches on the tiny island. Raven's lookout post was abandoned, and her men rejoined her at the campsite, where they found sixteen naked invaders tied to trees. Sixteen men were tied to sixteen Palms with their hands wrapped behind them and around the tree trunk. Raven chose sixteen of her crew to wear the clothing recently stripped from the invading sailors. Raven's crew gathered food, water barrels, and weapons to begin the trek back to the beach, where two dories awaited them.

Raven had prepared for this moment. Her men had made eight stretchers out of bamboo and rope netting. Four men carried each water barrel onto a stretcher and then through the jungle. Carrying the barrels on stretchers was much quicker than rolling them through the jungle.

An hour later, everyone gathered together on the beach. Raven's men loaded the water barrels onto the two dories, and Raven told the selected men and five women to get into the boats and begin rowing back to the ship. "Don't be too quick. Give us time to launch our boats before you approach the ship."

She told the women, "When you get close enough to see men on the ship, stand up and let them see you. They will be delighted to see women coming toward their ship."

Raven then led the rest of her people to another beach, a mile west of where the dories were. They pulled their canoes out of hiding and launched them into the sea. The long boats moved quickly through the open ocean. Raven hoped that the distraction she presented by sending the women on the dories would allow her long boats to sneak in undetected.

Pharaoh steered the tiller of the first dory. He kept his head down so those looking down from the ship might not be able to tell he was dark-skinned. All the other men kept their backs to the vessel as they approached. When his boat came within one hundred feet of the ship, Pharaoh told the three women in his boat, "Stand up and wave to the men on the ship. Show them how happy you are to see them."

The women did as Pharaoh told them. They stood, called out to the boat, and waved to the men standing beside the starboard rail. The men were shocked but delighted to see five naked women approaching their ship. The men began hooting and whistling as the dories came closer, which drew the attention of every man onboard the ship. Forty men stood at the starboard rail calling out to the women, waving to them, and inviting them to come aboard. Their captain was slightly amused but managed to remain stone-faced throughout the presentation.

Raven and the long boats reached the ship on the port side just minutes after the dories arrived. The canoes were tied to the *Scarlett Marie* as everyone climbed up the ship's port side and surrounded the ship's remaining crew.

Raven brandished her sword with Captain Billings clinging to her shoulder as she approached the captain and said, "My dear Captain, I have you at a disadvantage. Will you surrender?"

With a deep sigh and a lowered countenance, the captain replied, "Young lady, I fear I have no choice. What will you do with us?"

Raven replied, "I want only your ship and its cargo. You and your men may row to the island and join your men there."

The captain moved to the starboard rail to join his crew when Raven said, "No Captain! Your boats are on the port side."

The captain was confused by this announcement but walked over to the port side and looked down into the water, where he saw five canoes with outriggers.

Raven then told her men, "Cut away the outriggers. These men are excellent sailors, they won't need them."

The Africans laughed at Raven's comment as they followed her instructions and cut away the outriggers. Then, Raven had them remove a section of the port rail that was typically removed during the loading and unloading of merchant ships. As the captured sailors approached the rail, each was searched for weapons and relieved of them. Knives, clubs, pistols, and swords were collected and piled onto the deck of the newly captured ship. Thirty-two men were helped to enter the sea's salty water as each was pushed off the ship. They struggled to climb into the canoes, which continuously turned over whenever someone tried to climb onto the unstable boats. Ultimately, the best they could do was cling to the canoes While using them to aid them as they swam to shore.

The water barrels and food were loaded onto the ship, and the dories were brought aboard before they weighed anchor to begin their maiden voyage as a crew. Raven set up officers for her crew of amateur sailors. Pharaoh would be her first mate since he had the most experience aboard a ship. Caesar was assigned as the second mate. Attila, Nero, and Alexander were given ranks of first, second, and third officers, respectively. As second mate, Caesar would be in control of the helm for the most part. He was given two men to teach as his helmsmen.

Raven then instructed a few of the men and women to search the ship for anything of use that the sailors might have left behind. Raven searched through the captain's quarters and found everything she would need to help them navigate to any destination they might decide upon: charts, sextants, compasses, and more. She even found an extra captain's uniform in his sea chest. It was a little large, but she knew she could tailor it to fit her needs. Additional clothing was found below the decks where the sailors' sleeping quarters were located. The women returned on deck carrying a bolt of colorful cloth among the textiles slated to be sold or traded in Africa. The women began cutting and sewing the fabric together to make themselves clothes. Raven asked the women, "Did you see any red cloth while you were searching?"

Rose replied, "Yes, Raven. There are many bolts of red canvas."

Raven ordered some men to go down and retrieve all the red canvas they could find and one bolt of black fabric if it was there. Raven turned to Pharaoh and said, "I want new sails made for this ship. We will make her our own. Can you instruct the men and women to pattern them after the sails that are already flying?"

"Yes, Raven. I will see to it."

Raven said, "I want someone who can paint pictures to change the name on the ship's bow too. Please find him for me."

"Consider it done, Raven."

Chapter 20

Twenty-eight days had passed since Raven and her crew overtook the *Scarlett Marie*. Everyone was starting to feel comfortable in their duties as sailors and officers. Pharaoh and the other kings were quick learners and handled the crew well. It seemed they all felt at home on their new ship, now bound for Madagascar.

Pharaoh asked Raven, "Why do we go back to Madagascar? Will they not try to capture us and sell us again?"

Raven replied, "Don't worry. Señor Rivera doesn't have the man power to overtake us. Besides, he is a business man, not a fighter. We have goods to sell him and he has money to spend."

"What will you do with the money you make?"

"It isn't my money, it's our money. Everyone on this ship will have a share. Gather everyone together and let's discuss this with the crew."

Pharaoh did as she asked. He called everyone to the main deck so Raven could speak to them. All men and women stood on the main deck except Pharaoh, Caesar, and Raven, who stood on the quarterdeck. Caesar manned the helm for the moment while his helmsmen could join the others on the main deck.

Raven told her crew, "People of *Destiny*, I want to make you an offer. We are sailing to Madagascar, where we plan to trade our cargo. Madagascar is where many of you were taken to after you were captured by the men who would sell you into slavery. Many of you were captured somewhere on the mainland of Africa and taken to Madagascar. If any of you want to leave this ship to try to find your way back to your people, I will not stop you. I warn you that if you leave us, you will be in danger of being captured again. If that happens, I may not be there to save you again. Still, I will not stop you if that is what you wish. If you decide to stay with me, you will not be my slaves. You will have the ability to leave and go as you please. You will have a share in whatever enterprise we decide upon. We will draw up a statement of the ship's law for everyone to abide by, called Articles of Code. All will abide by those articles including your captain. If everyone will abide by the rules of these articles, we will have no problem in getting along with each other. However, if you break the code, you will be punished. If you are in agreement, you may continue to sail with me, otherwise you may leave the ship with no ill will from me."

The people were a little confused by Raven's speech. They knew nothing about official laws or documents, so they returned to their duties when Raven finished.

That night, Raven met with her officers and junior officers for a meal. Raven explained the Articles of Code more thoroughly to them. Once they finished their meal, Raven pulled out some parchment and began writing out the Articles of Code as they were discussed.

I. The Captain is to have two full shares; the first and second mates are to have one share and one half; the doctor, junior officers, gunner, and boatswain, one share and one quarter; and all other crew, one share.

II. He that shall be found guilty of taking up any unlawful weapon on board a privateer or any other ship by us taken, so as to strike or abuse one another in any regard, shall suffer what punishment the captain and the majority of the company shall see fit.

III. He that shall be found guilty of cowardice in the time of engagements, shall suffer what punishment the captain and the majority of the company shall think fit.

IV. If any gold, jewels, silver, etc., be found on board any ship to the value of a piece of eight, & the finder does not deliver it to the quartermaster in the space of 24 hours, he shall suffer what punishment the captain and the majority of the company shall think fit.

V. He that is found guilty of gaming or defrauding one another to the value of any amount shall suffer what punishment the captain and the majority of the company shall think fit.

VI. He that shall have the misfortune to lose a limb in time of engagement shall have the sum of six hundred pieces of eight and remain aboard as long as he shall think fit.

VII. He that sees a sail first shall have the best pistol or small arm aboard her.

VIII. He that shall be guilty of drunkenness in time of engagement shall suffer what punishment the captain and majority of the company shall think fit.

IX. No snapping of guns in the hold.

X. No man shall consort with any of the women on board, and no woman shall make themselves available to any man for consorting without the approval of the captain and the other officers. Anyone who violates shall suffer what punishment the captain and the majority of the company shall think fit.

The five kings agreed to the terms of the Articles of Code and made their mark at the bottom of the page alongside Raven's signature. The next morning, Raven gathered the crew once again and read the Articles of Code to them, explaining each one as she read. Then, she stated, "Know this, our mission on this ship will be two-fold. I am sick of seeing people captured and sent to the Americas to be sold into slavery. We will attack and raid any ship we find doing so. We will also raid ships who have already dropped their load and received payment for having dealt in the selling of slaves. Their profit shall be our gain."

The ship erupted in cheers from the crew. Men hugged men and raised their arms in triumph, and the women cheered as well.

On day forty-two, after overtaking the *Scarlett Marie*, Señor Rivera was awakened by one of his men that a new ship was arriving in the harbor.

"Señor Rivera, a ship is coming into harbor I have never seen before. It is called the *Raven's Destiny*! The ship, she has red sails!"

Rivera furrowed his brows as he spoke, "I have never heard of such a thing. Does it fly a flag?"

"No, Señor! There is no flag on the ship!"

"Well, let us see who has come to see us, then."

Rivera and several of his men stood on the dock waiting for the strange ship to arrive. With a closer look, Rivera noticed a black raven silhouette on the main sail. The ship itself was somewhat familiar, although it was like any other square-rigged sailing vessel. He noticed a young woman standing on the quarterdeck, her bright red curly locks of hair streaming behind her in the wind. Her face was familiar to him, although he could not place her. She wore a smartly tailored uniform that showed off her feminine figure. She wore a small pistol and a saber on her belt and presented herself as an individual who knew how to use them both.

As the ship moored at the dock, Rivera approached to greet the captain. Raven gave a few last orders to her officers and then stepped off the ship along with her first mate, Pharaoh.

Rivera stretched out his hand and greeted her, saying, "Welcome to Port St. Felix, Señorita. I am Oscar Alejandro Rivera. How may I be of service? Will your capitan be joining us?"

Raven replied, "Señor Rivera, you are looking at the captain of *Raven's Destiny*. They call me *The Red Raven*."

"Who does, Señorita?"

"My crew, and soon anyone who opposes me and lives through it."

Rivera then asked, "Is your ship, *Raven's Destiny*, a slave ship?"

"*Raven's Destiny* is *not*! In *fact*, just the opposite. Woe be to those vessels carrying men and women to places where they will be made to serve other men. I *abhor* slavery, Señor! I have little or no respect for those who participate in the trading of slavery including *you*."

"Señorita, have we met? You seem so familiar to me?"

"We have met. You once tried to hire me. I was once second mate of the merchant ship *Destiny* captained by Horatio Billings. You knew me as Richard Ashworth."

"Ah, yes! The negotiator! Tell me, how is Capitan Billings?"

"He died earlier this year. He went down with his ship along with about a hundred slaves. I rescued the others. While I did, the rest of *Destiny's* crew left us behind while they rowed away in boats leaving us for dead. Those *would-be* slaves are now my crew."

Rivera swallowed hard before asking, "Tell me Señorita Raven, what is it you want from me?"

"We have cargo to sell and we are in need of supplies, food, ammunition, and weapons. I'd like to look around your storage house. There might be something there that interest me."

"Of course, Señorita. Would you like to unload your cargo first?"

Raven turned to Pharaoh and nodded to him to have the crew unload the textiles from the ship. Caesar had already begun having the crew to bring the cargo from below and placed on the main deck to prepare for unloading. Pharaoh turned to the ship and shouted in Swahili, "Bring the cloth onto the docks!"

Rivera asked, "How many tons of textiles do you have?"

"I don't know. You'd have to ask the captain of the *Scarlett Marie*."

Rivera widened his eyes as he realized he had seen this ship before. "*The Scarlett Marie*? Capitan Logan, is he alive?"

"As far as I know. We sent him and his crew afloat off the coast of a tiny island in the Caribbean. He was alive when we left him."

Raven and Rivera continued to converse as the ship was unloaded. An hour later, the last few bolts of cloth were unloaded from the ship and placed on the dock for Rivera's inspection. Rivera had his men count and inspect the fabric. One man kept a tally as the others called out numbers to him. In the end, they reported to Rivera, a load of two tons of various colors and patterns of wool and cotton fabrics of excellent quality.

"Bueno!" said Rivera. "Señorita, tell me, how much do you want for the cargo?"

"Hmm, how does £12,000 sound?"

"That would be fine if you had brought me two tons of ready made clothing but this will need to be made into clothing before I could pay that much. I was thinking maybe £5,000."

Raven shook her head, playing the game she and Rivera were so good at. She paused while pursing her lips, then said, "£7,000 might be suitable."

Rivera returned her volley with a strenuous look on his face. "As usual Señorita, you do not make these negotiations easy for me. I will give you £6,000."

Raven allowed a slight smirk to appear on her face as she stretched out her hand and said, "Bueno! It's a deal!"

Rivera called out to his men to move the cargo to one of his warehouses before saying to Raven, "Now, how would you like to be paid?"

Some of it will need to be gold. I need to pay my men. We can trade the rest for food and supplies."

"Alright, let me take you to our storehouses and you can select what you need."

Raven followed Rivera up a path that led to his warehouses. There were six large huts along the path. The first warehouse on the right caught Raven's eye. There was a sign on the outside that read, *Peligro Explosivo!*

"What are those words, Señor?"

"It says, *Danger Explosive!*"

"What do you store in there?"

"I have all kinds of weapons, guns, swords, knives, canons…"

"Canons?"

"Si, Señorita! I have canons."

Raven requested, "May I see them, please?"

Rivera led Raven into the warehouse to show her the various weapons he had acquired through the years of trading. As they walked inside, Raven was in awe of the many canons Rivera had stored away. She stopped next to a group of brass canons standing together on their carriages. Each canon weighed about twelve hundred pounds, and because they were made of brass, not iron, they were in excellent condition. They would have likely already rusted away from the salt air if they had been made of iron.

Raven asked, "Where did you get these?"

"I have collected them from various ships throughout the years. I find it difficult to find a buyer for them. I could make you a good deal."

"Do you have any cannon balls?"

"Si, they are not in as good condition but I have them."

"How about black powder?"

"Si, I have it too. We make our own black powder here on the island."

Raven admired the cannons and asked, "What are these, eight-pounders?"

"Six!"

"They look so big! I would have guessed eight. But then, I have never actually seen one up close until now."

Rivera said, "Six pounders would be good on the deck of your ship. You can line them up on the main deck on either side."

Raven asked, "How about the bow and the stern?"

"No, Señorita! These guns would be too large for that. However, I have some four-pounders that will work nicely for the bow and stern."

"Alright, how much for four of the six-pounders, and two of the four-pounders with shot and powder. Oh, I need some rammers as well. Oh, and do you have any slow-match?"

"Si, I have it."

"Fine, how much for all of that?"

"Señorita, I am feeling generous today. For you, I will supply the cannons and all that you will need for them, food enough for your next voyage, and I will pay you £500 in gold and silver."

Raven contemplated his offer. She knew it probably wasn't the best deal, but since she was trading with goods she had not paid for, she felt she could live with it.

"Señor Rivera, If you will make me a promise not to reveal to anyone who I am or that we have traded, I will accept your offer."

Rivera asked, "Raven, are you planning on a new career in pirating?"

"I was thinking more along the lines of privateering."

"Oh, so what country have you accepted a commission from?"

"I represent the people of Africa. Señor Rivera, I know you are heavily involved in slave trading. I will make you a deal. I won't take that away from you as long as you keep my secrets. I plan to rescue as many slaves as I can from the merchant ships that sail along the coast of Africa and the Caribbean. If I find out that you have warned any of the merchant ship captains of me and my crew, we will come back and attack your little enterprise. You will be completely wiped away."

With the smile of a swindler, Rivera held out his hand to take Raven's, kissed her hand, and said, "We have a deal. Your secret is safe with me."

CHAPTER 21

For the next three days, Raven and her crew worked loading the new cannons onto *Raven's Destiny*. It took a while to load the twelve-hundred-pound guns onto the ship using a block and tackle, the crew rigged. Once the cannons were in place at their respective homes, they had to be secured using ropes tying them to the rail with enough slack to allow for recoil once the guns were fired. Two six-pound cannons were placed sixteen feet apart on the port rail. They built an ammunition station between the guns where cannonballs were stacked in a pyramid formation inside a wooden square built onto the deck. The station was capable of securely holding fifty-five cannonballs. The four-pound cannons were set up with one on the bow at the poop deck and the other at the stern on the quarterdeck. An ammunition station was set up at each of those cannons as well.

Once all the cannons were secured and the supplies were stowed, Raven ordered the ship to set sail. "Pharaoh, prepare to launch, let loose the bow line."

Pharaoh called out Raven's commands to the crew, "Let loose the bow line!"

Raven then ordered, "Let loose the stern line."

"Let loose the stern line!"

Raven's Destiny slowly moved away from the docks as Caesars's helmsman steered her into the bay. Her crew were standing on the yard-arms, ready to drop the sails when she ordered.

When the ship drifted fifty feet from the docks, Raven ordered, "Drop the Blood Sails."

Pharaoh sang out, "Drop the blood sails!

Raven's crew untied the ropes, holding the sails in place. One by one, the crimson sails dropped, billowing out as the wind caught them, causing the ship to thrust forward in the deep waters of the Atlantic. The image of a black raven was prominent on the top sail of the main mast, setting *Raven's Destiny* apart from any other square-rigged ship in the Atlantic.

Raven had Caesar steer *Destiny* up the west coast of Africa, looking for slavers exiting the coast near one of the tiny coves known as brights that were situated throughout the shores of the African Continent. The brights were perfect hiding places for slave ships to moor, where slaves could be loaded without much attention from other ships that might be looking for easy prey. Privateers from Spain, France, or Holland, as well as pirates, might be on the lookout for a ship loaded with cargo to capture. The Gulf of Guinea was brimming with brights where African slaves were being loaded onto ships to be delivered to the Americas.

While at sea, Raven taught her crew how to load and fire the cannons. She had never fired a cannon but had read about the big guns in one of the books aboard the original *Destiny*. She had also extensively questioned those men upon Billings' *Destiny* who had served on military ships and knew how to fire the guns very well.

Raven's crew practiced loading the powder bags daily, ramming the powder down the gun barrel, loading the cannonball into the barrel, aiming the cannon, and lighting the fuse. They limited firing the cannons to only once every four days while training. Raven had limited ammunition and didn't want to run out before they found themselves in a skirmish with another ship.

Raven's Destiny found herself just outside the Gulf of Guinea three weeks after they left Madagascar. Raven ordered the sails be raised so the ship could drift a while wherever the currents would carry her. They waited for any unsuspecting merchant carrier bound for the coast of Guinea. If a vessel was bound for this area, it carried goods to be traded for a load of slaves. If a ship were leaving these coasts, they would be carrying slaves. Either way, they would be targets for Raven and her crew. They intended to slow the slave trade in these waters, at least. If enough merchant ships lost their cargo or even their vessels, it would cause the merchants to think twice about how profitable slave trading might or might not be.

Raven's crew drifted in the gulf for days, waiting for a ship to come within sight. The ship used only minimal sails to avoid drifting too close to the shore. They used only the white sails so they wouldn't raise suspicions from approaching vessels. On the fifth day, when the sun was at its highest, a ship rolled in from the north, heading toward the gulf.

Raven sent her crew in to retrieve the ship. "Lower the blood sails!" she shouted.

Men scrambled to the tops and yardarms of the masts to drop the red sails, sending the ship at full speed in a direction that would cut off the approaching ship from reaching its destination. Raven looked through her spyglass to catch the ship's name, *Matilda*.

Matilda was a merchant ship sailing out of Bristol. She had a crew of forty men and was heavily laden with cargo to be traded in Guinea. She was a square-rigged ship similar in size to *Raven's Destiny*; only *Destiny* would be faster not having a load of cargo in her hull.

Matilda was captained by John Stinnett, a reasonably new captain who was the son of the ship's owner. Stinnett was about thirty years old, clean-shaven, well mannered, but not very brave. One of his crew called from the crow's nest and reported, "Ahoy! Ship off the starboard bow!"

The captain took out his spyglass and looked off the starboard bow to try to spot the ship. Then he called up to the lookout, "Is she a merchant vessel?"

"I think not, Captain! She be carrying guns on deck. Six pounders I'd say!"

Stinnett watched as they continued toward the coast of Guinea and saw that the approaching ship was indeed sailing at an angle that would intercept the *Matilda.* His ship was still at least ten miles from its destination, Accra, on the coast of Ghana. They had little hope of reaching the safety of their destination port.

Destiny was quickly gaining on the merchant ship. She came within a mile of the *Matilda* when the Captain looked through his spyglass again to see if he could make out the name of the ship approaching him so directly. He couldn't readily make out the name painted on the ship's bow, but he could see she was flying red sails. One of the sails displayed a black raven upon it. Stinnett began to worry that he was about to be overtaken by pirates. He made the call to his crew, "All hands on deck! Ship approaching appears to be pirates!"

The crew hurried about crewing their stations in preparation for the possibility of being attacked. However, there was little to do since they were an unarmed ship. They could only pray that their lives might be spared.

When *Destiny* reached about half a mile from *Matilda*, Raven ordered, "Fire the port bow gun over her bow! Caesar, turn her starboard thirty degrees!"

Destiny turned to the right, allowing the gun crew to aim the cannon and fire in front of the approaching ship without causing any damage to her. They had no intent of sinking the ship or even damaging her; they wanted her for a prize.

"***Boom!***" The cannon roared, sending the gun backward away from the port rail. The two-inch thick ropes that held her into position went taut as the gun retracted from its firing position. The gun crew quickly swabbed out the cannon and reloaded it in preparation for another shot, then moved the artillery back to the firing position at the port rail.

The cannonball whistled through the air, missing the bow of the *Matilda* by only five feet. Captain Stinnett's heart sank when he saw how close the shot was.

"All stop!" he called. "Raise the sails and send up the white flag!"

There would be no battle. *Matilda* surrendered before the fight even began.

Raven's Destiny pulled alongside *Matilda,* where Raven's crew tossed grappling hooks over the side and pulled *Matilda* closer so Raven and her escorts could transfer to the other ship. Twelve heavily armed men followed Raven to the other ship to parle with Captain Stinnett.

Stinnett was shocked to see a young woman leading the rabble of the attacking ship.

"Good evening, Captain. May I ask your name, please?"

Stinnett was stunned by the good manners of the young pirate girl who had captured his ship. "I am Captain John Stinnett. My father is Henry Stinnett, the owner of this vessel."

Raven replied, "Quite wrong my dear Captain. I am now the owner of this ship."

"That's preposterous! You can't just take what is not yours! Who are you, young woman?"

"They call me the Red Raven."

"Who does?"

"My crew and all those who encounter me on the high seas."

"What do you plan to do with us?"

Raven replied, "Your crew has a choice to make. They may serve on my crew or they will be left here in the Gulf of Guinea. You, Captain, well I hope you can swim."

Stinnett was shocked by her comment. Surely, she didn't expect him to swim from their location to the coast of Guinea. The swim would be at least five miles. "I beg of you, young Captain, please don't send me overboard. Why are you doing this?"

"No doubt, Captain Stinnett, you've taken notice of my crew. As you can see they are all Africans, Africans taken unwillingly from their homes with the intent to sell them as slaves. I intend to free everyone of them I can. You no doubt were intent on trading goods here in Guinea to receive a load of slaves. Your days of being a slave trader are over. You can either take your chances in the sea or my men will hang you from your own yardarm. Which will it be?"

Stinnett replied, "As you wish."

Stinnett stepped to the starboard side of *Matilda*, where the rail had been removed. He stepped off the ship's deck into the chilly waters of the sea.

Raven turned to the crew of *Matilda* and said, "You men have a choice to make. You may remain onboard and serve as my crew or you may follow your captain into the sea."

Many of the men murmured among themselves. One man stated, "I'll not be made to work along side these black savages!"

Raven grabbed the man by his collar and dragged him to the rail. She took out her knife and carved a letter R into the right side of his face. "Then you will be food for the sharks!" She pushed him into the water.

Raven asked, "Who else?"

She saw shoving among the men of *Matilda* as some of them wrestled with one another about their decision. One man was pushed forward and landed in Raven's arms.

"What about you?"

"I'll not serve any girl!"

"Fine!"

Raven also gave him an R on his face and tossed him into the waters below.

Thirty-three men abandoned the ship with their faces bleeding from a red R. Seven remained behind. Raven turned to those remaining and announced, "If you men choose to stay, you must understand this; these men are not slaves. You are no better than they are. You will sleep together, you will eat together, you will work together, and you will fight together. You are mates! Understand?"

Each man responded, "*Aye, Captain!*"

One of the men who remained from the *Matilda* was a young second mate named Jeffrey Hamilton. Hamilton was only seventeen but was serving his fourth year aboard the merchant ship, working his way through the ranks just as Raven had done. Raven saw that he wore an officer's uniform, so she approached him and asked, "first mate?"

"Second."

"Why didn't you join your Captain overboard?"

"My face!"

"Your face?"

"Yes, my face! It's too pretty to be marred with your knife. I rather like it, don't you?"

Raven stared into his eyes as if searching for his intentions. Without indicating her thoughts, she replied, "You'll do." and walked away.

CHAPTER 22

Raven followed Jeffery down into the hull to inspect her cargo. Like most merchant ships, there were three decks, two below the main. The sleeping area for the crew and the food stores was on the mid-deck. The stores were dwindling because they were near the end of their voyage from Bristol. Raven would need to resupply soon.

They went down into the lowest deck to inspect, and Raven found several barrels of rum, what she estimated to be fifty bales of cotton, and ten crates of long rifles with ammunition. Raven called up to one of her men on the main deck, "Daktari! Daktari!"

He responded, "Yes, Raven?"

"Daktari, have Pharaoh send over ten men to retrieve this cargo and take it over to *Destiny*."

"Yes, Raven."

Ten more men climbed over from *Destiny* onto *Matilda* as Raven instructed. They climbed into the lowest deck and carried up the ten crates of rifles and ammunition. Raven had them moved to the main deck, then sent five containers to her flagship, *Destiny*.

"Pharaoh, I want you to captain this ship. You will command half the crew while I take the other half with me. We will sail together in our quest to free your brothers from slavery."

Pharaoh smiled only with his eyes as he realized the great faith Raven must have had in him to offer him a captainship under her command. He replied, "I will do as you command."

Raven said, "We need to supply *Matilda* and sell off her cargo—well, maybe not all of it. We might keep some of the rum for special occasions." She smiled. "Move one of the barrels of rum over to *Destiny,* and we will keep one here on *Matilda.* The rest we will sell."

"Aye, Raven!"

Raven split her crew; half would remain onboard *Destiny* while the other would transfer to *Matilda.* She also split the remaining crew members of *Matilda,* with three staying onboard her, while Jeffrey and three others would transfer to *Destiny.*

Raven temporarily appointed Caesar her first mate while continuing to man the helm. She thought she might make Jeffrey her first mate, but she wanted to scrutinize his abilities first. Jeffrey stayed by her side most of the time while she interrogated his knowledge of the seas and sailing.

Raven instructed Attila, "Prepare to sail. Lower the white sails and take up the crimson."

Attila gave the order to change sails so they would be inconspicuous as they rolled into port. They sailed for Port Harcourt off the coast of Nigeria, deep in the heart of the Gulf of Guinea. Jacque Le Fleur, a French trader, had set up a post there ten years earlier. He was heavily into slave trading. Raven could just remove each slave trading post rather than going to the trouble of attacking those who would trade with them. However, in doing so, she would endanger the lives of Africans being held captive. They might be killed if she fired her guns upon the trading post. Instead, she chose to eliminate those who sought to trade with them. If no one came to deal with them, the demand for slaves would no longer exist, thus no more slave trading, or, so she hoped.

Both ships docked at Harcourt, and Raven left her ship to meet with Le Fleur for the first time.

Jacque Le Fleur was a well-traveled man from Marseille on the Mediterranean. He grew up the son of a French soldier, destitute after his father was killed in battle while Jacque was only twelve. Le Fleur survived by stealing whatever he could to feed or clothe himself. He soon developed a reputation as a confidence man before reaching the age of eighteen. Wanted by the French police, Jacque fled Marseille by working on a French frigate. The ship's captain, Jean Le Vasseu, later known as Francois, continually beat Le Fleur for his seemingly never-ending thievery.

Jacque fled the frigate once it stopped in Guinea, and he set up shop in Harcourt, eventually building a small trade empire. Over the years, Le Fleur gathered a band of like-minded young men to rob, steal, and defraud anyone in their path. Over the years, Jacque discovered that slaves were a hot commodity. He sent his men into the small nearby villages around Nigeria and captured whomever he could, to be sold into slavery to the highest bidder.

Raven despised such men who would take the lives of others and force them into service far away from their homes. However, her plan required her to deal with these unscrupulous men to ruin them eventually. With Le Fleur, she planned to con the con man.

The Red Raven moored her ships at Port Harcourt and waited to be approached by Le Fleur or one of his representatives. A burly man named Titus, who wore an extensive beard, approached the ship and called out to anyone onboard; it happened to be Nero.

"You there! Slave! Who is your master?"

Nero cursed the man in Swahili, then replied, "I am no slave. I am an officer aboard this ship. What do you want?"

"Are you here to trade?"

"That is not for me to say. Our captain makes those decisions."

"Well, where is he?"

Nero scoffed, "Hmph. *She* will be with you when she is ready."

"She? You mean your captain is a woman?"

"Aye, she is, and the most capable of all who sail these waters."

It was Titus' turn to scoff, "I'll believe it when I see it."

Raven then stepped out onto the deck from her quarters. She wore her tailored uniform, which showed off every curve of her body. She wore a saber on her left hip and a pistol on her right. Jeffrey accompanied her as she walked to the rail to greet the burly man with all the questions.

Titus was dumbfounded when he saw how beautiful and young the captain of *Raven's Destiny* was. Somehow, he had expected to see someone much older and uglier.

"Are you the Captain?"

"I am. They call me Red Raven. Who might you be?"

"Titus. I represent Monsieur Le Fleur, who owns this trading post."

Titus looked around and noticed a second ship, "I've never seen your ship before. The *Matilda* has been here on occasion. What is she doing with you?"

"I recently acquired *Matilda*. I am here to trade her cargo. Will I be negotiating with you or Monsieur Le Fleur?"

"I'll take you to Le Fleur. He makes all the transactions. Are you looking for slaves? We've got a good load of them ready to go."

"I'll be discussing that with Monsieur Le Fleur."

"Of course. Follow me, I'll take you to him."

Late in the evening, Captain John Stinnett and twelve of his crew from *Matilda* reached the beach of San-Pedro on the coast of Côte d'Ivoire. The rest of his men drowned, having never learned to swim. Spanish soldiers approached the men as they walked onto the beach.

"Alto! Who are you? What are you doing here?"

Stinnett asked, "Where is here?"

"You are in San-Pedro. Property of the sovereignty of Spain whose king is His Majesty Philip the Fifth of Anjou. Now, who are you?"

"I'm Captain John Stinnett of the merchant vessel, *Matilda*. We were on our way to Accra to trade our cargo when we were overrun by pirates being led by a young female who called herself, the Red Raven."

"Pirates! Did they sink your ship?"

"No, she took it from me!"

"Where is she now?"

"The last I saw her she was heading east with my ship."

"Uh! Too bad! What about the rest of your crew? Did you try to fight and lose your men?"

"No! We were defenseless. We had only small arms while she had artillery. She seized us, took all our weapons, our cargo, and left us to drown in the sea. All except seven of my men, and if I ever catch them they will hang for mutiny and desertion."

"Mmm, I suppose you are looking for refuge? I will take you to General Don Pedro Leon. He will decide what to do with you."

"Thank-you, sir."

"Follow me!"

Raven was taken to a large wood-framed house a quarter mile from the beach. She and Jeffrey were led into a large open room, finely furnished, and were asked to wait. Five minutes later, a short, light-skinned man with a finely trimmed mustache entered the room.

"I am Jacque Le Fleur. I understand you wish to speak to me about some cargo you have brought."

Raven replied, "I have cargo to sell for the right price."

"What kind of cargo?"

"Mostly cotton but also rum."

Le Fleur asked, "You said you have cargo to sell, would you be interested in trading? I have some very fine slaves available to trade."

"I don't buy slaves, I free them."

Le Fleur was shocked at her comment, "What do you mean, free them?"

"Just what I said. My crew is made up mostly of Africans that I have freed from slavery."

"So, you buy them and then free them? That doesn't sound very profitable to me."

"I didn't say I buy them. Quite the contrary. I just free them from their captives. Now, do you want to look at my cargo or should I find another port?"

Le Fleur replied, "Oui, I will look at your cargo; then we can discuss what it is worth."

Raven, Jeffrey, and Le Fleur walked together back to the docks. While on the path, Le Fleur commented, "By the way, I don't recall you giving your name."

She replied, "I am the Red Raven."

"Red Raven? Should I have heard of you?"

"Probably not. But you will hear much of me in the near future."

Le Fleur looked her over as they walked, noticing the saber and pistol on her waist.

"Do you know how to use those weapons you wear around your waist?"

"Pray you never have the occasion to find out."

Jeffrey walked behind the two as they conversed. He found the conversation quite comical. He had already witnessed Raven's ability to use a knife. He was sure she also knew how to use a sword and gun.

When they reached the docks, Raven led Le Fleur onto *Matilda* to show him the cargo. They climbed down to the lower hold, and she allowed Le Fleur to inspect the bales of cotton and taste the rum. Satisfied, Le Fleur said, "You may unload your cargo. I'm sure we can make a suitable deal."

He then climbed out of the hull and left the ship. When Raven came out of the hull, she ordered her men to unload the cargo. Raven and Le Fleur stood by and watched as her crew unloaded the goods from *Matilda*. Once everything had been placed on the docks, Le Fleur made a pretense of counting the bales and barrels, then said to her, "Very well. You have delivered me an excellent load. You make take your ships and leave."

Raven's eyes burned into his as she realized what he had said. "Do you think I'm just going to leave my cargo here without payment?"

"I do! As you can see, I have the advantage."

Le Fleur waved his hand to reveal one hundred armed men scattered among the buildings and trees along the beach. Raven looked around and saw that she was outmanned. One of Le Fleur's men came up behind Raven and pinned her arms behind her. She struggled to free herself, but his grip was too tight. Raven bent her head forward and raised her left foot; she stomped on the man's foot with the heel of her boot. The man released his grip, allowing Raven to go into action. She kicked him between his legs, then rammed the heel of her hand into his windpipe. The man fell to the ground dazed, not knowing whether to grab his crotch or throat, for both ached severely.

Raven then called out, "Fire!"

Destiny's starboard guns fired upon the men hiding in the trees. Bits of trees, sand, and men flew everywhere from the explosion.

Raven drew her sword and confronted Le Fleur. He drew his blade and returned her attack. They danced in the sand, striking at each other while the edges of their blades sang as they crossed. Le Fleur was shocked at how accomplished the young woman was with the blade. However, he felt he was better. Le Fleur backed Raven away with each thrust of his sword until she finally fell over a fallen tree on the beach. Raven didn't let the fall deter her. As she fell, she grabbed a handful of sand and flung it into Le Fleur's face. As he choked and struggled to wipe away the sand from his eyes, mouth, and nose, Raven took the opportunity to thrust her sword into his chest. Le Fleur fell backward into the sand and struggled to catch his breath because she had punctured one of his lungs. Raven seized the opportunity and hacked at his throat with her sword, nearly severing his head from his body.

All around her, men were battling one another. Raven called to her men operating the guns on the ship and said, "Don't fire on the buildings!"

The cannons fired on the trees around the beach, hitting men and knocking them unconscious or killing them. A man called out in French when he noticed that Le Fleur was dead on the beach. Slowly, the number of men attacking from the trees dwindled until no one was left.

Chapter 23

Raven discovered she had lost two of her men in the skirmish. She gathered her men at the docks to give further instructions. "Pharaoh, man the ships with twenty of the crew while the rest of us search the buildings for supplies and anything of value.

Raven took twenty men with her to Le Fleur's house to search it for any gold or other valuables he might have had. The rest of the men searched the huts and storage barns around the beach.

Le Fleur's servants were startled by Raven and her band as they entered the house without notice. A man-servant stood in front of three women to protect them. He held a rifle in his hands. Raven spoke to him in Swahili, saying, "Usiogope, Hatutakudhuru! (Don't fear, we won't harm you.)"

The man lowered his gun and spoke to Raven in English, "Who are you?"

"I am the Red Raven. I'm here to free you from your captors. Le Fleur is dead."

The slaves rejoiced at her announcement.

Raven asked, "Do you know where he kept his valuables?"

"In his office. I'll show you."

The man said, "My name is Pierre, or at least that is what Le Fleur called me."

Pierre led her into the office, where a large ornate desk sat. He took her to a wall behind the desk where a huge tapestry was hung. Pierre pulled back the tapestry and revealed a doorway leading into another room. Raven and her men followed him into the hidden room and saw more treasure than she had ever dreamed could be there. Gold, diamonds, silver, and jewels of all sorts were kept in small sea chests throughout the room. Raven took a quick count and estimated at least fifty small chests filled with loot.

"Pierre, are there any wagons or carts about?"

"Yes, ma'am. Over at the docks there's a barn with several wagons. Horses too."

Raven sent Daktari back to the docks, "Tell Pharaoh what we have found. Have him bring wagons and horses to haul the treasure back to the ships."

Daktari ran back to the docks and found Pharaoh, who was busy discovering a different kind of treasure. In several barns scattered around the area behind the docks, Pharaoh discovered captive Africans waiting to be sold. They were all shackled together and to the posts which supported the structures. The would-be slaves were shocked to see Pharaoh as he entered the barns, a black man like themselves, only dressed in white man's attire. Pharaoh spoke to the people in Swahili and said, "Don't be afraid. We will set you free."

The people began speaking all at once, asking questions of Pharaoh that he could not comprehend because they all spoke simultaneously.

"Please! Please! I know you all have questions, but there will be time for answers later. We must get you out of here first."

Pharaoh's men began unlocking the shackles and releasing the people when Daktari ran into the area shouting Pharaoh's name.

Pharaoh stepped out to see what the matter was.

Daktari said while panting, "Pharaoh, Raven has found much treasure. She wants you to bring wagons and horses to haul it all to the ships. Come quick!"

Pharaoh and Daktari located the barn where the wagons were stored and had the horses hitched to the wagons. Pharaoh then sent Daktari and five men to return the wagons to Raven. Pharaoh remained behind to continue releasing the enslaved people.

Back at Le Fleur's house, Raven had her men begin carrying the chests out of the secret room, and they stacked them on the porch to await the wagons. Meanwhile, Raven searched the rest of the house with Jeffrey to see what else of value there might be. Raven found several knives of various styles, many of which were ornate. She found a pair of dueling pistols, many swords, and a wardrobe filled with fancy suits. She had them all gathered up to be taken to the ships.

Daktari soon arrived with the wagons and extra help. He and the other men quickly began loading the wagons with the chests and all Raven had gathered from the house. Once they had finished loading the wagons, Raven turned to Pierre and asked, "Where is your home?"

"It is many days from here in the direction that the sun rises in the morning."

"Will you go back? You are free now."

"It has been many years since I have been there. All of my people are gone."

"You can join us if you like."

"What about these women? What will become of them?"

Raven replied, "They are welcome too. I have other women on my ships. Know this however, I have rules that you must all abide by. If you are willing to serve on my crew, you will be entitled to a share in whatever we capture, like the rest of my men and women."

Pierre looked back at the women who heard Raven's words. They responded with hopeful eyes and nodded to Pierre.

"Thank you, ma'am. We will come with you."

"You may call me Captain, or Raven."

"Thank you, Raven."

They all followed on foot while Daktari and the other drivers moved the wagons back to the beach. When they arrived on the beach, they found a large congregation of Africans waiting outside the barns. Raven searched for Pharaoh as she approached them. She finally found him near the docks, instructing his men about loading supplies onto the ships. Pharaoh's men had discovered a warehouse of food supplies, including barrels of salted meat. He had his men split the supplies between the two ships.

Raven approached Pharaoh and asked, "I see you found more than just supplies."

"Aye! I have counted one hundred and twelve people who were being held captive. What do you want to do with them?"

"Well, we can't take that many with us. They can't have been far removed from their homes. We will supply them and arm them, then send them back home."

"Will you speak with them?"

Raven paused before answering, "Yes. I'll talk to them."

Pharaoh called out to silence the people who were gathered around. He spoke to them in Swahili, saying, "People of Africa, listen to me. This is our great leader, the Red Raven. She will speak to you and help you return to your homes. Please listen."

Raven asked Pharaoh, "Will you translate for me, please?"

Pharaoh nodded.

"I'm sure all of you are frightened by what has happened to you by these white men over the past days. You may not realize it, but their intent was to sell you to other white men as slaves. You would have been taken into a large ship like one of these, and taken many days across the ocean to a place where you would be forced to serve in hard labor. You would no longer be allowed to come and go as you please. You would only be allowed to do whatever your master told you to do. But you are free now! Go back to your homes. Warn your people. Make preparations, because more of the white men will come and try to take more of your people. You must fight against them. Don't let them take you because even if you die while trying to escape, death is better than what they have in store for you. We will give you food and weapons for your journey home. Be careful, the men we attacked this day are still about and they might try to take you again. Fight them! Fight them! May God be with you on your journey home."

Raven turned to Pharaoh and said, "See that they are all supplied and armed."

"Yes, Raven."

Then Pharaoh saw the chest being loaded onto the ship and asked her, "What did you find?"

Raven smiled and replied, "More treasure than you could spend in a lifetime."

The people began to leave in small groups as Pharaoh's men passed out food and machetes or swords to them. They left the beach, heading east and north to find their way home. Raven could hear the people sing as they walked along the paths through the jungles of Guinea.

Raven had all of the treasure placed on *Destiny* so that it could be counted and divided. She approached Jeffrey and asked, "How would you like to be my quartermaster?"

Jeffrey smiled and asked, "So, you trust me now?"

"I'm willing to give you the benefit of the doubt. Don't make me regret this. I have a document onboard telling how the treasure should be split. You, as quartermaster will receive one and a half shares. When we pass out the treasure to the men make sure each man and woman have their own sea chest to store their shares. I will give instructions to them about consequences of thievery among them."

"Aye, Captain."

Destiny and *Matilda* remained in Port Harcourt while they were continually supplied, and the treasure was counted and divided. Two days later, Raven had all the men and women gather around the docks to distribute the prize. Raven stood on the deck of *Destiny* as she spoke to the people.

"People of *Destiny* and *Matilda,* we have made our first capture which has yielded us much treasure. Before you receive your bounty, I want to remind those of you who have been with me from the beginning and instruct those new to our number the Articles of Code have given instruction about how you will handle yourselves concerning your share of the treasure. Article I of the Code states that 'The captain is to have two full shares; the first and second mates are to have one share and one half; The doctor, junior officers, gunner and boatswain, one share and one quarter. All other crew, one share.' Let me say that anyone who is found to have stolen from any one else aboard these ships will be punished severely. You will be whipped, your share of treasure will be divided among the others, and you will be marooned on the nearest island I can find. I will not abide to thievery within our ranks. You new men and women should also know that Article X states, 'No man shall consort with any of the women onboard and no woman shall make themselves available to any man for consorting without approval of the captain and the other officers. Anyone who violates shall suffer what punishment the captain and the majority of the company shall think fit.' All of the Articles of Code are available should you have any questions.

It all comes down to this: treat each other the way you want to be treated. If you find you can't abide by the code, you are welcome to leave at any time. After you receive your share today, anyone who wants to remain here is welcome. Let Mr. Hamilton know your decision once he has dispersed your share. One other thing, I have instructed Mr. Hamilton to hold out two shares each for *Raven's Destiny* and *Matilda* to keep them outfitted and provisioned."

Pharaoh stood next to Jeffrey and called out the names of each man or woman on the crew. As they approached, Pharaoh indicated to Mr. Hamilton that man or woman's rank on the ship. A chest was issued to each of the crew when they came forward. Each chest contained approximately twenty pounds of gold, silver, and gems. The number of crew now stood at seventy-five men and women. After the treasure was handed out, seventy-five men and women who would stay and sail with Raven remained.

Chapter 24

On the third day after the raid on Port Harcourt, both ships pulled out to sea. Pierre and his female companions were placed on *Matilda* to serve as cooks for Pharaoh and his crew.

Pharaoh directed his helmsmen to follow Raven's ship into the gulf and out into the open waters of the Atlantic. Raven was once again bound for Madagascar to trade with Señor Rivera. She intended to buy more cannons to arm *Matilda* for their next voyage. As they left the Gulf of Guinea, they spotted two more ships entering the gulf, undoubtedly looking to trade. Whether they were going to Port Harcourt or not, she did not know. If they were, they would be disappointed.

The skies were clear, the winds were crisp, and sailing was smooth around the Cape of Good Hope. Twenty-one days later, they drifted into Port St. Felix. Señor Rivera must have spotted them coming from a distance because he was waiting at the docks as they pulled into port.

Raven met Rivera as she walked off the ship, and the two extended greetings as if they were old friends.

"Señorita Raven, I see you have come back very soon. I hope you have had a successful journey."

"Well enough, Señor Rivera. It is good to see you."

"Have you come back to St Felix to trade again?"

Raven replied, "I'm here to purchase more cannons if you still have some available. I need to outfit my new ship."

Rivera looked surprised as he realized she now had not one but two ships at her disposal.

"My, you have had a successful journey, haven't you? What is her name?"

"*Matilda!*"

Rivera was momentarily speechless when he heard the name.

"*Matilda* did you say? What has happened to Capitan Stinnett?"

Raven replied, "Last I saw him he was swimming toward the coast of Nigeria with most of his crew. The rest of them decided to join my crew. Is he a friend of yours?"

"We have done business together, si, but I would not say we are amigos."

"Well then, how about those guns? Do you have anymore that I can buy for *Matilda?*"

"I have cannons. Do you have money?"

"I have some gold and silver. I also have rubies, diamonds, and sapphires if you would be interested in any of them."

"Si, Señorita Raven! I would like to see them!"

"Let's walk over to the *Matilda*, then."

They walked together to the gangplank leading to *Matilda's* deck and boarded her. Pharaoh met them at the starboard rail, and Raven said, "Pharaoh, this is Señor Rivera. He would like to see some of the gems we have to trade. Would you have someone bring out one of the chests, please?"

"Aye, Raven!"

Pharaoh led Raven and Rivera to the quarterdeck to a small table used occasionally to spread out charts. Two of Pharaoh's men brought out one of the sea chests containing treasure. When they opened the chest, Rivera gawked as he said, "Oh my! These are very nice!"

He pulled several gems out of the chest to examine them more closely. Some jewels were inset into gold and silver necklaces, bracelets, and broaches.

"Where did you get these, Señorita?"

"I... inherited them."

Rivera looked at her, puzzled. "Hmm?"

Raven asked, "Have you heard of Jacque Le Fleur?"

"Si! He is a trader in Guinea is he not?"

"Not anymore. He double-crossed me on a deal, so I shut down his operation for him. He's dead and his post is no longer occupied."

Rivera was shocked by her words, and Raven could see it.

"Did you kill him, Señorita?"

"I told you, Señor Rivera, anyone who opposes my efforts will pay dearly."

"Did he have slaves?"

"He did. Four of them are now serving on this ship. The other one hundred and twelve are on their way back to their villages, armed and ready to fight for their freedom."

"Be assured, Señorita Raven, I will never go against you. We are amigos are we not?"

Raven smirked and replied, "For now."

Raven and Rivera settled on a price for the six cannons to be purchased for the *Matilda*. Raven set her men immediately to loading and securing the new guns and the ammunition. It took three days to load and secure the cannons onto the ship, along with the gunpowder and ammunition. Once everything was secured, Raven allowed her people two days to lounge around the port and spend their newly earned money. When they returned to the ship, more than a few were intoxicated. Most of them wore new clothes and brought back trinkets of some sort for their pleasure. The men and women who made up Raven's crew had never had money of any kind and were never taught what to do with it if they acquired it, so they spent it as quickly as they could, like little children looking for a new toy.

Once everyone was back on their respective ships, Raven confined them to the ships for twelve hours before launching. She wanted her crews to be sober and ready to work when they headed out to sea.

At noon the next day, Raven set sail out of Port St. Felix, heading back to the Gulf of Guinea. *Raven's Destiny* led the way, with *Matilda* following behind. Ten days out, intense storms moved in from the northwest. Raven could see them moving in and directed her ships to sail westward to avoid the strong winds sweeping through. They escaped the worst part of the storms but were still pelted with heavy rain. The waves rocked the ships back and forth and, at times, tossed them very close to one another. Pharaoh decided to separate from Raven's ship to decrease the chances of a collision.

The seas rolled, and the skies rumbled all through the night. Because of the cloud cover, the moon and stars were invisible. The two ships could only try to stay within sight of each other throughout the night. Aside from their compass, there was no way to tell where they were heading until the clouds cleared to reveal the stars or until sunlight returned.

The next morning, the clouds continued to hover above the ships, and rain continued to fall, but the storms had moved away. Raven was able to use the sextant to find their location and discovered they had drifted about fifty miles off course. She instructed Caesar to correct the course, and they again sailed toward the Gulf of Guinea. It took them a week to once again reach the mouth of the gulf.

Raven signaled for Pharaoh to bring his ship closer so she could devise a plan with him. Pharaoh brought *Matilda* alongside *Destiny*, then climbed onto *Destiny* to meet with Raven.

"When we see a ship I want you to cut them off. Fire a shot over their bow to make them stop. If they don't stop, I will come up from behind and fire from the rear. They will be forced to stop or fight for they will not be able to flee us."

"As you wish, Raven."

"We want to capture the ship if possible. But if they decide to make a run for it, we will disable their ship."

"I understand."

"Good luck to you, my friend."

"And to you, Red Raven."

The two ships glided through the waters with only light sails to carry them. They patrolled the mouth of the Gulf of Guinea back and forth, sailing north, then south. On the third day, a young man sat in the crow's nest atop the main mast of *Destiny*. As they sailed southeasterly, he spotted a ship sailing westward from Port Gentil off the coast of Gabon.

The young man Raven had dubbed Gabriel pointed to the horizon and called out, "Ship ahoy, off the starboard bow!"

Raven used her spyglass while standing on the quarterdeck to search the direction Gabriel was pointing. She spotted a merchant ship running low in the water. It was heavily laden, probably carrying slaves in her hull. Raven searched the bow of the ship, looking for a name. The ship was still too far away to see it. She signaled to Pharaoh to come about and head off the approaching ship without going into the gulf any deeper. Pharaoh sailed southward casually, attempting to seem nonchalant and unthreatening.

After an hour, the ship's name became clear enough for Raven to read. It was the *Tryton*, an English vessel sailing out of Bristol.

Raven had seen her before. She was captained by an old sailor named Joshua Taggert. Taggert must have been sixty years old, much older than most captains sailing the Atlantic waters. He was a blistery old man who took no guff from anyone.

As the *Tryton* sailed a mile off the coast of Gabon, she turned west, heading out into open water. One of Taggert's crew spotted *Matilda* off the starboard bow and called out to the captain. Captain Taggert pulled out his spyglass and pointed toward the approaching ship. He soon discovered it to be *Matilda*.

"No worries, lads. It's only the *Matilda* making her way to the coast."

As Taggert continued watching the ship through his spyglass, he began to second guess himself, wondering, "When did *Matilda* start carrying artillery?"

Taggert became worried when he witnessed *Matilda* turning to apprehend his ship. She moved closer and closer, and then suddenly, "*Boom!*" a shot rang out from *Matilda's* bow gun, throwing a four-pound cannonball into *Tryton's* path. Taggert immediately knew what it meant. *Matilda* had been overtaken at some point by pirates, and she was now coming to take *Tryton*.

Taggert was a salty old dog who would not allow his ship to be taken so easily. He called out from the quarterdeck, "Full sails! We've got to make a run for it, lads!"

Taggert's crew fleetly began lowering the ship's sails, trying to outrun the *Matilda*, when suddenly, a call came from the stern of Taggert's ship.

"Ship ahoy off the starboard stern!"

Taggert swung around to see what his spotter had seen. Half a mile behind *Tryton* was a ship with crimson sails following. On the top sail of the mizenmast was an image of a black bird of some sort. Taggert was quite puzzled by the spectacle of a ship with red sails following behind him. The approaching ship flew no flag, but he could only assume it was a second pirate ship coming to capture the *Tryton*.

Taggert looked again at the ship's bow on his tail with his spyglass. He finally made out the name *"Raven's Destiny."* He had never heard of such a ship by that name nor of a ship flying crimson sails. A chill ran up his stiff spine, and he doubted that he and his crew could escape. Two armed vessels had him cut off from escape, one at his bow and one at his stern. Nevertheless, he intended to outrun them if at all possible.

Raven quickly gained on the fleeing ship, reaching within a quarter mile in only a few minutes. She determined that the master of the ship had decidedly chosen to run away rather than surrender. Raven was determined as well. She would not let her prize escape, even if it meant sinking her. She sent one of her runners to deliver a message to the gunner on the bow.

The young man ran from the quarterdeck to the bow and delivered Raven's message.

"Raven says to take out the rudder so it can not steer."

The gunner acknowledged Raven's order and sent his men into action. They loaded the bow gun and prepared to fire. He waited until Raven's helmsman lined up *Destiny* behind the fleeing ship. The gunner measured in his mind the placement of the gun and the timing of the wake being created by the prize ship in front of them. When he was finally satisfied, he called out, "Fire!"

The gunner's mate, who held a long stick with a slow-burning wick at the end, called out, "Fire in the hole!"

He dropped the wick into the hole at the top of the cannon tube, igniting the black powder inside the cylinder. ***Boom!***

A four-pound cannonball flew through the air, striking the stern of *Tryton* and knocking out her rudder.

CHAPTER 25

Both ships converged on the *Tryton*. With no way to steer his ship, Taggert had no choice but to raise his sails and surrender. *Destiny* reached the *Tryton* first. She pulled alongside the disabled ship, grappling her with their hooks, bringing her closer so they could board her. *Matilda* was soon grappled on the opposite side, leaving *Tryton* sandwiched between the two ships.

Raven met Pharaoh on Taggert's ship along with her and Pharaoh's boarding crew. They held Taggert's men at gunpoint while Raven spoke to Taggert.

"Captain, you have been captured!"

Taggert was shocked to see the young woman leading the band of pirates before him.

"What do you want?"

Raven asked, "What is your cargo?"

"I have nothing of value."

"Really? Then, why is your ship riding so low in the water?"

"There are only a few slaves below, nothing else! Who are you, young miss?"

"I am the Red Raven. Now, Captain Taggert, how many slaves is a few?"

"You know who I am?"

"Aye, I know the *Tryton*. I know you sail out of Bristol which happens to be my home. I know you're in the business of buying and selling slaves and I know that you have sailed your last voyage as a slave trader."

Taggert wasn't sure what she meant by that. Did she intend to end his life? His mouth suddenly went dry. He began to sweat. His salty demeanor was no more.

Raven asked, "How many crew are aboard?"

"There are only twenty-five, including me."

"Have them all assemble here on deck, now."

Taggert nodded to his first mate, who stood nearby, and then called out to the men.

"All hands assemble on deck! All hands!"

The crew of the *Tryton* gathered together in the middle of the main deck, surrounded by forty of Raven's crew. Raven moved up to the quarterdeck so everyone could see and hear her as she spoke.

"I am the Red Raven! You men are now my prisoners. You need have no fear of me or my men unless you decide to resist. I am not blood-thirsty, however, I will not hesitate to cut you down if you come at me. Now, all of you will transfer to *Raven's Destiny* and descend yourselves into the lower deck where you will reside until we reach our destination. While you are down there, decide what you want to do with your lives. You may come along with me as your new captain, or you may stay with Captain Taggert and his officers. We will be at our destination in three days. That's how long you have to make your decision."

Raven's crew pressed the captives over to *Destiny*, where they were taken below and shackled on the lowest deck where so many slaves had been shackled before. They would be treated much like the men and women they had hauled through the open sea so many times, with little food or water to consume and lying in their own filth.

Raven had Pharaoh and his crew tow the *Tryton* to the nearest shore on the coast of Gabon, where they ran her aground. They intended to careen her to her port side so that repairs could be made to the helm. First, they unloaded the slaves being held below decks. The people traveling below had no idea that another crew had overtaken their captors. Raven's crew reassured the people that they were in no danger.

Pharaoh discovered that Captain Taggert exaggerated about having only a few slaves onboard. Pharaoh counted three hundred and twelve African men and women in the ship's hull.

Raven sailed her ship nearby, protecting the crew of *Matilda* while they worked on the repairs of the *Tryton*. Once Pharaoh's men had the ship careened, it took four hours for them to make the repairs and bring the ship upright again. During the hours of dusk, all three ships were back in the sea sailing westward toward an uninhabited island Raven had found on her charts. The island had no name, so Raven decided to call it Captive's Cay. It took two days of fast sailing for them to reach the island. When they were half a mile off the beach of the cay, Raven had the prisoners brought back up on deck. The former crew of the *Tryton* came on deck looking ragged, dirty, and sweaty. They looked around and saw their former ship coming along beside *Destiny*. On deck, they watched as three hundred twelve angry black faces stared at them from the deck of the *Tryton*.

With Captain Billings clinging to her left shoulder, Raven addressed the former crew. "Well, you men have had time to think about your dilemma. If any of you decide to serve with me, know this, most of my crew is made up of men who are like those looking at you now. I rescued them to serve as my crew and they are faithful and true. If you are willing to serve alongside them as equals, you are welcome to stay as a part of our crew. If this displeases you, then there lies your new home."

Raven pointed at the island lying in the distance. She then commanded her men to remove the starboard rail and extend the gangplank.

"Captain Taggert, you will be first to exit the ship and proceed to your new home."

"What? Aren't you going to at least let us have our dories?"

"You are seamen are you not? You can swim I should think. Besides, all of you could certainly use a bath after being in that hull for three days. Now, off with you!"

Raven drew her sword and pressed Taggert to the plank. Taggert tiptoed over the plank, searching the dark waters below him. He crept over the plank at the point of Raven's blade until he finally ran out of plank. Raven gave him one last poke in his derriere, sending him into the waters below. Taggert cried out as he fell sixteen feet to the drink. He plunged beneath the surface, and when he rose again, he spattered and sputtered to cough up the seawater that had entered his mouth.

Raven sent each of the four other officers into the sea behind Captain Taggert. Each of them fumed in anger as they walked the plank. When they were all gone, Raven turned to the remaining crew of the *Tryton*.

"Alright, then. Who will be next?"

A young man, about twenty-two years old, stepped forward and said, "Begging the Captain's pardon, ma'am, you mentioned you might want some of us to stay to serve on your crew."

Raven looked them all over. They were all young except one. One man was about forty years old and stood next to a younger boy of about thirteen. Raven supposed they were father and son.

"Are all of you willing to serve alongside my crew without malice? You realize no one on this crew is better than anyone else no matter the color of their skin. I have officers who are dark skinned who you will be expected to take orders from and serve just as you would me. You understand this?"

The men all looked at one another, shook their heads, and muttered their agreement.

"Each of you will be required to sign the Articles of Code and abide by them. Consider yourselves crew to the Red Raven."

Everyone on board *Destiny*, including the new crew members, cheered and raised their hands in triumph and jubilee. The black men welcomed the new white men, shaking their hands and patting them on the back.

Raven raised her hands to quiet the crew, then said, "Make ready the ships! We sail for Gabon!"

Raven placed Caesar on the *Tryton* to command as her Captain. Attila was sent to serve as Pharaoh's first mate onboard *Matilda*. Nero was sent to serve with Caesar as his first mate on the *Tryton*, and Alexander remained on *Destiny* as Raven's first mate. The former crew of *Tryton* was split between the three ships. The older man with his son stayed on *Destiny*. Raven wanted to know more about them. They reminded her of herself with her papa.

As the ships returned to Gabon, Raven summoned the father and son to her quarters.

"What are your names?"

The man spoke up and answered. "I'm Isaac Finch, ma'am, and this is my son, Jeremy."

"How old are you Jeremy?"

The boy was timid and not quick to answer.

"Go ahead son, answer the Captain."

The boy almost whispered as he replied, "I'm thirteen, ma'am."

Raven asked, "Are you frightened of me, Jeremy?"

The boy hesitated to answer her. He shook his head slightly without looking at her.

Raven knelt in front of the boy and looked him in the eye. While still smiling, she said, "You have nothing to fear from me or my crew. As long as you work hard and do as you're told, no one will hurt you. Do you understand?"

Again, Jeremy only slightly nodded his head.

"We shall have to find that voice that lives deep inside you."

Then Raven turned back to Isaac and asked, "What were your duties aboard *Tryton*?"

"I was helmsman, Captain."

"Wonderful!" said Raven. "I could use an experienced helmsman on my ship. Many of my crew are very inexperienced. Report to Alexander. He is my first mate. Tell him I sent you to the helm."

"Aye, Captain!"

Isaac and Jeremy turned to leave when Raven interrupted, "Oh, Isaac, we aren't so formal here on my ships. You may call me Captain if you like, or you may simply call me, Raven."

"Aye, Raven!"

Just as they were exiting the hatch, Raven spoke to the boy.

"Jeremy, I would like you to report to the galley to serve as ship's boy. Everyday at noon I want you to report to me here in my quarters. I'm going to teach you to be a sailor."

Jeremy smiled ever so slightly as he nodded.

Three ships sailed together in formation, with *Destiny* in the lead. Two days after they left Captive's Cay, they approached Port Gentil on the shore of Gabon. The port was not significant, much like Port Harcourt. It was operated by another Frenchman named Andre Noel Arsenault. Arsenault was a descendant of a long line of weapons makers who began making swords, knives, and armor centuries ago. Through the years, they modernized their weaponry and produced firearms of all sorts. Although he still participated in manufacturing guns, Andre branched out and decided to enter slave trading as well.

The village at Port Gentil was made up of several little homes where his men lived, some having families. A large building near the rear of the village contained a forge where swords and guns were made. Another even larger building where slaves were housed until they could be disposed of by selling them to some greedy tradesman. Arsenault's manor sat atop a small hill on the south end of the village about a quarter mile away.

Raven moored her ships half a mile offshore from the port. Her timing could not have been better because they arrived three hours past dusk. Most of the village was asleep, and only a few guards patrolled the docks and the town. Raven ordered all lamps to be extinguished. She wanted to know as much as possible about the port village, so she sent a team to spy out the situation. Raven put Jeffrey in charge of the team, sending him out with six men from *Destiny's* crew in a dory.

Raven told Jeffrey, "I need to know what they have in the way of firepower. Do they have cannons, if so, what size are they. Do they have other weapons and how many. How many men do they have to fight us. Find their weakness."

"Aye, Raven!"

Jeffrey and his crew scrambled down into one of the dories and rowed to the shore, taking a route that would land them to the west of the village so they could come to shore unseen. They ran from tree to tree, crouched over as they ran to hide themselves from any lookouts that might be around. When they reached the tiny village, they discovered it to be made up of several grass and bamboo huts.

The crew quietly slinked through the village, counting the number of huts that existed as they went. As they made their way through the center of the village, Jeffrey spotted a guard standing next to a larger structure. Jeffrey motioned for his men to back-track to take a different route. They came around behind the barn and found it unguarded. Jeffrey removed his knife and cut away the bindings on the structure's outer wall, allowing him to make a temporary hole. He carefully poked his head inside but could see nothing because it was completely dark inside. However, he could hear someone inside. It sounded like someone was sleeping, but not just one person, many. Jeffrey pulled his head out and looked around. He noticed a small campfire burning in front of one of the huts nearby. He motioned to one of his men and sent him to retrieve a burning stick from the fire as a small torch. The young man did as Jeffrey requested and soon returned with a short stick of wood and a burning flame.

Jeffery took the torch and carefully poked it through the hole in the wall as he moved his head through and looked inside. In the dark, there lay nearly one hundred Africans shackled to posts that held up the barn's roof. They all slept, and no one saw him as he carefully walked through to get a closer look. There were no windows in the structure, only one door, and the inside smelled of urine and feces. Jeffrey quickly crawled back through the hole, then covered it up as best he could.

They proceeded to the next building, which was more substantially built—a wood-frame structure with a chimney in the center. Smoke rose from the chimney, and the smell of hot iron lingered in the air. The front of the barn, where the forge was located, was open. Behind the chimney stood a large door that was locked.

They moved to the back of the barn and discovered that although the walls were strongly built, no foundation was underneath. It was built on the sand. Jeffrey had four of his men start digging a hole next to the base of a wall to tunnel under the wall. Within minutes, they had dug a big enough tunnel for Jeffrey to squeeze through. He took his torch and crawled under the wall to look inside. Jeffrey found an armory filled with various weapons: swords, knives, long guns, pistols, and cannons. There was enough to start a revolution. He found crates stacked on another wall that, when opened, revealed ammunition for the rifles and pistols.

Jeffrey crawled back out of the barn and instructed his men to refill the hole, trying to leave no trace that anyone had been there. They crept back through town, returned to the dory, and rowed away from the shore.

Chapter 26

Jeffrey and his crew reported back to Raven four hours after they had left to spy out the island village. When Jeffrey arrived and knocked on her door, Raven was asleep in her bed with Captain Billings at her side.

"Enter!"

Jeffrey entered Raven's quarters as she rose from her bed.

"How did it go?"

"Very well! There are twelve huts scattered throughout the village. Two large buildings near the rear, one of them is a frame building. That one is a factory of sorts with a forge. They make all kinds of weapons including cannons. The other barn is where they keep the slaves. They keep them shackled to the post inside but the structure is flimsy."

"Was the building where they make the weapons left open? How did you get in?"

"No, it's locked. But, there isn't any foundation, we simply dug through the sand and crawled underneath. Raven, there must be a thousand weapons in there; swords, knives, guns, cannons and ammunition too."

"You said they had cannons, were there any protecting the coast?"

"None that I could find."

"Alright, Jeffrey. Good work! I'll think on it tonight and come up with a plan. Thank you!"

Jeffrey excused himself and left Raven to her thoughts. Raven lay on her bed and contemplated what Jeffrey had relayed to her. She saw two possibilities before her. They could sail into port in the guise of coming to trade, then find a way to release the prisoners or attack the village and plunder it. As Raven considered her choices, she eventually drifted to sleep.

The next morning, Raven signaled for her other Captains to meet with her aboard *Destiny*. Pharaoh and Caesar rowed over from their respective ships and climbed aboard. They met Raven and Jeffrey in her cabin and sat at a table together to discuss a plan of attack.

Raven made a drawing to simulate the village based on Jeffrey's description. She pointed out the locations of the living quarters, the armory, the prison, and Arsenault's Manor.

"We will begin at mid-night. Pharaoh, you will lead the first group into the village to capture the night guards. You will take the dory's into port and hide them away from the docks. Tell your men not to kill unless absolutely necessary. Carry them to the prison and shackle them. By that time, Caesar's men will join you."

"Aye, Raven."

"We will follow in the ships bringing them into dock an hour after you row your boat into shore. Caesar, your group will move in capturing those who are sleeping in those huts. Take them to the prison barn and free the people inside, put their chains on our prisoners and bring the freed people to the docks."

"Aye, Raven."

"Jeffrey, you and I will lead the last group to the armory. By that time, Pharaoh and anyone else who is available will meet us there. I want to empty it of every weapon they have. Everyone, leave your experienced white sailors onboard your ships. They will remain with the ships at the dock to protect them, and so that none of our men harm them by mistake. Are there any questions?"

Everyone remained quiet.

"Good! Now, everyone back to your ships and get some rest. I will see you at midnight.'

Raven's men nervously waited for midnight to come. They rested in their hammocks, but sleep was fleeting. Most of them bided their time by sharpening the blades of their machetes or knives.

Just before midnight, Pharaoh gathered his men and instructed them on what to do. Ten men followed Pharaoh down into two dories and rowed to shore. They landed near the spot Jeffrey had the previous night, tied their boats out of sight, and slinked into the village. Pharaoh divided them into pairs and instructed them to capture the guards quietly.

"Kill only if you must. Gag them, tie them up and take them to the big barn at the rear of the village."

Pharaoh took one pair of men with him. They moved from hut to hut, hiding and peeking around corners, searching for anyone outside. They discovered their first victim at the dock. They watched him as he stood near the beach, watching three ships moored in the distance. Pharaoh motioned to one of his men to take out the guard. The African crept up behind the guard and bounced the hilt of his machete off the back of the guard's head, knocking him unconscious. They bound the guard's hands behind him and gagged him, then carried him to the prison barn.

When they reached the prison, Pharaoh saw two other pairs already waiting for him with victims in hand. Moments later, the fourth pair showed up without a prisoner.

"We searched everywhere but found no other guards."

The last couple then joined Pharaoh and the others. They had an unconscious guard with them. The barn door had a lock. Pharaoh said, "Search them! See if one of them has the key."

They all searched their prisoners and finally found a key in the pocket of the man Pharaoh's men had captured. Pharaoh unlocked the door and opened it. It was dark inside, but he could tell people occupied the darkness. Pharaoh turned to one of his men and said, "We need light."

The man scrambled to the nearest campfire, retrieved a burning stick, and brought it to Pharaoh. Pharaoh stepped into the barn and saw nearly one hundred frightened black faces staring at him.

"Don't be afraid, my people. We are here to rescue you."

The people began to speak at once, and Pharaoh was afraid they would rouse the men sleeping in the huts outside. He raised his forefinger to his lips and said, "Please, keep quiet. There are other guards we must capture. Remain here until I return."

Pharaoh turned to four of his men and said, "Stay here and shackle these men we have captured. Do the same with the others when they are brought in. You may free our people, but keep them inside until I return."

He took the rest of his men to join Caesar in clearing the huts of its occupants. Caesar and his men were coming toward the village from the ships. He and Pharaoh coordinated their attack on the huts. They wanted all the huts entered and cleared at the same time. Once the attack groups were in place at all twelve huts, Caesar blew his conch, and the attack began. They entered the huts carrying torches and quickly captured each cabin's occupants. Some held two men, and others had only one man with families inside. They brought the captives to the prison, where they were gagged and shackled with the others.

Once the village was secured, Everyone joined Raven and her crew, who were already raiding the armory. They hadn't bothered searching for a key to the door; they chose to break the door down instead. They removed every crate of ammunition, every gun, and every blade from the warehouse. They left the cannons, not knowing if they were complete or not. All the weapons were placed in Destiny's hull, which *would la*ter be divided.

When they finished stowing everything on board, Raven gathered the people released from the prison and the three hundred and twelve from *Tryton* on the beach in front of the dock. She spoke to them as Pharaoh translated.

"People of Africa, you have been wronged by these white men who have invaded your land. They intended to sell you into slavery, but you will be no man's slave. My men and I have freed you. You are free to go back to your homes. If you have no home to return to, or if you simply would like to, you may join me and my crew as we continue to free others from their white captives. Those of you who decide to go home will be armed so that you may fight your way if necessary. All men who remain will be treated as equals in my crew but you must be allegiant to us all. I don't have room for everyone, so only the most capable men will be allowed to join us. Those of you who want to be considered for service on one of my ships, please move toward the docks and line up. The rest of you should move back to the village and receive your weapons for your trip home."

Raven put Caesar in charge of arming those people who would be going home. Raven and Pharaoh interviewed the candidates to serve on the ships. Daylight was approaching, and Raven still had much to do since she had not yet dealt with Arsenault. She and Pharaoh quickly filtered out fifty men who wanted to join them. They were too young and too slight of stature or too tall or bulky. Raven was looking for strong, athletic men to serve on her ships. She narrowed the candidates to one hundred, then walked the line asking questions until she could cut out twenty-five more. Seventy-five men were selected and quickly indoctrinated into her crew.

Dawn approached, and Raven moved everyone out of the area before starting her next phase of the takeover of Port Gentil. She lined up her newly armed men in front of the docks and most of her existing crew. Raven ordered six cannons be loaded with gunpowder only. When all six guns were ready, she ordered them to fire in succession.

"Boom!" "Boom!" "Boom!" "Boom!" "Boom!" "Boom!"

Andre Arsenault suddenly awoke hearing the blast coming from the beach.

"Henri! Henri!"

A servant entered Arsenault's bedroom and replied, "What is it, Monsieur?"

"That is what I want to know, idiot! Who is firing upon us?"

"I do not know, Monsieur."

"Well, find out!"

Henri left the house and quickly ran to the village to ask one of the guards what was happening. Who was firing on their little community?

Andre quickly dressed, stalked out of the house, and followed the path to the beach.

As he ran toward the village, Henri thought he heard someone walking through the jungle. He stopped to see who it might be. In the distance, he spotted many people carrying swords and machetes as they trudged through the jungle without speaking.

"Who are these people and why are they firing on us?" he asked himself.

Andre soon caught up with Henri and asked him loudly, "Why have you stopped? What are you looking at?"

Henri whispered to his master, "Monsieur, there are many people moving through the jungle away from the village. I think maybe the slaves have escaped."

"We shall see about this!"

Andre yelled out, "You there! Where do you think you are going?"

Henri tried to quiet Andre. "Shh! Monsieur, they are armed!

"What? How did this happen?"

Andre led the way as he and Henri trudged the path leading to the village. When he accessed the clearing where the tiny community lay, Andre was shocked to see it empty. He walked a little farther and found more than one hundred armed men standing at the docks in front of three large armed ships. He marched forward, determined to discover what nonsense had awakened him this morning.

"Who are you people and what are you doing here?"

Raven stepped forward and replied, "I am the Red Raven! My crew and I thought we might do a little trading."

"Is this what you call trading? What have you done with my men?"

"Your men are well enough. Some of them will awake with a headache, but they are not dead. You will find they have traded places with the people you had intended to sell as slaves."

"What? Henri, go and free the men! Send them to me right away!"

Raven replied, "Never mind, Henri. Stay where you are."

"What do you intend to do with us?"

Raven explained, "I'm here to make you a deal."

"What sort of deal?"

"I know you are a talented arms maker. I've seen your forge. I will allow you to stay here and continue making your weapons and selling them to whomever you like, under one condition."

"What might that be?"

Raven raised her voice so that all could hear her, "You will no longer engage in slave trading. You may make and sell all the weapons you like, I might even buy some from you from time to time. However, if I find out you are selling or buying slaves again, I will come back and utterly destroy your operation and hang you and your men."

"Who are you to say who can and cannot own slaves? Do you intend to free all slaves?"

"As I said before, I am Red Raven and yes, I plan to free every last slave I come across. No man or woman should be owned by another. Tell me, Henri. Are you a free man?"

"No, Mademoiselle. I have served the Arsenault family for forty years."

"Would you like to come with me and be a free man?"

Henri looked at his feet as he kicked at the sand and replied, "Oui Mademoiselle, I would love to."

"Then, come aboard, Henri!"

Henri smiled as he approached the ships and made his way onto *Destiny*.

"Alright, Monsieur Arsenault. You may now free your men from their bonds. But so you will remember to honor our agreement, I have one more thing for you to see."

Raven pointed behind Arsenault to the village huts. Raven's men had just ignited all of them, and they were engulfed with flames reaching twenty feet high.

"Au revoir, Arsenault!"

CHAPTER 27

*R*aven's *Destiny, Matilda,* and *Tryton* all set out to sea. Raven stood next to Alexander on the quarterdeck as he commanded the helm. Isaac stood at the wheel, steering *Destiny* into the wind, making corrections at Alexander's command. They sailed south from the equator, moving from summer into winter without notice. The weather was mild, and the temperature remained warm as they sailed away from the Gulf of Guinea.

Raven noticed how Isaac handled the helm; he was gentle with his steering, not making sudden moves. Most novices would make abrupt changes, turning the wheel too quickly when given commands to alter direction. But Isaac was no novice. He was as gentle with the helm as she had witnessed with his son, Jeremy. She began to wonder what might have happened to her papa. Did he and the crew of *Destiny* survive? If so, where are they now?

Just as they entered the deep waters of the Atlantic, a call came from the crow's nest of *Matilda*. "Ship ahoy! Starboard stern!"

Raven turned around to see what the spotter from *Matilda* had seen. She took out her spyglass, searched the horizon to the north, and spotted a vessel flying a French flag. Raven told Alexander, "Raise the mainmast!"

Alexander cried out to the crew, "Raise the mainmast!"

The crew scrambled up the mainmast's net ladders and began gathering the white canvas sail to tie it up along the yardarm.

Destiny slowed considerably as the crew bound the sail against the yardarm.

Alexander asked, "What is it, Raven?"

"I want to get a closer look at that ship. It looks like a frigate, but I can't be sure."

"Do you plan to attack a French frigate? They are much faster than we. We won't be able to outrun them if they pursue."

"No, I don't want to attack. I'm just curious about it. I don't think they would be after us. There hasn't been enough time since we attacked Port Harcourt for the French navy to have received word. I think they are going into the gulf to resupply. The French frigate is much smaller than the British frigate. It can't hold as much to supply the crew so they have to find a place to resupply. If they turn into the gulf, then we will continue to St. Felix. If they follow, we will need to prepare for battle because there is no way we can outrun them however much of a head start we have."

Matilda and *Tryton* took a cue from *Destiny* and raised their sails to match Raven's. Raven watched through her spyglass as the frigate quickly gained on the three ships. Raven found herself holding her breath and reminded herself to breathe.

Slowly, the frigate began to turn eastward, heading into the Gulf of Guinea. Raven turned to Alexander and smiled.

"We're clear. They are not after us, at least not yet. Lower the mainsail and make for St. Felix. "

"Aye, Raven!"

Three weeks later, Raven's fleet pulled into Port St. Felix on the west coast of Madagascar. They docked all three ships at the port, and as usual, Señor Rivera was waiting to greet them.

"Señorita Raven, you are back so soon? How good it is to see you. I see you have captured another ship. Do you need more cannons?"

"I do, Señor."

"Well, as usual you have come to the right place. Are we paying with gold?"

"I was hoping we could make a trade this time."

"Oh? What do you want to trade?"

"I have acquired some weapons I thought you might like. Pistols, long guns, swords, knives…"

Rivera interrupted, "You expect me to outfit you with six cannons for a few weapons?"

"No, I was thinking more like five hundred long guns, two hundred pistols, and maybe two hundred swords. They are all quality weapons made by Andre Arsenault."

Rivera raised his eyebrows and asked, "Did you say, Andre Arsenault? His family has made excellent weapons for many years. Where did you get them?"

"Señor, I don't ask where you get your slaves. Why would you ask me where I got my weapons?"

Rivera asked, "Is he still alive?"

"He is. And he will remain alive as long as he abides by our agreement."

"May I ask what that agreement entails?"

"He is to continue making weapons but he may no longer participate in slave trading."

"I see, and he has agreed to these terms?"

"I believe he will honor our terms. If not, he will pay the price."

"And may I ask, what is that price?"

"He and his men will dance from a tall tree on a short rope."

Rivera's eyes widened with her comment made in such a matter-of-fact fashion.

"Well Señorita Raven, let us look at these weapons and see if we can make a trade."

Raven had her crew bring a sample of the weapons to the main deck and opened the crates to reveal them to Rivera. He picked up and examined several rifles, pistols, and swords.

"Bueno, bueno, muy bueno! Señorita Raven, we have a deal."

Raven asked, "What, no bartering?"

"Si, I think it is a good deal for both of us. There is no need for games between us. Maybe another time I will not be so generous."

Raven replied, "Something tells me you already have a buyer for these weapons."

"Ah! You know me so well, Señorita Raven."

They exchanged smiles and then shook hands to seal the deal. Rivera's men began unloading the weapons from Raven's ship while her crew loaded the new cannons onto *Tryton*.

Raven sent Pierre and some of the women into the village to buy supplies for the ships while Raven and Captain Billings casually strolled along the docks.

Four hours later, the cannons were installed on *Tryton*. Some of the men asked about leaving the ship for a few hours. Raven wasn't keen to have her crew return unfit for duty after drinking themselves without constraint. Instead, she suggested they have a little party onboard the ships.

"We will break out a keg of rum for each ship and you can celebrate our good fortune together here."

Everyone was elated by her suggestion and cheered as the rum kegs were brought up from below decks. They sang, danced, and drank until the rum was finished. By that time, night had fallen, and eyelids were becoming heavy. The crew retired to their hammocks and dreamt the night away.

The next morning, Raven awoke to the sound of another ship pulling into port. She quickly dressed and left her cabin with Captain Billings clinging to her shoulder. As she stood on the main deck, she watched the ship as it tied up to the docks. Raven read the name of the ship on its bow, *Charming Betty*, a vessel larger than any of the ships in her fleet.

Raven climbed to the quarterdeck for a better look as *Betty's* crew prepared to unload its cargo. She watched as the captain and first mate of the ship conversed on their quarterdeck. Raven looked to her left and spotted Rivera walking toward *Betty* with a concerned look. She wondered why. Usually, a new ship coming into port meant money in his pocket. Why was he not happy to see this ship?

Raven then watched as the first mate and someone she thought might be their helmsman stepped down from the quarterdeck and left the ship together to meet Rivera on the dock. She saw them all speaking together but could not hear anything they were saying. The helmsman seemed familiar to Raven; however, she could not make out his face from a distance.

She continued to watch as the first mate seemed to introduce himself to Rivera, then introduced the helmsman.

"Buenos Dias, Señor Jones! It is good to see you and your crew again." Rivera said nervously.

Kevin Barker Jones had sailed on the *Charming Betty* for ten years, starting by serving as a ship's boy and moving his way up through the ranks. He was tall and well-built. Serving ten years at sea had made him look much older than his twenty-five years should have.

Jones replied, "Good morning, Señor Rivera. This is my helmsman, Mr. Ashworth."

"Ah, yes. Nice to meet you, Señor. Now what can I do for you today?"

Jones said, "Well, we're here to trade as usual."

"And, what have you brought for me?"

"Rum, tobacco, and cotton from the Carolinas."

"Yes, of course. I can buy it all from you. I'm sure we can reach a suitable price."

Jones replied, "Buy? We're here to trade. Don't you have any slaves to trade?"

"Regrettably no, Señor Jones. I have no slaves to trade right now."

Jones was puzzled. Rivera was acting odd. He had always preferred trading over outright purchase.

"Where are we supposed to get our slaves, then?"

"I don't know, Señor. I hear Guinea might have some for sale."

"Guinea? That's three weeks sailing from here. I'll have to talk to the captain about this. Mr. Ashworth, don't let anyone off-load the ship until I get back. "

"Aye, Mr. Jones!"

Jones walked back up the gangplank to seek out the captain and give him the bad news. Rivera then asked Mr. Ashworth, "Pardon me, but didn't you use to sail on a ship called *Destiny*?"

Ashworth was a little confused by the question, "I...I did. How did you know?"

"I am a man who observes much, Señor. Did you not have a young boy?"

"Yes, my son Richard."

Rivera asked, "And where is he now?"

Ashworth's continence fell as he replied, "Lost at sea when *Destiny* went down."

"Oh Señor, I am sorry to hear this. But, don't give up hope, you may see him one day, no?"

Suddenly, Rivera turned to Raven, who was watching from afar and beckoned her over to him. Raven turned and looked behind to see who he was motioning to. When she realized he meant for her to come over, she stepped down from the quarterdeck, onto the gangplank, and onto the docks to meet him and the stranger. Ashworth's back was turned toward her as he spoke to Rivera. As Raven approached slowly, a lump came into her throat. The stranger looked so familiar.

Rivera took Ashworth by the shoulder and said, "I want you to meet a friend of mine, Señor. This is the Red Raven, capitan of *Raven's Destiny*."

John was shocked to see the young woman standing behind him, whom he hadn't seen in over a year. Her beautiful curly red hair spilled around her shoulders, with a tiny monkey clinging to the curls.

Raven was also shocked to see her papa standing before her when she feared he might be dead.

"Papa?"

"Raven!"

The two embraced and cried together as John kissed his daughter on her forehead.

"I was so afraid you perished at sea. Where have you been?"

"It's a long story, but come with me and I shall tell you."

"Wait! I have my duties aboard the *Betty*!"

"Would you not rather sail with me on one of my ships?"

"Ships!"

"Yes, Papa. I am a captain now, or rather more like a commodore. I have a small fleet of ships and I need good men."

Raven turned to Rivera and said, "Thank you, Señor!"

"It is my pleasure, Señora Raven. And do not worry, I have already told Señor Jones I have no slaves for him."

"Thank you, again!"

Raven and John walked arm in arm together up the gangplank and went to Raven's cabin to talk.

"What happened to you, Papa?"

"We rowed in those dories for weeks. We were finally picked up a hundred miles from Charlestown by the *Betty*. Most of us signed on with her, Mr. Gant, Hardy and Mr. Greer are all there."

Raven replied, "Maybe we can get them to join us as well."

"Us?"

"Papa, I want you to come sail with me and my crew. Bring the others with you if they like."

"Have you become a merchant?"

"Not exactly. More like a privateer."

"What do you mean?"

"We are in the business of freeing slaves from other merchant ships or from those who trade them. We recently captured Port Harcourt and Port Gentil in the Gulf of Guinea. We also freed slaves from the *Matilda* and *Tryton*."

"Sounds more like piracy the privateering!"

"We serve the people of Africa! We are their privateers. We free them from slavery and provide them with weapons to fight for themselves against slavery."

"So you kill innocent men?"

"I haven't killed anyone who hasn't tried to kill me first, Papa. I will shut them down, however. Every last one of them!"

"What about Rivera? You seem to be on good terms with him."

"He and I have an understanding. He keeps my identity secret and I allow him to continue with his ventures. Out of respect for me, however, he doesn't trade slaves while I am in St. Felix."

"What do you do with the slaves after you free them?"

"Most of them are sent back to their homes, armed and ready for battle. Some of them stay and serve on my ships. Most of my crew are made up of Africans."

They sat silent for a while before Raven asked, "Well, will you come with me?"

"It seems like a strange venture but, yes I'll come with you."

Raven smiled at her papa and asked, "Will you talk to the others and see if they will join us as well?"

"Certainly!"

CHAPTER 28

When first mate Kevin Jones informed Captain Bennett that Rivera didn't have any slaves to trade for their cargo, Bennett was irate. Bennett instructed Jones to sell the cargo to Rivera, and they would head to another location he knew of to buy their slaves.

Once Bennett was finished with Jones, a knock came on his door.

"Enter!"

John Ashworth, Louis Hardy, and Andrew Greer, who served as *Destiny's* doctor, entered the cabin.

"Pardon us, Captain."

"What is it, Mr. Ashworth?"

"Captain, the three of us have been offered a place on one of the other ships here in St. Felix. All three of us served with the officers of that ship before we came to work for you."

"And I suppose you want to go back to them, am I correct?"

"Well, yes Sir."

"Permission denied!"

"May I ask why, Sir?"

"Ashworth, how do you expect this ship to operate if I lose one of my helmsmen, my cook, and the doctor? There isn't anyone here to replace you men. If we were in Bristol, it might be different, but I'm not likely to find any replacements here in the middle of nowhere."

"I understand, sir. May I at least go back and tell them we won't be able to join them?"

"What, so you can abandon me? If I let you off this ship I'll never see you again. No sir!"

"Yes, sir. Thank you, sir."

The three men left the captain's cabin with disappointment on their faces. Hardy asked, "What do we do now?"

John replied, "If I can get a note over to Raven she can come and get us."

Hardy asked, "Raven? Who is Raven?"

"Do you remember my son, Richard?"

"Yes, fine young lad he was!"

"Well, the truth is, he wasn't my son, he was my daughter and her name is Raven."

"What? Richard is a girl? Come to think of it, that does explain some things."

"Like what? Asked John.

"Like why he never took his shirt off when he worked like the other sailors did. He never bathed with the men. And that day when the captain had him whipped when he was very young, he wouldn't take his shirt all the way off to receive his lashes."

John looked at Mr. Greer, who didn't seem shocked at all, "You don't seem surprised, Mr. Greer."

"I'm not. I have known almost from the beginning that Richard was a girl."

"How?" John asked.

"The day Richard was whipped, I tended to his wounds, I caught a glimpse of his chest as he dressed. I could see he was not a boy, but a girl."

"And you said nothing?"

"I saw no reason to say anything. I liked Richard from the start. He was sharp, intelligent, and hard working. Whatever secret he or she had was my secret as well."

John smiled at Greer and shook his hand. "Thank you Mr. Greer. I know Raven will be excited to see you."

Hardy asked, "So, you have a plan?"

"Aye, I'll get in line with the crew unloading the cargo and try to pass a note to Señor Rivera. She has a special relationship with him evidently. Then it will be up to Raven. Just be ready to go when the time comes."

Rivera and Kevin Jones stood conversing on the docks as the men of *Charming Betty* began unloading the cargo. John placed a keg on his left shoulder to hide his face from the captain should he be watching. As he walked past Jones, he handed Rivera a folded piece of paper and said, "Here is some seed for your bird, Señor Rivera." Then, he continued to walk away.

Rivera was caught off guard as he accepted the paper. "What?"

The man was already gone. Rivera looked at the folded piece of paper with the word "Raven" written on the outside.

"Oh, thank you, Señor!"

Rivera then asked Jones, "Would you please excuse me, Señor Jones? I have to attend to something."

"Of course."

Jones stepped away to keep an eye on his men unloading *Betty*. Rivera casually walked to *Raven's Destiny* and made his way up the gangplank. Isaac stood beside the rail as Rivera approached, "Excuse me, Señor. Would you be so kind as to ask Capitan Raven if I might have a word with her?"

Isaac replied, "Wait here, please."

Isaac went to Raven's cabin and told her Rivera requested to speak with her.

"Show him to my cabin please, Isaac."

"Aye, Raven."

Isaac returned to the gangplank and said to Rivera, "Follow me, please."

He led Rivera to Raven's cabin and knocked.

"Enter!"

Isaac opened the door and allowed Rivera to walk into Raven's cabin; then, he returned to his place at the ship's rail.

Raven asked, "What can I do for you, Señor Rivera?"

"I have something for you. Your papa passed this to me discreetly while he was unloading cargo from the neighboring ship."

Raven took the folded paper and read its contents.

Dear Raven;

Captain Bennett has refused to allow Hardy, Greer, or me to transfer to your ship. Mr. Gant opted not to come with us. I'm afraid we cannot go with you at this time. He won't even allow me to say goodbye to you in person. He plans to set sail at dusk once the ship has been unloaded.

Farewell;

Papa

Raven looked at Rivera and said, "I'm afraid there will be trouble this evening."

"Oh, Señorita? What kind of trouble?"

My papa would accompany two other men and join me on my ships. Captain Bennett has refused their request. Papa says they will leave port tonight at dusk, so I must hurry if I am to rescue him. It would be best if you went back to your hacienda, Señor. It could be dangerous for you."

"I see what you mean. Then, I shall finish my business with them and leave them to you."

"Gracias, Señor Rivera!"

"Adios, Señorita Raven. Until we meet again."

Raven moved quickly. She called Pharaoh and Caesar to meet her on *Destiny*. Each captain left their ship and walked down the docks to walk aboard Raven's ship. Raven met them on the main deck and quickly instructed them on what she wanted them to do.

"Go, now! We have no time to waste!"

Each of the three ships slowly pulled away from the docks and set sail toward the Cape. After sailing for an hour, Raven ordered her crew to raise the sails. The three ships moored together a quarter mile apart from one another, then waited.

Another hour passed, and the sun began to sink into the western sky aft of the ships. Daktari called from the crow's nest, "Ship ahoy! Due east!"

Raven pulled out her spyglass and searched the eastern waters. She found *Charming Betty* sailing with full sails directly toward her. Raven told Alexander, "Give the order to standby."

"Standby, prepare to make sail!"

Raven's men and the crews aboard *Matilda* and *Tryton* prepared to lower their sails to make the pursuit of the approaching ship. Raven didn't want to raise her sails until *Betty* passed by them. She knew that a ship as large as the *Charming Betty* would be no match in speed with her smaller vessels. Her ships could outrun and outmaneuver *Betty*.

Half an hour passed while they waited for *Betty* to come into range. Caesar moved *Tryton* into a position east of the other ships and pointed her bow southward. *Destiny* and *Matilda* pointed their bows westward, ready for pursuit if needed.

Caesar stood by the gunner on the ship's bow, ready to give the order to fire. *Betty* was at full sail as she moved into the blockade she was unaware of. Caesar patiently waited for the right time, then yelled, "Fire!"

The fuse was lit, and "***Boom!***" The cannon erupted, shooting its ball across the *Betty's* bow.

Caesar heard someone from the approaching ship call out, "Raise the sails! All stop!"

Caesar then called out, "Lower the foresails!"

Tryton soon pulled in behind *Betty* to pursue should she not stop. Raven ordered, "Lower the blood foresail!"

Her men dropped the crimson sails of the foremast and pulled along a path that would glide her ship parallel to the *Betty*. Pharaoh ordered his ship to do the same from the opposite side of the prey ship.

Bennett knew trying to outrun the three ships in his wake was useless. He ordered his men to slow the ship so his pursuers could board them. Pharaoh moved in along the port side of *Betty*, and his men threw their grappling hooks to secure her. The crew aboard *Betty* stared at thirty men, mostly Africans, who were pointing long guns at them.

Raven's crew threw their hooks on the starboard side and captured *Betty*, too. However, Raven's men boarded the other ship and held the men at bay using swords and knives. Raven swung herself over to join her men while carrying a pistol in her left hand and a knife in her belt. She looked around the ship as she landed on deck, searching for the captain.

Captain Bennett stepped down from the quarterdeck and stood before Raven. He was quite disgusted to see a young woman in man's clothing. He asked, "What is it you want?"

"You have three of my men aboard your ship and I want them back."

"I believe you are mistaken."

"Possibly, but I think not."

Bennett spat out, "I have no pirates aboard my ship other than your rabble you brought on board just now.

Raven replied, "I beg to differ, Captain."

Then Raven announced, "John Ashworth, Louis Hardy, Andrew Greer, step forward please!"

The three men picked up their packs containing their belongings and walked toward Raven. As they approached, she turned her head and motioned for them to climb aboard *Destiny*.

Raven looked around and noticed a familiar face.

"Hello, Mr. Gant!"

Henry Gant was shocked. Who was this young woman who called him by name?

"Don't you recognize me?"

Gant stepped forward for a closer look. His eyes squinted as he realized he recognized who she was, but she was once a he.

"Richard? Richard Ashworth?"

"Aye, Mr. Gant! Only it's Raven Ashworth."

Gant smiled a sneaky little smile of defiance as he said, "I always knew there be something odd about you."

"And I always knew you were a sniveling little rat!"

Raven took out her knife and slashed his right cheek. Gant backed away, gathering himself before grabbing his knife and pursuing Raven. Suddenly, Twelve sword points were held against his torso, keeping him at bay. Gant sneered at Raven as he tossed his knife to the deck.

Bennett then arrogantly asked, "Will that be all?"

"No! There is the matter of a toll."

"What toll?"

Raven replied, "All slave ships sailing through these waters must pay me a toll."

"But, we have no slaves aboard this ship!"

"Yes, but only because Rivera refused to sell you any. Your sole purpose in sailing into Port Felix was to purchase slaves.

"Well why does that concern you?"

Raven replied, "Captain, have you not seen my crew? It is made up mostly of men and women who were taken as slaves by men like you. Now they help me free their kind from your kind. Now, pay the toll!"

Bennett exasperatedly asked, "How much?"

"All of it."

"What? What do you mean all of it?"

"I mean every last doubloon! And, anything else of value you might have."

Raven signaled her men standing by on *Destiny*, and they swung aboard the *Betty* and began ransacking the captain's quarters and everywhere below decks, searching for anything of value. Two of her men carried a sea chest from the captain's cabin containing money and jewels.

While the ship was being searched, Caesar's men moved up behind the *Betty* in a dory and began sawing through the helm's ropes. They quickly returned to the *Tryton* and signaled to Raven that the rudder was disabled.

Raven then turned and swung back aboard her ship along with her men. They cut loose the *Betty* and all three ships sailed away to the west.

CHAPTER 29

Raven's fleet again sailed toward the Gulf of Guinea to see what other merchant ships they might find there. Along the way, Raven was able to catch up with her papa.

"What happened to you, Papa? Where did the dories take you after *Destiny* sank?"

"We rowed for a week heading west in hopes of being found by another merchant vessel or any vessel for that matter. We lost a few men along the way. Some went out of the head from drinking sea water. We tried to tell them not to, but they were so thirsty, they wouldn't listen. We were finally picked up by a schooner fishing off the coast of Charlestown. They took us ashore and we were fed and cared for until we were able to recover. Some of the men wanted nothing more to do with the sea; they found jobs in Charlestown. The four of us signed on with Captain Bennett doing what we knew how to do. He wasn't a bad captain. I've seen much worse. But he wasn't Captain Billings, that's for sure. What about you? How did you become a ship's captain?"

"When *Destiny* sank, she broke apart. My five men and I tried to free as many of the slaves in the hold as we could before she did. We ended up with about seventy men and women. Captain Billings and Mr. McGuire went down to the sea. We tied planks together using two of the masts as floats. We floated along for days, fighting off sharks. Two men were eaten by sharks. We finally caught sight of a small island and began paddling our raft toward it. We lived on that island for more than a month or so, long enough that we built huts for us to live in. Then we built canoes and waited for a ship to come our way. A ship finally came. They stopped at the island to collect fresh water, so we seized the opportunity and overtook them. We left them on the island while we took their ship. They had over a hundred slaves onboard; they now sail with me."

John asked, "So, what's your plan?"

"We'll do what we've been doing ever since. We captured two more ships, we overthrew Port Harcourt and freed their slaves. I had to kill the leader of that post, a Frenchman. We landed on Port Gentil and freed three hundred slaves there. I told the trader there if he agreed to no longer capture and sell Africans he could live and continue his business of producing firearms."

"Where are we going now?"

"Back to the Gulf. There are several more trading posts and ships there that need to be purged of their sins."

Raven saw the concerned look on her papa's face, "What is it, Papa?"

"I was just wondering, do you realize how grave the circumstances you are putting you and your crew into? I admire that you want to free these people, I really do. But, you're disrupting more than just people's lifestyle. Slavery isn't just about having someone to do your work for you, it's about greed. When you start taking away someone's money, eventually you will be the one to pay. These aren't just merchants that you are effecting; we're talking about royalty, and not just English, but French, Spanish, Dutch, they all have a hand in it."

"I know, Papa. But I can't let it go on in good conscience any longer. These people deserve lives of freedom, and it isn't only them. The English, with their "*Indentured Servants*," must also be stopped. No one should have to live under the thumb of another individual no matter who they are."

John replied, "I just hope you realize what a grave situation you have put yourself into. I could at least understand if you were robbing these people of their riches, but taking away how they make their money seems to be the slow and dangerous way to go about it.'

Raven walked over to one of three sea chests on the floor near her bed and kicked it open.

"Who said I'm not robbing them?"

Raven's ships arrived at the mouth of the Gulf of Guinea twenty days later. They patrolled the waters on the north side of the Gulf, searching for merchant ships entering or exiting any ports that lay off the coast of Africa.

On the third morning, Pharaoh's seeker called from the crow's nest, "Ship ahoy! Port stern!"

Pharaoh looked over his left shoulder and discovered a vessel sailing toward the Gulf. The ship carried only two masts. Pharaoh signaled to Raven, who was watching the vessel through her spyglass. John stood beside her and asked, "Is it a merchant?"

"No, it looks like a schooner. There are only two masts. Tell Pharaoh to let it pass."

Alexander signaled to Pharaoh to let the ship pass. They all watched from a quarter mile away as the schooner sailed past and entered a port called Abidjan on the coast of Côte d'Ivoire, an African country bordering Liberia on its eastern side.

The ship flew a French flag and carried twelve guns on each side of her hull. Raven decided it was most likely a French navy vessel, which she wanted no part of. The schooner had more firepower and was faster than any of her merchant vessels.

As Raven watched the schooner dock at Abidjan, she moved farther into the Gulf and looked for prospects elsewhere. She signaled the other ships, and they set sail, heading east. Raven decided to try her hand at the port of Lomé, a coastal town in Ghana. They sailed four hours before reaching Lomé. As they sailed into port, they saw that the docks were empty.

Raven decided that since there were no merchant ships to pillage, she would send spies to see what the town held. She suspected they were like most other African ports owned by the French or the Spanish, hoarding slaves to be sold and shipped to the Americas.

Five groups were sent out from the ships. Only white men were sent so that no one was suspicious of seeing three ships manned by African sailors. Raven instructed everyone onboard the ships to remain out of sight as much as possible until dusk.

John Ashworth led one of the groups that was sent into town. The others were led by Jeffrey Hamilton, Andrew Greer, Isaac, who took his son Jeremy, and Nathan Coates, who had been one of the crew on *Matilda* when it was captured.

Raven met with them all before they were sent out to spy.

"Your mission is to gain information about what is traded here. Don't get into any trouble, and don't get drunk. That goes especially for you, Jeremy." Raven said with a smile, looking at the boy she had become so fond of.

The men chuckled at Raven's joke and then settled for the rest of her orders.

"Look for any sign of slave trading. Are there any warehouses or barns that are holding slaves? If not, what kind of trading do they have here? I want to know if it is worth spending our time here, or should we move along. Alright? Good luck, everyone!"

Raven waited on the quarterdeck as her men spied out of the town. After a while, a man approached her ship. He was nicely dressed, wearing a felt hat and carrying a cane. He called up to her from the dock, speaking to her in French.

Raven called down to him, "Je ne parle pas Français. Un instant s'il vous plaît."

"Oui, Mademoiselle!"

Raven sent one of her crew over to find Pierre to come and translate for her. Henri had been transferred to the *Tryton* to serve as their cook, so Raven sent for Pierre, who was closer. Within moments, Pierre trotted over to *Destiny* and met Raven at the bottom of the gangplank.

"Pierre, can you please translate for me?"

"Oui, Mademoiselle!"

Pierre and the stranger conversed for a while before Pierre finally translated to Raven: "He says he is Jean Claude Bastian, a businessman here in Lomé. He supplies many of the ships that come to port here."

"What kind of supplies?"

Pierre listened again, then translated, "Food, rum, ship's gear, weapons, slaves..."

Raven interrupted, "He has slaves to sell?"

"Oui, Mademoiselle!"

"How many does he have to sell right now?"

Pierre asked, then answered, "He has approximately six hundred slaves, Mademoiselle."

"Ask him if anyone else here has slaves to sell. Tell him I have three ships to fill."

"No, Raven. He is the only supplier here. He said his papa settled this town and owned just about everything here. He died a year ago, so now Monsieur Bastian owns it all."

Bastian spoke again, then Pierre translated, "He says he can take you to his warehouse where they are located. You can look them over before you purchase."

Something in the pit of Raven's stomach told her Bastian might not be legitimate. Raven told Pierre, "Ask him if I can meet him at his warehouse later today."

Pierre translated, and Bastian seemed disappointed she wasn't willing to leave immediately. Bastian gave Pierre directions on how to find the warehouse and asked when he could expect her."

"Tell him I will meet him in two hours."

Raven heard Bastian reply, "Tres bien!" and then he walked away.

Raven walked back onboard *Destiny* with Pierre by her side.

"Pierre, I would like you to remain with me for the remainder of the day in case I need you to translate for me again."

"Oui, Mademoiselle."

"Excuse me while I go to my cabin, please. I will call for you when I'm ready for you."

"Oui, Mademoiselle."

Raven entered her cabin and found Captain Billings nibbling on an orange. When he saw Raven enter the room, he squealed, leaped onto her shoulder, and began fingering her hair as if looking for lice or fleas to nibble on.

Raven lay on her bed to rest for a while, waiting for her men to return.

Someone rapped on the door, waking Raven from a deep sleep. She raised herself up and sat at the edge of her bed. *"Knock, knock, knock!"* she heard again, then answered, "Enter!"

Jeffrey stood before her with one of the other men at his back. Jeffrey's face was pale as if he had stood at death's doorpost.

"What is it, Jeffrey?"

"Raven, as we were searching through town we came across a poster on a tree near the center of town. I removed it and brought it to you."

Jeffrey handed Raven a rolled-up piece of parchment and waited for her to read it. It was written in French, but she immediately knew it was a wanted poster. There was a drawing of a young woman's face on it. She had long curly hair. It wasn't a very good likeness, but Raven knew it was supposed to be her portrait. She tried to read the print but could only make out a few words.

"Call Pierre to come back to me!"

The man who had accompanied Jeffrey stepped out and found Pierre sitting on one of the steps leading up to the quarterdeck. He called out to him, "Pierre! Pierre, Raven needs you right away."

Pierre quickly walked to Raven's cabin and entered. Raven handed Pierre the poster and asked, "Can you translate this for me?"

Pierre examined the poster momentarily, then replied, "No, Mademoiselle. I can't read. If you can read the words to me, I can tell you what they mean."

Raven took the poster back and read the words as best she could.

"Recherché pour piraterie et crimes contre la France."

Pierre translated, "It says, wanted for piracy and crimes against France."

"Environ seize ans, cheveux roux et yeux bleus."

"Approximately sixteen years old, red hair, and blue eyes."

"Le Corbeau Rouge."

"The Red Raven."

"Toute personne ayant des informations doit contacter les autorités locale."

"Anyone with information should contact the local authorities."

Raven felt panic as she heard the words translated.

"We have to get out of here! Pierre, get back to your ship and tell Pharaoh to prepare to launch the ship. Tell him to ready his men for battle in case we are attacked. Go, quickly!"

"Oui, Mademoiselle!"

Pierre turned, ran out of her cabin, down the gangplank, and then sprinted to *Matilda*.

"Jeffrey, tell Alexander to call back our men!"

"Right away, Raven!"

Jeffrey and his companion left her quarters and found Alexander on the quarterdeck.

"Alexander, Raven says to call back our men and prepare to sail!"

Alexander flew into action. He called out to his men in Swahili to prepare to sail away. He then took his conch shell out and began to blow long blasts, one after the other, to signal their crew to return to the ships immediately.

Caesar and Pharaoh began barking orders to their crews to set sail. The crews snapped to, untying the lines that held them to the docks, and men began climbing the rope ladders to let down the sails once the order came.

Raven met Alexander on the quarterdeck with Captain Billings on her shoulder. She used her spyglass to search for her men. The buildings and tall trees throughout the town made it difficult for her to see. Alexander cried out and pointed to one of the streets, "There! It is your papa!"

Raven searched where Alexander had pointed, and her heart flipped as she realized Papa was running with his companion to reach the ship. As she watched, she heard Alexander say, "And there is Mr. Greer!"

Andrew and his partner sprinted to the ship. People came out of their homes and shops to see what was happening. Nathan Coates and his companion nearly knocked over a woman as they rounded the corner of her house, trying to get to *Matilda*.

All that was left was for Isaac and Jeremy to arrive. Raven anxiously waited, searching every street for Isaac and his son. Alexander blew his conch repeatedly, hoping the two would hear and return quickly.

Men carrying weapons began arriving from the streets of Lomé. Alexander saw them and told Raven, "We can not wait any longer. It is too late!"

Raven said nothing as she continued to search and hope for their return. Alexander called his men to begin their departure. "Raise the gangplank! Shove off!"

The sailors of *Destiny* retracted the gangplank and pushed the ship away from the dock. *Matilda* and *Tryton* had already moved out and began stretching their sails into the wind.

Suddenly, Raven spotted someone running from the east end of the docks. It was Isaac and Jeremey.

"There they are!"

Raven pointed to the father and son, who were running as fast as possible, dodging people and obstacles along the way. They finally reached the dock where *Destiny* had been tied, but it was too late. The gangplank was gone. Isaac snatched up the thirteen-year-old boy and flung him as hard as he could toward the ship. Jeremy flew into the arms of two crewmen and knocked them down, all three rolling onto the deck. Isaac took five steps backward, ran as fast as he could, and leaped. He caught hold of the rail, but then his feet slipped, leaving him hanging with only his fingertips. Two men caught his arms before he could slip away into the water. They brought him onboard to safety, and everyone momentarily celebrated before returning to their duties.

Raven called John, Andrew, Isaac, and Jeffrey to share the news that she was now a wanted woman.

John asked his daughter, "What do you intend to do?"

"The French are searching for me, so we will go where they don't have any authority. We'll make our way to the Americas."

Chapter 30

Raven's ships sailed westward, making good speed. She constantly looked over her shoulder to see if anyone was following her. The more Raven thought about it, the more she was convinced that Lomé was a trap. Monsieur Bastian was luring her into town with the promise of slaves so she could be captured and he could win the reward set on her head. She boiled in anger and fear at the thought.

As they sailed through the Atlantic, Raven contemplated her next move for days. She realized her crew, especially the white men, would not continue to sail with her to free other men from slavery. If there was no profit in it for the men, they would soon grow tired of her crusade.

The days dragged by with no other vessels in sight. They sailed west along the equator, thinking they might find a merchant ship heading for Brazil. One hundred miles east of Brazil, Raven directed her ships to turn northwest up the coast of South America. Ten days later, they found themselves in Caribbean waters.

One day, Raven decided to meet with the older sailors of her crew, John, Andrew Greer, Louis Hardy, and Nathan Coates. They all gathered in Raven's quarters as she drilled them with questions about islands in the Caribbean.

"I have been thinking lately about our situation. I know now that my hopes of releasing all slaves being taken from Africa is unrealistic. My friendship with Pharaoh and the others caused me to be overwhelmed by the thought of another human being living in servitude to another. However, saving more slaves from the French, Spanish, or even English, won't feed my men. We have no place to deliver the freed ones so that will be safe. They will likely be recaptured. So, what are your thoughts?"

No one spoke for a long time. Finally, Louis Hardy said, "Well, Raven, the way I see it, the French see you as a pirate. Am I right?"

"Yes."

"So, why not let them continue thinking that. You'll never convince them otherwise. You can pay your African friends by giving them enough money to eventually buy themselves the kind of living they want. With enough money they can buy land, or a boat of their own, or whatever they want."

"Are you saying, we should become pirates?"

"Why not? There are hundreds of Spanish ships sailing these waters filled with gold and silver traveling from Mexico, Panama, and Colombia. There's a place I have heard of on the north end of the Bahamas that we could use as a base to sail from."

Raven asked, "You mean New Providence?"

"Right!"

"But doesn't New Providence already have a lot of pirates living there?"

"Well, we'll fit right in won't we?"

Raven looked around the room and searched for answers from the other men who had remained silent.

"Does anyone else have an idea?"

Nathan said, "I've never thought of myself as being someone who would ever enter into piracy, but I've never thought I might some day be a rich man either. Having more money than would fit in my pockets appeals to me."

Raven looked at her papa. "What do you think?"

John looked into his daughter's blue eyes and smiled, "Raven, I would follow you to the ends of the earth no matter how much money I might make. But, I think you may have left someone out on this little meeting."

Raven was quiet, then responded, "Yes, of course."

She opened her cabin door and called for Jeremy, who promptly ran to her.

"Jeremy, get Alexander and tell him to come to my cabin, then signal the other ships that I need the Captains and first officers to join me in my quarters."

Jeremy nodded, then ran to find Alexander.

As they waited, Raven asked the men in attendance, "Would you men mind standing and allowing my officers to sit at the table, please?"

They all did as Raven asked.

In less than a minute, Alexander knocked on Raven's door.

"Enter!"

Alexander entered and saw the other men already in attendance. He began to wonder what this was all about.

"It's alright, Alexander. Have a seat. I'll explain as soon as the others get here."

Jeremy picked up a conch shell and blew the signal for officers to meet together, just as Raven had shown him. Each ship returned a blow of the conch to him, acknowledging, "*Signal received.*"

Almost immediately, a dory began rowing from *Matilda* and *Tryton* to *Destiny*. Jeremy met the dories and instructed Pharaoh and the others, "Raven is in her cabin."

All four officers walked into the entry of Raven's quarters and knocked.

"Enter!"

Just as Alexander had done, all four men wondered what might be happening when they saw Raven, John, Jeffrey, Andrew, and Nathan standing around Alexander's table.

Raven said, "Please have a seat."

Each man sat down nervously, wondering what they had done wrong.

Raven began, "I've been talking to Papa and these other men about our future. It was pointed out that I should have included you men into this conversation, so I have summoned you to consult you as well."

Raven put the wanted poster on the table before them and said, "It seems that I am a wanted fugitive by the French government. That is why we fled so quickly from the Gulf of Guinea. Since we left there, I have been contemplating what we should do next. I have come to realize my desire to free all the African slaves being sold and sent to the Americas was a bit too ambitious. As much as I would like to free them all, I now know, that would be impossible. So, what will we do? We have three ships at our disposal. How should we use them?"

They all sat around the table, looking at each other and then at Raven. Pharaoh shrugged his shoulders, saying, "Raven, from the beginning, I have been here to serve you. I will continue to serve you until the end."

The others muttered their agreement.

"But don't you understand, you are free men! If you want to stay with me, that's fine, I'm glad to have you. But, if you want to go back to your homes or start new homes somewhere, you are welcome to do that."

Caesar replied, "I have no home to go back to. I will stay with you."

The others muttered their agreement again.

"Don't you want to take your money and find a place of your own? Maybe start a family?"

Pharaoh replied, "Maybe someday, but I would like to make more money first. I don't know where I will be in the end, but I will know where I want to be when I see it. Then, I might leave and start a new life. Not until then."

Raven replied, "Alright then, a suggestion has been made. It seems the French, Dutch, and especially the Spanish make treasure runs through these waters carrying gold, silver, and more. There is a place called New Providence in the Bahamas where other sailors like us are setting up a base of operations. We will go there and see if it might be suitable for us. Then, we will begin raiding the ships traveling through these waters."

Everyone began showing their excitement at the prospect of capturing treasure ships and making out with three shiploads of gold and silver.

Raven ordered, "Let's get to it then!"

Everyone left her room carrying new attitudes and new purposes.

Raven's ships arrived in New Providence a week later. As they neared the port, they saw two ships already there: a square-rigged ship and a brigantine. The brigantine was a much smaller ship than the square-rigged ships. It had only two masts but was built for battle, carrying twenty guns in her hull.

As the ships approached the docks, several men gathered along the beach, watching the three ships come into port, one of which was flying crimson sails. Two men broke through the crowd to meet the vessels. The first was a man about thirty years old, wearing a captain's uniform. He was clean-shaven and tied his brown hair behind his head underneath his three-cornered hat. The other man was younger and a bit frightful. He had black hair and a beard that hadn't been trimmed or combed in quite a while. The two of them met Raven as she stepped down from her ship.

The two men were unsurprised to see Raven, as so many had before them. However, they were a little surprised to see that her crew was mostly Africans.

The first man held out his hand to Raven and said, "Welcome to New Providence, I'm Benjamin Hornigold. This is my first mate, Edward Teach. You must be the Raven we have heard so much about."

"That I am, gentlemen."

"What brings you to New Providence?"

"My men and I are looking for a place to lay up for a while. Maybe resupply, maybe see what kind of mischief we can discover."

Benjamin replied, "Ah, mischief. I love it indeed. Well, we can offer you a place here in New Providence where you can stay while you are not involved in mischief, but not for free."

Raven inquired, "How much?"

"Two shares in whatever you take, and if you capture a ship, I will buy it from you. I'm looking to expand my fleet."

"How many ships do you have now?"

"Just one, that's why I want to expand."

Raven replied, "I have no need for anymore ships, so here's what I offer; whatever ship we take next I will give you instead of the two shares. The deal holds true for any ships we take thereafter."

Benjamin pondered Raven's offer, then replied, "Deal! Now Raven, would you join me for some refreshment at my house?"

"May I bring my captains along?"

"But of course. Bring them along."

Raven walked back to *Destiny* and gave Jeffry orders to settle the crew. Then, she walked to each ship and asked Pharaoh and Caesar to join her. Hornigold was caught off guard when he saw that Raven's captains were African. As they approached Hornigold, he commented, "I have never seen black captains before."

Raven replied, "Well, now you have. This is Pharaoh and Caesar. They are my most trusted men. Pharaoh has been with me since I was twelve years old serving as ship's boy on the original *Destiny*."

"So, you used to be a boy?"

"When my mother died, I started dressing as a boy so that I could go to sea with my papa."

They continued to talk as they walked to Benjamin's house.

"How many ships have you taken?"

"Why do you want to know? Do you want to collect the reward for me?"

"There is a reward for you?"

"Sure! Don't you have bounties offered for your capture?"

"I do, but I've been at this a little longer than you. How much are you worth?"

Raven replied, "Let me put it this way, I'm worth a lot more to you working with you than I would be if you turned me into the French."

Benjamin smiled at her as they continued to walk along.

CHAPTER 31

Raven, with Captain Billings on her shoulder, Pharaoh and Caesar followed Hornigold into his house. They sat at a table where they were served refreshments of fruit and rum.

Hornigold asked, "Do you always carry that furry little creature on your shoulder?"

"This is Captain Billings. He is master of *Raven's Destiny.*"

Raven began asking questions about their prospects of finding treasure.

"When can we expect the Spanish treasure ships to come through?"

"Not for a while. You just missed the first fleet by a few months. They sail through this area between March and April. The next fleet won't be here until sometime between August and September."

"Do you just sit here and wait, or are there other ships to raid?"

Benjamin replied, "There are others, most of them sailing into Charles Town carrying slaves. Have you been to Charles Town?"

Raven handed Captain Billings a piece of banana and replied, "That's where *Destiny* used to sell her slaves when I served onboard her under Captain Billings."

"Then you know, ships coming out of Charles Town are easily taken, but have little to give in the way of gold or silver. Most of their money gained from the sale of slaves is then spent on other cargo like cotton and rum. Here, this rum that we drink came from Charles Town."

Raven raised her mug to make a toast and said, "Well, I guess Charles Town isn't all bad."

They drank their rum, and Raven asked, "How long will it take to get to Charles Town from here?"

"Two and a half days. Charles Town was built inside a cove that leaves them vulnerable on three sides. The ocean side, the south and east, and two rivers on the east and west. I have often thought of setting up a blockade there to rob the ships coming in and going out, but I do not have enough ships yet."

"How many ships do you need?"

"Six or seven would be ideal, but I could manage it with five."

"How many do you have?"

"I have can find four ships ready for battle, one of them being my ship, the *Ranger*."

"Well, with my three you have enough do you not?"

Benjamin smiled slightly and replied, "Indeed."

Raven asked, "When do we start?"

"We should work out the details of the attack first. The captains of the other ships should be here within the next two or three days. I'll talk to them, then."

Raven said, "We should work out the split as well."

"What split?"

"Since we're working together, I was thinking we should split the loot rather than you just take two shares of what I capture. Maybe...50–50?"

Hornigold raised his eyebrows before replying, "I think not. It is my plan and I have to pay the other ships. I'll go 70–30."

"Oh, how generous of you. Let's make it 60–40."

Benjamin responded, "You tire me young lady, 65–35."

"No, 60–40 and you keep any captured ships."

Hornigold stared at her momentarily and noticed she was very good at this negotiation game. "Alright, deal."

They shook hands and then drank to the deal.

Benjamin commented, "You should have held out for 50-50. I would have taken it."

"No you wouldn't."

"You're right, I wouldn't."

They both chuckled.

They wasted the next few days on the island waiting for Hornigold's other ships to arrive. Another square-rigged ship and two schooners finally arrived after two weeks at sea searching for other ships to prey upon. Once each vessel's captains were informed of the plan, they set out to sail together.

They sailed out of port early one morning and arrived at midnight on the third day. Seven ships lined up at the mouth of the bay leading into Charles Town. No ship leaving or going to Charles Town could go through the blockade without having been boarded and searched for anything of value, including slaves. If a ship had slaves aboard, the boarding crew captured it and sailed back to New Providence, confiscating the ship.

Raven quickly grew bored by the waiting game they were playing. She longed to be out on the open sea searching for a prize ship that would provide the kind of payoff that all sailors dreamed of finding.

A month passed while they blocked the path leading to Charles Town. Town leaders began to panic because the slave trade had slowed to a halt, and the goods from England that they sorely needed were not making it into port. The governor of South Carolina, Edward Tynte, was notified of the blockade and summoned the leader of the Carolina Militia to come to the aid of the citizens of Charles Town.

Early one morning, as the sun began to rise over the bay, a barrage of cannon fire filled the sky from the coast of Charles Town. Twenty cannons futilely fired upon the blockade from the shore. Sixteen-pound guns threw shots into the air toward the floating embargo, but the cannonballs never reached their marks. The ships were all moored outside of firing range for the big guns so that the militia could do little from the beach.

Wealthy merchants contacted Governor Tynte, informing him that the situation was becoming dire. If supplies were not allowed to reach port soon, all trade in Carolina would end. Tynte suggested that the merchants band together and arm their vessels so they could attack the blockade since a navy had not yet been established to help them.

Five merchant vessels were held in port because the owners didn't want to risk losing their cargo to marauders. Alexander Trammel, a wealthy merchant based in Charles Town, owned three ships, and he located and armed them with six twelve-pound cannons. Trammel then instructed the captains of the vessels to attack the blockade and clear a path for approaching merchant vessels.

Most of the merchant captains were unskilled in naval tactics of war. Their men knew little about loading and firing large artillery weapons. When they attacked the blockade, one of Hornigold's vessels was absent, taking a load of spoils to the island. Hornigold saw the five merchant vessels leaving the port and noticed they were now armed. He signaled to Raven to prepare for battle.

Raven moved her ships into position to point her guns directly at the approaching ships. Hornigold lined his ships next to Raven's ships. Each vessel was scattered about a quarter of a mile from each other.

When the first merchant vessel reached a distance its captain thought would be firing distance, he ordered his guns to fire upon the blockade.

Boom! The first cannon blasted its shot, but instead of the cannonball flying through the air, it remained in the cannon's barrel. The inexperienced gunmen had overloaded gunpowder and improperly packed the cannon's barrel. Instead of shooting the cannonball from its tube, it exploded on the ship's deck, blowing shrapnel and fire in all directions. Several of the crew were impacted by the blasts, catching their clothes on fire, burning their skin, lighting up their beards, and causing general panic. The explosion then set off a sequence of explosions throughout the ship by igniting the powder stored beneath the deck.

Raven's crew watched as the first ship was engulfed in flames. Many men cheered as they watched the ship burn. More explosions ignited as the flames reached beneath the ship's hull, lighting the gunpowder below decks. Then, they watched as the ship slowly sank into the bay.

Four merchant vessels remained sailing toward the blockade. After witnessing the casualty of the first ship, the other captains ensured their guns were loaded correctly. When they reached the point they thought was within cannon shot of the blockade, they began to fire ***Boom! Boom! Boom! Boom!***

Shot after shot erupted from the approaching ships, sending numerous cannonballs at the blockade. Two shots were fired toward *Destiny*, one falling only ten feet short, the other arched over the bow, missing its target.

Raven ordered the crew, "Prepare to return fire!"

The gun crews on the port side prepared their guns as Alexander turned the ship so the guns could aim at their target. Pharaoh and Caesar also prepared their gun crews, turning their ships either to starboard or port and presenting their guns to the approaching vessels.

Hornigold's three remaining ships began firing from their bow guns as they pointed their bows at the attacking ships. Benjamin's ships presented less of a target, but his four-pound guns could do less damage than Raven's six-pounders that she intended to fire upon the opponents. Hornigold fired his bow guns at the enemy. The four-pound cannonballs hit their targets but did minor damage as they hit three merchant ships' decks. The cannonballs bounced upon the deck, cracking the deck boards but not wholly.

Raven fired her rail guns at one of the remaining ships in the bay. The six-pound ball of the first shot tore through the lower part of their main sail and then put a hole into the captain's cabin below the quarterdeck. The second shot knocked out the foremast of that same ship, bringing down its foresail and rigging onto the deck. Two of their crew lay pinned to the deck underneath the mast, the sail draped over them so no one could see them.

Pharaoh's crew fired on the second vessel. The first shot damaged the ship's rudder, while the second shot blew a large hole in the starboard hull just above the waterline. With each dip, the ship took into the water's waves, the ship took in more and more water. The ship didn't immediately sink; however, it continuously filled the hull with water, slowing the ship to a near halt. Pharaoh continued to fire, aiming again for the hull. Two more shots hit the starboard hull. One of the shots hit just below the waterline, causing extensive damage to the hull causing the ship to sink quickly. Men began jumping from the vessel, swimming toward the shore or one of the other ships.

With three ships damaged or sinking, the other two vessels returned to the shore to save themselves. The battle was soon over, for now.

A schooner was sent out into the bay the next day, hoisting a white flag of surrender. Hornigold and the others allowed the ship to approach unmolested. When the ship arrived, it pulled alongside Hornigold's vessel. Raven took a dory over to Benjamin's ship to witness what was being said.

The governor sent Colonel Evan Gray of the Carolina Militia to negotiate a cease to the blockade. When Raven arrived, the Colonel and Benjamin were already in heavy discussion.

Gray said, "What is it you seek from us to open the bay back up to trade vessels?"

Horniglod replied, "Might I suggest a protection tax?"

"Protection tax? What is that?"

"My ships will patrol this bay. Every ship that enters cannot leave without paying a twenty percent tax on all the goods they sell while here in Charles Town. Each will be inspected upon arrival and an estimate made as to the value of its goods. Once the goods are sold, the tax must be paid to one of my representatives before the ship leaves the bay."

Gray replied, "Twenty percent? That's a very high tax indeed. Not even the King requires that much tax."

"Ah but Colonel, wouldn't it be worth it to see that your supplies make it into port? Your merchants will simply need to charge more for their goods. They charge more, they collect more, I get paid more, everyone is happy."

The colonel frowned at the suggestion but relinquished and said, "I will present your suggestion to the governor."

"Fine. While you are discussing it with him, let him know we will remain in port until he pays us £1000 in gold or silver. That payment will seal our deal. You deliver the £1000 when you bring me his answer, and I will pull out all but one of my ships."

Gray returned to his schooner and then sailed back to port.

Raven returned to her dory and rowed back to *Destiny*. She was beginning to think aligning herself with Hornigold was not such a good idea. She had little expectation of ever seeing her forty percent cut.

The next day, Colonel Gray returned to Hornigold's ship carrying a small chest containing £1000 silver. He had his men set the chest on the deck of Hornigold's ship, then said," The governor has agreed to your terms. Here is your payment of £1000 silver."

"Very good, Colonel. I will pull my ships back immediately. One of my ships will dock at your port and check each ship leaving or coming to make sure my fee is paid."

Gray glared at Hornigold but said nothing. He turned, climbed over to his schooner, and sailed back to port.

Hornigold sent Raven a message advising she and her ships could return to New Providence. Raven set sail out of the bay but didn't sail back to New Providence. Instead, she pulled north of the Bahamas to meet with Pharaoh and Caesar. She summoned them to meet her on *Destiny* to discuss their next steps.

Pharaoh and Caesar met Raven in her quarters with Jeffrey to discuss their plans for the future.

Raven said, "I think it's a mistake to partner up with Hornigold and his crew. I don't trust any of them."

Pharaoh replied, "I think you are right, Raven. These men are not to be trusted. They will turn you in for the reward as soon as they get the chance and then take all of your ships, too."

Raven asked, "Do you have a suggestion of where we should go or what we should do?"

Caesar suggested, "We only saw one French ship at the Gulf of Guinea. Why can we not go back there to search for more merchant ships. We had good success there. We should go back there and try again."

Raven thought for a moment before replying, "Why not? One French navy vessel shouldn't frighten us away. Let's go back and see what we can stir up for ourselves."

Everyone agreed and raised a glass of ale to toast their next adventure.

CHAPTER 32

Raven's ships sailed eastward, catching the tradewinds that would carry them to the west coast of Europe. Fifteen days later, they changed course, sailing south along the coast of West Africa. Eleven days later, they sailed into the Gulf of Guinea. Raven checked in at Port Gentil to see how things faired with Andre Arsenault.

As they pulled into port, Raven saw that Arsenault had rebuilt most of the huts that had existed before she had them burned. Other places were still under construction. Raven rested her ships along the docks, and she left *Destiny* to have a look around. She took twenty armed men with her. Almost as soon as she reached the beach, Raven was met by Arsenault and a band of his men.

"Mademoiselle, I see you have returned. What is your business here?"

"I'm just checking up on you, Monsieur Arsenault. I want to make sure you aren't dealing in slave trading anymore."

"I am not, Mademoiselle. Only firearms and ammunition, as before."

"I'm glad to hear it. You don't mind if we look around just to make sure?"

"Be my guest, s'il vous plaît. I have nothing to hide."

Raven motioned for her men to spread out by twos to search the area for slaves. They searched the huts, the large barn, and the forge where Arsenault's firearms were made. Then, they proceeded toward Arsenault's residence. They searched Arsenault's house and outbuildings and found nothing. As they began to walk back to where Raven was waiting, Daktari noticed a path leading in the opposite direction from the house. He led the men down the trail for about a quarter of a mile until they reached a clearing in the jungle where another large structure stood. Before stepping into the clearing, Daktari waited to see if anyone was patrolling the area. The structure was larger than the one they had freed Arsenault's slaves from before; it was twice as big. One of the men standing behind Daktari nudged him in the ribs, then pointed in the distance at a man standing under a shade tree. They found another man resting under a tree on the opposite side of the building. Daktari spoke to the men following him.

"You four, go around that way and get behind that man. You other four, do the same with the other man. The rest of us will walk out to distract them. We will capture them, then look inside the building."

The men split up as Daktari had instructed and surrounded the guards, relaxing in the shade. Once Daktari's men were in position, each group signaled him by making a bird call, first from the west side, then one from the east. Daktari returned the call and led the remaining men into the clearing. They reached the halfway point to the barn before the guards noticed them. The guard on the west side jumped up when he saw ten men walking toward the barn. He called out to the other guard, who jumped up and began walking toward the men approaching. Suddenly, each guard was surrounded and disarmed by Raven's men. Each man was then led to the barn, where they met Daktari.

"Open the door," Daktari ordered.

The two guards were young, barely in their twenties. Neither was brave enough to try to take on a band of eighteen well-armed

Africans. One of the guards fumbled around, looking for the key to the lock that sealed the barn door. He shakily presented the key to Daktari and waited for further instructions from the tall black man.

Daktari unlocked the door and then opened it. A wave of stench erupted from the barn; the smell of urine and feces made everyone choke and cough as it wandered out of the building. It was dark inside, but the light allowed into the barn from the opened door was enough for Daktari and his men to see that Arsenault was once again hoarding men and women to sell.

Daktari turned to one of his men and said, "Quickly! Go and get Raven!"

The young African ran as fast as he could through the clearing and down the path that had led them from Arsenault's house. He ran down the next path to the beach, where he found Raven conversing with Arsenault.

The young man spoke to Raven in Swahili so the French man would not understand his words. "Raven! Come quickly! There is a large building half a mile from here. Many people are being kept there."

Raven glared at Arsenault. "Well Monsieur, it seems you're hiding something from me."

Raven signaled to Pharaoh and Caesar, who were waiting on their respective ships. Each captain sent down twenty more armed men to escort Raven. Two of her men bound Arsenault's hands behind his back and led him away, following Raven as she walked the path to where her young man took her. Twenty minutes later, they entered the clearing where Arsenault had hidden his slave barn.

Daktari had already begun unchaining the captives held inside the barn. The people slowly strolled around the clearing, shading their eyes from the bright sunlight. As their chains were removed, more and more people walked out of the building.

An hour later, all the people had been freed from their bonds. They counted four hundred and thirty-two enslaved people. Raven asked them to gather around so she could speak to them. Daktari translated so everyone could understand.

"I am the Red Raven. I and my men have come here to deliver you from a fate more terrible than death. These men intend to sell you to other men who will take you to a far away place where you will no longer see your families. A place where you will be forced to work and not be paid. A place where you will not be allowed to come and go as you please. My men were faced with that same fate. I took them out of bondage and gave them their freedom. I am now giving you your freedom. You may return to your homes. Warn your people, your families. Avoid traveling in small packs. Arm yourselves and be ready to fight for your freedom. Don't be afraid to fight these men who come looking to capture you, because death is better than a life of slavery. Death is quick, whereas slavery is forever."

The people murmured as Raven finished speaking. They asked in one voice, "What will you do with these men?"

Raven raised her hands to quiet the crowd before she said, "Come and see what I will do with these men."

Raven and her men led Arsenault and his men back to the beach. All the people quietly followed. When they reached the shore, Raven saw that her captains had already retrieved the rest of Arsenault's crew and had bound them. They were kneeling in the sand near the docks.

Raven called out to her men as she approached, "Rope!"

Several of her men scattered around the camp, looking for lengths of rope. Others went onboard the ships and searched for rope.

When Raven and the entourage reached the beach, she ordered her men to hang Arsenault's men from the trees scattered throughout the encampment in sight of any passersby.

Each of Arsenault's men was taken to a tree with low-hanging branches. Some hung as high as twenty feet from the ground while others as little as ten feet. A rope was looped around each man's neck while his hands were bound behind him. Then, three men began tugging on the rope, raising the condemned man off the ground. Their bodies wriggled, jerked, and convulsed as they tried to free themselves. Their faces turned red as air failed to enter their lungs. Each man slowly died at the end of a rope while Arsenault watched with contempt on his face.

Raven turned to Arsenault and said, "Your turn!"

Arsenault's eyes began to water, and he sobbed as he realized his life was about to end. He remained quiet, saying nothing to Raven nor anyone else as they led him to a tree and placed the noose around his neck. As her men stood ready to hoist Arsenault off the ground, Raven's last words to him were, "I warned you what would happen. You ignored my warning and now you must pay."

Raven nodded to her men, and they pulled against the rope, lifting his feet off the ground. Arsenault grunted, convulsed, and whimpered as his body was lifted twenty feet from the ground. They tied off his rope at the base of the tree's trunk and watched as his body swayed back and forth.

Pharaoh asked, "Do you want to burn it again?"

"No. We will leave it as a warning for anyone who passes by here. Bring me a door from one of the huts so I can make a sign."

They did as she asked. Raven had them bring her some red paint from the hull of one of the ships, and she wrote these words on the door."

"Beware the Fate of Slave Traders!"

They set the sign up underneath Arsenault's hanging body. Then, Raven sent her men to loot Arsenault's house and all the huts, including the forge where all the weapons were made.

Raven's men found three small sea chests filled with gold and silver coins in a room in Arsenault's house. They brought it out to Raven and showed her what they had discovered.

"Well, at least we get paid for this dirty deed. Take it to Jeffrey so he can hand out the shares!"

The men cheered as they picked up the chests and carried them onto *Destiny* to present to Jeffrey.

Everything looted from the huts, and the forge was also taken aboard *Destiny*. Any food, weapons, and other supplies were immediately divided and parceled out to all three ships.

The crew were in high spirits as they set sail once again. Having extra coins in their pockets always made them happier. Raven decided they would sail up the coast to see what else might be available. The next port would be at Mbini, which was on the coast of Equatorial Guinea. The Portuguese had settled the area in the 1400s.

Raven knew little of the town but thought it might be promising since it was so close. She would allow the crew to leave the ships and spend some of their money while they scoped out the town to see what it might offer.

It took only seventeen hours to reach Mbini, so they arrived mid-morning the next day. The skies were filled with a blanket of gray clouds hiding the sunlight. The wind blew strong out of the north, chilling the air with an arctic blast.

There was just enough room at the docks for the three ships to moor, indicating that Mbini was not a place where much commerce occurred. Nonetheless, Raven wanted to explore the little town to see what might be available.

Group after group left the ships, wanting to explore the little town east of the beach. Raven watched them leave the boats as she enjoyed the cold wind blowing through her hair. As usual, Captain Billings sat atop Raven's shoulder, clinging to one of her curls.

Raven noticed that some of her crew had paired up with one another. Pharaoh walked with Rose as they stepped from *Matilda* onto the dock. Caesar and Birdie left *Tryton* together and walked hand in hand. Attila walked with April while Alexander and Melody left together. Nero had paired up with Whisper, which Raven thought was appropriate since both were so shy. Although, since Nero had been made first mate aboard *Tryton*, he had come out of his shell and become more assertive at the encouragement of Caesar.

John Ashworth approached Raven and asked, "Are you not going into the village?"

"No, Papa. I think I will stay on the ship for now. Someone has to keep an eye on our vessels and everyone needs a day where they can be carefree."

"What about you? Don't you deserve to be carefree?"

"Oh, I am, Papa! Everyday for me is a carefree day. I love being at sea. That is where I am happiest. And, to see my friends have a moment of happiness is all I can hope for. They all need to feel free to do as they please if only for a short while. I enjoy watching their happy faces as they leave the ships," she said and smiled.

John asked, "Would you like me to stay with you?"

"No, Papa. Go and enjoy yourself. Captain Billings will keep me company."

John nodded, then stepped away from his daughter to join the others in the little village. A few moments later, Jeffrey walked up and stood next to Raven but said nothing. They stood side by side at the rail, watching the others leave the ships. Their hands were so close as they stood together that they couldn't help but feel each other's touch. Jeffrey noticed that Raven didn't pull away from the touch of his pinky finger touching hers. He lingered there for a long while, still saying nothing. Finally, Raven took Jeffrey's hand and led him away from the rail. They walked hand–in–hand to the port rail on the ship's opposite side and stood together once more. Raven reached behind Jeffrey with her right hand and held him around the waist. Jeffrey wrapped his left arm around Raven and pulled her close as they stood side by side, watching the gray clouds roll through the sky. Captain Billings reached up and tugged at Jeffrey's ear as to tell him he was too close.

Chapter 33

Mbini proved to be quite the respite for Raven's crew. They spent a week in the little village, visiting the friendly people. The locals had developed a fermented drink they called Sirop Ivre. It was made from bananas and honey and was delicious and intoxicating.

After a week of relaxation, Raven decided it was time to leave. She called her crew back to the ships, and they weighed anchor, heading east, deeper into the Gulf of Guinea. There was little in the way of civilization as they sailed up the coast on the western shores of Africa. For five days, they sailed along the coast of the Gulf without much to see. There were no villages within sight of the beach. The lands were uninhabited.

On the fifth day, a young man sitting in the crow's nest of the *Tryton* called out, "I see something shining through the trees! The light flashes like a star in the night sky." He pointed toward the shore where only tall trees and a distant mountain stood.

Caesar relayed the message to Raven that something had been spotted. Raven took one of the dories along with John and Jeffrey and rowed to *Tryton*. When they reached the other ship, Caesar called down to her from the rail.

"Timlani has seen something on the shore. It sparkles like the stars he said. Up on that mountainside."

Raven asked, "Were you able to see it?"

"No, I haven't. I think we must climb up to the crow's nest if we are going to see it."

"I'll be right up!"

Raven climbed out of the dory and onto the Tryton. Caesar grabbed her hand to help her over the rail as she swung over it. Raven asked, "Do you have your spyglass?"

"Aye, Raven."

"Let me have it."

Caesar handed her the spyglass, and she immediately began climbing the rope ladder up the side of the mast leading to the crow's nest. Raven greeted Timlani as she climbed into the nest with him.

"Which direction?"

Timlani pointed to the mountain and said, "There, just between those two mountain peaks."

Raven pointed her spyglass at the notch in the mountain created by the twin peaks and searched for any light. *Tryton* bobbed up and down in the water as the waves hit her hull. Suddenly, a sparkle of light flashed in the eyepiece of the glass as Raven swung it slowly over the horizon. Raven froze as the light once again disappeared. She pointed the glass in the direction she thought she had witnessed the flash. Just as the flash returned, Raven heard Timlani say, "Look! There it is again! Did you see it?"

Raven saw the light flash, but only for a second. She waited again, and when the movement of the waves against *Tryton's* hull hit the ideal position, the light flashed again.

"There it is!"

Timlani asked, "What do you think it is?"

"I don't know! It could be anything reflecting the sun's rays. Maybe someone on the mountain carrying a polished sword, or it could be diamonds, or maybe even..."

Timlani impatiently waited for her to continue, "What, Raven? What could it be?"

"Gold."

Raven pulled out her compass and took a reading of the location of the light before climbing down the rope ladder. She then told Caesar, "Find a place to anchor the ships, we're going ashore!"

Caesar blew the conch to signal the other ships to follow him to a place suitable to moor the ships. Each ship returned a signal and followed as *Tryton* sailed closer to land. The tide was low, so they moored about one hundred yards from the beach. Each ship lowered its dories and filled them with men and weapons before rowing to shore. Six dories carried fifty men and Raven to the sandbar that served as a beach. The dories had to be dragged the last twenty yards to reach dry sand because the water was so shallow. Crabs scurried across the sand, trying to escape the feet of the men tugging on the boats as they pulled them ashore.

Raven pulled out her compass again and took another reading while she searched for an entry into the jungle. "That way!" she pointed as she and Caesar led the way into the jungle.

Caesar led the way, swinging a machete to clear a path they could travel. Raven kept an eye on her compass and redirected Caesar from time to time. Although the temperature wasn't too extreme, the humidity made it seem much worse. Mosquitos were rampant and unrelenting as they traveled down the path that Caesar cleared. Rats crossed the trail before the travelers as they walked down the track. Various kinds of snakes clung to low tree branches that hung above the path. Occasionally, one of the snakes would drop from a tree, landing on an inattentive traveler on the trail. Men would gasp or even cry out as a snake found itself on the shoulder of one of them.

Caesar called back to the men behind him, "Don't worry about the snakes! They are after the rats."

Three hours passed as the safari traveled through the jungle, trying to find the mountain where the light had been. The mountain grew as they got closer but still seemed far away. Suddenly, Caesar stopped in his tracks to listen. In the distance, he heard **Boom, Boom, Boom, Boom, Boom.**

He turned to Raven and said, "Drums. They know we are here."

"Do you see them?"

"No. But they see us. They will come to us, soon."

Caesar continued clearing the path for a while longer; suddenly, a man appeared in front of him. The man had long hair that stood up on top of his head. He had a bone piercing his nose, running horizontally to the ground as he stood there. He carried a long spear and a shield of a hardened animal hide. The man was naked except for a loin cloth worn around his waist. The man mumbled words in his native language, his eyes wide with anger. Caesar shrugged his shoulders to the man. The man spoke again, and Caesar realized the language was similar to his but not the same. Caesar tried talking to the man as best he could using Swahili. Eventually, they figured out what each one was trying to say.

"He says we are not wanted here. We must go."

Raven said, "Tell him, we are not here to harm them. We only want to help them."

After babbling back and forth, Caesar said, "He wants to know how we can help. We have nothing they need."

Raven thought for a while about what these people might want that she could supply.

"Caesar, what do you think they might want that we could get for them?"

"These are simple people. They have not been exposed to the things we have seen. Maybe some of the colorful textiles, weapons, rum…"

"Rum!"

Raven looked behind her to find someone near the middle of the line.

"Joku!"

Everyone behind Raven began to call his name, "Joku! Joku! Joku!"

Joku pushed his way forward to meet Raven.

"Aye, Raven?"

"Joku, may I borrow your flask?"

"My flask, Raven? Why do you want it."

"Joku, everyone knows what you carry is that flask. Don't be coy with me."

"Aye, Raven."

Joku lowered his head in shame as he handed Raven the flask. Raven took the flask and stepped forward to the warrior who was waiting. She opened the flask and took a swig to show she could be trusted. Raven winced a little as the liquid fire burned her throat. Then she offered it to the man. Curious, he took the flask from Raven and smelled of its contents. He raised his eyebrows as he realized the liquid had a sweet yet fermented smell. He took a sip and smiled as the liquid filled his mouth with happiness. He took another longer drink, and Joku gasped as he watched his rum disappear.

Caesar and the man conversed some more, this time in a more friendly manner. Then Caesar told Raven, "He wants to know if we have more?"

"Tell him we have more and can get even more if we can find something to trade."

Caesar translated, and the man nodded in agreement.

"He says his name is Abobtu and he wants us to follow him to his village."

"Tell him I will send men back to our ships to bring more rum for him and his people."

Caesar translated, and Abobtu seemed pleased to hear it. He nodded to Raven and then began to lead them through the jungle. Raven turned to Joku and said, "Go back to the ships and tell Pharaoh to send two barrels of rum. Also, tell him to send as many bolts of textiles as we have. We are going to trade with these people."

"Aye, Raven!"

Joku took five men with him, and they ran back to the beach. Even though the trail was clearly cut, it took them more than an hour to reach the dories. They rowed back to the ships, where Pharaoh saw the men rowing toward him and began to panic.

"What is it, Joku? Where is Raven?"

"She has sent me back. She wants us to bring two barrels of rum and any textiles that we might have. She wants to set up a trade with these people."

"Raven is not in any trouble?"

"No, it does not appear so."

"What are they willing to trade?"

"I do not know. We will find out when we reach their village."

Pharaoh ordered two rum barrels be brought up from the ship's lower deck. He called out to the other vessels and instructed them to bring out any textiles that they still had onboard. Pharaoh had two barrels of rum and twenty bolts of fabric loaded onto the dory and sent six more men with Joku and his crew to help deliver the goods. Before they rowed away, Pharaoh said, "Here! You might need this!" He tossed them a tap for the barrels and anxiously waited for Raven's return.

Joku and the other men landed on the beach and began rolling the barrels and carrying the fabric down the path. The barrels were cumbersome, but with two men per barrel, they quickly moved them through the jungle. Still, it took three hours for them to finally reach the small village at the trail's end.

Raven met them as they entered the village, where everyone anxiously awaited their arrival. The tall man with the bone in his nose stood beside Raven as they rolled the barrels up to her. Joku looked around the village and noticed everyone standing around them as they entered. He then saw something else: the whole village was decorated with gold. Tall staffs covered in gold, small statues of animals covered in gold, and the women wore earrings and necklaces made of gold. Joku's eyes widened at the sight of the gold.

At the base of the mountain, there was an elaborate structure encrusted with gold. It was like no other village anyone had ever seen before—a city of gold.

Raven asked, "Did you happen to bring a tap with you?"

"Aye, Raven. Pharaoh remembered it just as we were leaving."

Joku handed Raven the tap, and she showed the natives how to drive the tap into the barrel to retrieve the rum. The men of the village all lined up holding golden cups to taste the unique concoction brought to them.

The whole village partook in the special liquid and made a feast to celebrate with their new friends. Caesar sat next to Raven and the village chief, the father of Abobtu. The Chief's name was Al Bagani.

They communicated well enough to work out a deal and make both parties happy. Raven would bring them more rum, textiles, weapons, and tools, which Al Bagani's people would trade for gold bars. In the meantime, Al Bagani sent enough gold with them when they left that evening that each man struggled to carry his load back to the ship. Three hours past dusk, Raven and her men loaded all the gold into the dories and rowed back to the ships.

When they reached the ships, Raven had the men divide the gold between the three ships for storage. She called her officers together so she and Caesar could tell of all that had happened. Raven then ordered another keg of rum to be opened so they could celebrate their good fortune.

Chapter 34

Raven knew that if they were going to continue trading with Al Bagani and his people, they would need to find more rum, textiles, weapons, and tools—mostly rum. The closest place she knew to get the things she needed would be Port St. Felix with Señor Rivera, so they set sail for Madagascar.

Sailing was smooth as they traveled west out of the Gulf of Guinea. However, two weeks later, when they turned south toward the Cape, the weather took a turn for the worse. Thunderstorms rocked the ships for three days. Rough waters rolled the ships through the seas, creating non-stop bobbing up and down the entire time. Even the more seasoned sailors of the group succumbed to motion sickness. Steering of the ships was difficult as well. The ships had to separate so they weren't in danger of running into one another.

On day thirty-five, *Destiny* finally made port at St. Felix with neither Tryton nor Matilda in sight. Raven had not seen them for days and didn't even know if either ship was still afloat. As usual, she tied her ship at the dock and had half-expected to be met by Señor Rivera, but he was nowhere about.

Raven asked around the village if anyone had seen Rivera, but no one seemed to know where he might be. She asked a man on the docks if he had seen any other ships in port lately, thinking maybe her other ships had already come and gone. It wasn't likely because Raven would have expected them to wait for her here.

The unknown man said, "I have only seen one ship in the past two weeks. It was a French vessel, heavily armed. The capitan spoke to Señor Rivera many times while they were here, but we have seen little of him since the ship left three days ago."

Raven asked, "Was it a French merchant ship?"

"No, Señorita. It was heavily armed. Lots of cannons. Many soldiers."

"Which way did they sail?"

"They were sailing west, up the eastern shore of Africa. The capitan, he said he would be back in a few days."

That made Raven nervous. Was the French vessel looking for her or just patrolling the waters around Africa? Raven decided to go to Rivera's hacienda to see if she could find him. She was still puzzled by his absence. Jeffrey and John accompanied Raven as they walked through town, heading toward Rivera's villa on the opposite side of town. People seemed frightful to see them as they strolled through the village. Some closed their doors and hid inside as the trio walked by their homes.

The hairs on the back of Raven's neck stood up on end. She got a bad feeling in the pit of her stomach. Something was wrong. Raven slowed her pace, carefully checking her surroundings as she walked. Then she said to the others, "Be watchful. Something isn't right here."

Jeffrey asked, "What do you mean?"

"These people know us. They have seen us many times but for some reason they are avoiding us."

As they reached the rear edge of the village, shy of Rivera's villa, Raven understood what was wrong. Rivera's home was guarded by French soldiers. Raven surmised that a trap had been laid for her, and the French were expecting her.

Raven balked, held out her arms to stop her companions, and said, "Wait. It's a trap. We've got to get back to *Destiny*. Everyone split up. We'll meet back at the ship."

John refused, "No, Raven! We need to stay together!"

"No, Papa! If we all get captured then they will capture *Destiny* too. Who knows, they may have already taken *Matilda* and *Tryton*. If not, one of us needs to be available to warn them. Now, go!"

John turned and went back the way they had come. Jeffrey chose a different route, moving southward for a while before heading directly for the ship. Raven moved north and then west toward the beach. She ran from house to house, hiding behind each other, searching ahead for anything suspicious.

Jeffrey reached the ship first. He went directly to Alexander and told him, "Raven suspects it is a trap. Everyone in town is avoiding us. She wants us to be ready to sail right away and be prepared for a fight."

Alexander called for all hands on deck and gave instructions to prepare to sail. Then he ordered all men to gather near the port rail, armed and ready for an attack. He sent only a few to watch the starboard rail in case a ship came behind them. They prepared the cannons on the starboard rail in case they were attacked by sea.

As soon as the men began mustering to their stations, John arrived at *Destiny* half out of breath. He found Pharaoh and Jeffrey on the quarter-deck and asked, "Where's Raven?"

Pharaoh answered, "She has not yet returned."

John grew worrisome for his daughter. He knew she was very capable of fighting if attacked, but if she were outnumbered, she might fall prey to her attackers.

A call came from the starboard rail, "Look! Two ships! I think it is *Matilda* and *Tryton*!"

Alexander took out his spyglass to see if he could determine who it might be. The first ship was Tryton and she was coming full sails. However, the ship behind her was not *Matilda*. It appeared to be a frigate, and it was well-armed. Pharaoh checked the mast for a flag. There it was. France's red, white, and blue bands flew above the ship. It was behind *Tryton* by half a mile, but it was closing fast.

Suddenly, Alexander heard a familiar voice call out from behind. It was Raven running toward the ship. She was still a quarter of a mile away, but she was waving her arms at him and calling to him. He couldn't quite tell what she was saying, but then he saw why she was running. Six French soldiers were chasing her through the streets. Alexander called out to his men, "Cast off!"

Then he took a rifle and began aiming at Raven's attackers. He took careful aim so that Raven would not be hit. **Boom!** The shot rang out and caused everyone to turn to see who had fired. Then they turned and saw one of the men chasing Raven fall. Daktari took up a rifle and aimed from the port rail. Just as he was about to fire, Alexander yelled to him, "Daktari, make sure you don't hit Raven! She will be very angry if you do!"

Daktari fired his weapon, and another soldier hit the ground. Raven continued running to the ship, but her legs grew weary. Suddenly, as she had cleared the town and was approaching the beach, ten more soldiers simultaneously appeared from the north and south. They surrounded Raven so she could do nothing except surrender. Again, she called out to the ship and said, "Get out of here! Save yourselves!"

John stood on the quarterdeck, watching as his daughter was bound and taken away. Tears ran down his cheeks, and he whispered, "Raven."

Tryton continued toward the port as the frigate pursued her. Suddenly, a cannon fired from the frigate and struck *Tryton's* bow, knocking out her rudder. Caesar ordered his men to fire upon the frigate as best they could. Since they had no rudder, it was difficult to position the guns to fire at the approaching ship. Nevertheless, Caesar's crew worked furiously at loading and firing the cannons from their bow and port rail as best they could. The young men who worked as powder monkeys quickly stuffed canvas bags with black powder below decks and transported them to the cannons above decks.

Tryton fired shot after shot at the frigate, but little damage was done. One shot from the four-pounder stern gun managed to rupture a hole in the French ship's forecastle, leaving only minor damage.

Caesar's crew fired repeatedly at the French vessel, but it was useless. Without a proper rudder, they couldn't position *Tryton* to give a clear shot at the enemy. They were like injured fish flailing in the water.

Suddenly, a cannon blast from the frigate sent an eight-pounder cannonball at *Tryton,* striking her port hull. The ball tore through the hull and knocked over a lit oil lantern, which fell to the lower deck and erupted into flames. The flames quickly spread throughout the deck, where all the black powder was stored. Any powder spilled by the powder monkeys quickly ignited and caused one explosion after another.

Ten barrels of black powder exploded below decks one after the other until the whole ship finally erupted into flames and splinters that flew twenty feet into the air. Men and women screamed as their skin was scorched and blown apart from their bodies. However, the screams were short-lived. No one survived as blast after blast sent *Tryton* into the depths of the sea.

Alexander watched in terror as he saw his friend Caesar go down with his ship and crew. He quickly turned his attention back to his own crew and ordered them to drop all sails. They would make a run for it.

As the frigate turned its sights on *Destiny*, Alexander decided to go north. He would loop around the island of Madagascar and sail through the Indian Ocean, then back toward the Cape of Good Hope. Alexander hoped that he would find Pharaoh and *Matilda* there. If not, they would go back to the Gulf of Guinea to a cove that Raven had pointed out to each of her captains as a place of refuge should they all become separated. Raven had dubbed it The Robin's Nest.

As *Destiny* sailed northward, Alexander kept an eye on the frigate behind them. He soon felt relief as he surmised the French vessel was slowing and moving into port instead of pursuing *Destiny*.

They sailed four thousand miles around Madagascar before reaching the Cape. *Destiny* took a wide berth around the island's south end to avoid running into the French. Thirty-one days after leaving Port St. Felix, they sailed into The Robin's Nest inside the Gulf of Guinea.

As *Destiny* slowly entered the cove, Alexander spotted *Matilda* mooring inside. He blew on his conch shell to let Pharaoh and his crew know who was approaching. *Destiny* was moored closely by *Matilda*, and then Alexander and his crew began traveling by dory to the beach where Pharaoh and his crew were camping.

When Alexander approached Pharaoh who was waiting for him at the edge of the water, Alexander said, "I have bad news. Raven had been captured by the French."

"How did this happen?"

"They were waiting for us at Port St. Felix. Raven went to speak to Señor Rivera but she, John, and Jeffrey were ambushed before they could talk to Rivera. The three of them split up and only John and Jeffrey made it back safely. We watched as they captured Raven and took her away."

"You did not try to rescue her?" Pharaoh asked angrily.

"We tried! We killed two of them before they took her away, while we had other things to worry about and beside, Raven ordered us to escape."

"What other things did you have to worry about?"

"As we were preparing to leave, *Tryton* approached from the Cape. She was being chased by a French frigate. It was heavily armed and it sank *Tryton* and all her crew."

"Caesar is gone?"

"Yes, my friend. Caesar and thirty of his men."

They paused for a moment as John approached them.

"What do you plan to do about Raven?" he asked them both.

Pharaoh said, "We should go to some of the French ports in the Gulf. Spy them out and see if we can get information about Raven. I will take John with me if you can spare him at the helm. It would be better to have a white man asking questions about such things rather than an African. We will go to Abidjan to ask around. You can send Jeffrey into the port to ask questions. I suggest you go back to Lomé. Maybe someone is still there that has heard about Raven. We will meet back here in two weeks."

Alexander replied, "We will leave in the morning. I need to resupply the ship before I sail again. We are running low on fresh water and food."

Pharaoh shook Alexander's hand and said, "Good luck, my friend. Until we meet again."

CHAPTER 35

Raven struggled against her bonds as the soldiers led her away. They marched her through the village down a street leading back to Rivera's villa. They opened the door and led Raven inside, where she found Señor Rivera sitting at a table in his office. He looked very uncomfortable as Raven was shown into his office. She also noticed his face was marked as if he had been beaten.

A man was standing next to Rivera, who seemed to be the leader of the French troops. As Raven was brought in, he began to speak with a heavy French accent.

"Well, Mademoiselle Raven I presume. You have made quite the name for yourself in such a short time. My name is Colonel Francois Michaud, and I want you to know that you are under arrest for crimes against France and her citizens."

Raven erupted in disdain as she asked, "For what? Freeing Africans from being forced into slavery? It is France who should be arrested for such atrocities! France, England, Holland, Spain, and all other countries who would force people into slavery should be arrested and hanged!"

"Not only did you interfere with the commerce of slavery, you committed murder. The murder of several French citizens!"

"I murdered no one! If you're talking about Monsieur Jacque Le Fleur, he attacked me. I was only defending myself and my men."

Michaud asked, "And Monsieur Arsenault? Were you defending yourself when you hanged him and all his men on Port Gentil's beach?"

"No! I was keeping a promise I made to him. I told him he would live as long as he stopped working in the slave trade. He was free to continue making his weapons and selling them. But, I also told him if I caught him capturing Africans to sell as slaves I would hang him with all of his men."

"So, you confess to your crimes!"

"I confess, but it was no crime! I warned him what would happen. He chose his own fate!"

"And you, Mademoiselle, have chosen yours. You will be taken back to France where you will be tried for your crimes."

Michaud looked at his guards and said, "Take her away!"

He looked at Rivera and asked, "And now, mon ami, what to do with you?"

Rivera replied, "I have committed no crime. I am a business man operating a trading post."

"Perhaps. However, should evidence come forth that you have conspired with this, Red Raven, your fate will be the same as hers."

Michaud left Rivera with his men and returned to their ship. Raven was led through the streets of the village in chains. She tried to walk proudly alongside her captives with all her might, but the heavy chains made it difficult for her to stand fully erect.

Once on the frigate, Raven was shackled in the lowermost deck, where she shared a space with the rats and roaches that scurried around looking for food crumbs. The space smelled of dead animals, rotting meat and produce, and human waste. Darkness filled the hull, with only thin light streams entering through cracks in the deck above her.

Raven began to sob. She had not cried since she was very young when she lost her mother to illness. She had always been strong and didn't give in to emotions other than anger. Her anger and hate of those who would mistreat other people is what drove her to be who she was. She loved her papa, but love was never expressed between them. She loved her men and her crew, but it was only represented by treating them with respect and generosity whenever she could. She began to think about love. Did she love Jeffrey? She wasn't sure. She wasn't even sure if she knew what love was. Raven had fond feelings for Jeffrey. She enjoyed his presence. She liked how he looked, the touch of his hand against hers. But was it love?

Suddenly, Raven wiped away her tears. She would not allow her captives to see her sorrow or even her fear. Hate? Oh, yes! They would definitely see that in her.

No one ever came down to check on her except for the one time each night when she was presented with a bowl of swill to eat. She was allowed a cup of mush and a cup of water every day. But that was all. She grew increasingly hungry daily, so much so that she began eating the cock roaches that crawled too close to her. It was the only protein she received while being held captive. The only one she ever saw while residing on the ship was the young boy who brought her food. No men were allowed down below for fear of what they might do to the attractive young woman in man's clothing. Many of the men were frightened of her anyway, although none would admit it. They called her a Chat Sauvage, Wild Cat.

Matilda landed at Abidjan ten hours after they set sail from the hidden cove they called The Robin's Nest. Pharaoh sent John Ashworth and Pierre into town to see if they could discover where Raven might have been taken.

John and Pierre walked through the streets looking for a pub that might be suitable for finding information. Pubs were notorious for being hubs of gossip. If anyone had heard of the Red Raven, the news would have likely returned to one of the pubs.

It was just past noon when John and Pierre stepped inside one of the pubs, a small place called La dame qui danse (The Dancing Lady). John looked around as they entered and saw the barkeeper, a young woman serving tables, and six patrons sitting at three tables. Four small tables remained vacant, so John and Pierre chose one near the center of the room where they could converse with more than one table at a time.

The young lady came to their table and asked in French, "What can I get you?"

John deferred to Pierre, who spoke French, to converse with her.

"We would like two ales, please."

"Oui."

When she returned with their ale, Pierre tried to strike up a conversation with her, "I heard they captured that girl called Red Raven."

The maiden, whose name was Jolie, replied, "Really? I had not heard that." Then she turned and walked away.

The men two tables away heard Pierre's statement and joined in the conversation. The first was an older man with a white beard dressed like a docker. He probably worked the docks unloading and loading cargo. The second man was younger and clean-shaven but also dressed like a docker. The younger of the two was more talkative. He spoke up and replied to Pierre, "I have not heard about the Red Raven's capture, but I know the French government was looking for her earnestly. She was disrupting their trade."

Pierre asked, "Really? Have you ever seen her?"

"Only the picture on the wanted poster. She looked very pretty to me. I would like to meet her someday."

Pierre nodded and smiled at the young man. "I hear she's a dangerous female. I'm not sure I ever want to meet her."

"Oh, I could handle her. She would melt in my arms."

Again, Pierre chuckled at the young man. "I wonder what will happen when they capture her?"

"She is a pirate. All the pirates captured by the French government are taken to La Rochelle. They have a prison there. If they capture her, she will be taken there and executed. It is a shame. Such a pretty young thing."

Pierre looked at John without saying anything. John could tell Pierre had the information they needed. They finished their drinks and then got up from the table. John placed money on their table to pay for the drinks, then walked over and paid for the young man's drink and his companion's. John nodded to the two, smiled, and walked away. Pierre followed after saying, "Nice talking with you. Enjoy your drinks."

The young man raised his glass and said, "Merci! Au revoir!"

John and Pierre casually left the pub and slowly walked together down the street, heading back to the dock.

John asked, "Well?"

"The young man said the French take pirates to a place called La Rochelle. There is a prison there. She will be held there until trial, then execution."

John replied, "Let's get back to the ship and tell Pharaoh."

They hurried, winding through the streets until they reached the dock. When they reached the port, they saw two soldiers walking together along the docks. John and Pierre stopped for a moment to watch the soldiers.

The soldiers looked at *Matilda* as they passed by but took very little interest in her.

John said, "Come on."

They walked together casually to the ship, crossed the gangplank, and went directly to Pharaoh's quarters. Pharaoh's door was open, so they entered unannounced.

John said to him, "Pharaoh, we think we know where they are taking her."

"Where?"

"There is a place called, La Rochelle. They have a prison there. We heard that's where they take pirates when they are captured."

Pharaoh pulled out several charts and began searching through them. He also handed John some. Pharaoh said, "La Rochelle must either be a colony of France or a city within France's border.

John found a chart of the colonies around the Gulf of Guinea that he searched, while Pharaoh searched for a chart of France itself. Pharaoh finally found a chart of the western coast of Europe from France through Portugal. He pulled out a magnifying glass and searched through the chart along the coast of France.

"I have it!"

Pharaoh pointed at a place on the western edge of France near the coast.

"Let's get back to The Robin's Nest! We must meet with Alexander and come up with a plan."

John suggested, "We aren't suppose to meet him for another two weeks. Why don't we sail up the coast and try to find him? It might be quicker."

"Yes, of course. We will try that. If we don't find him within the week, we will go back to the original plan."

Pharaoh ordered his men to make ready to sail. They untied from the dock and pushed away. Once the ship had drifted into the bay, they lowered their sails and headed east toward Lomé. Two hours in, a young man called from the crow's nest, "Ship ahoy!"

Pharaoh took out his spyglass and looked over the bow; it was *Raven's Destiny. Destiny* was still half a mile from *Matilda,* so there was no way to signal her. They continued to sail toward her, and twenty minutes later, they found themselves close enough to signal her. Pharaoh blew his conch shell and waited for Alexander to return the call. Almost immediately, the call was returned.

The ships came together and threw grappling hooks to bring them closer. Sandbags were tied to the sides of the vessels to keep them from damaging each other as the sea tossed them together. Pharaoh met Alexander at the rails of the ships to converse.

"Alexander, did you find out anything?"

"No, Pharaoh. No one seems to know anything about the Raven being captured. How about you?"

"We found out where they take prisoners who are captured for piracy. It is a place called La Rochelle. I found it on the charts. It is 46.2° north, 1.2° west. Do you have enough supplies for twenty days?"

"I have enough for at least thirty days."

"Good. We will sail together. If we get separated we will meet on a peninsula southwest of La Rochelle. It looks like a peacock sticking his head out and looking west on the charts. Signal me if we need to meet along the way."

"I will. Good luck to you!"

"Good luck to us all!"

CHAPTER 36

THE TRIAL

The frigate arrived early one morning at the port of La Rochelle. The port was inside a bay at the innermost part between two peninsulas. La Rochelle was a large city with tall stone buildings scattered throughout. Small apartment buildings and shops filled in the gaps between all the larger buildings. People were already going about their daily routines when the ship arrived.

Raven could hear the muffled sounds of people yelling above her on the upper deck as they prepared for docking. She became anxious as to where they might have brought her. She had no idea what direction they had traveled or how long they had been at sea.

Hours passed while the ship was secured and made ready for the crew to disembark. Raven thought maybe they had forgotten about her. However, her question was short-lived. It wasn't long before two soldiers climbed down to retrieve her. They unlocked her shackles and then led her up to the top deck. Once there, they put new bonds on her wrists and ankles. The guards led her away, down the gangplank, onto the docks, then into the streets of La Rochelle.

No less than twenty guards escorted Raven as they moved her down through the city center, where the government offices were. People gathered throughout the streets to see the hardened criminal who had been captured and brought into their fair city. A multi-level stone building stood before her as she was displayed ceremoniously along the way. When they reached the steps of the tall building, she noticed words were carved in the building's stone front.

Palais de Justice et Prison de La Rochelle

Raven didn't need to speak French to know what it said; Justice and Prison were all she needed to see.

They led her up the courthouse steps, her chains rattling with every step. She counted thirty-nine steps to the top of the portico. She was led through two large wooden doors, each at least twelve feet high. Inside, the floors were made of marble, and the walls were the exact stones that she saw on the outside. Eighteen guards remained outside, while two led her into the courthouse along with Colonel Michaud. It was cold inside the building, and each step she took echoed throughout the halls of the structure.

Raven was led into a spacious room near the center of the courthouse. At the far end stood a large wooden podium where an older gentleman sat. He wore a long powdered wig, a long black robe, and a white collar. His face was stern as he impatiently waited for the accused to take her place before him.

A conversation took place between the man behind the podium and the Colonel, with Raven standing alone and confused before them. She didn't understand most of the conversation, yet waited for her turn to speak.

After several minutes of dialogue between the two officials, the judge picked up a gavel, banged it on the podium, and said, "Coupable!"

He then began a long diatribe that she couldn't understand. Then once again, he banged his gavel and said, "Le tribunal est ajourné!"

Raven understood this time. The court was adjourned, and her fate had been sealed without her being allowed to declare her innocence. The Colonel signaled for the guards to take her away, but Raven interrupted and asked, "Do I not have an opportunity to speak?"

The Colonel replied, "You can speak to the walls of your cell while you await your execution."

"Execution! For what?"

"Mademoiselle, the French have strict laws concerning piracy and murder. You will be executed on the 30th of September."

"What is today's date?"

"September 5th."

Michaud took the opportunity to motion for his guards to lead Raven away while she stood stunned by the news. Tears began to well up in her eyes as she sobbed. Her guards dragged her from the courtroom back out into the hallway. From there, she was taken to the back of the building to a stairway leading down into a dark, dank area where the holding cells were located.

Raven heard noises from some cells: coughing, crying, sniffling. They led her to the last cell on the right, opened the door, and removed her shackles. They shoved her into the cell, and one spoke in French as he pointed to a chamber pot in the corner. Raven understood the gist. He closed the door and locked it.

Raven's cell was tiny, five feet wide and eight feet deep—stone walls and a stone floor made for a damp, cold place to sleep. A slit in the outer wall allowed fresh air and sunlight to enter the room. At six inches wide, it was too small for anyone to fit through and too high up the wall for anyone to look out. There was no cot or blanket to sleep on or keep her warm.

Raven paced the floor from one end to the other, then back again. She had not had any exercise in over a month since being chained in the hull of the frigate. It felt good to stretch her legs, even in her tiny cell.

The moans, cries, and coughs continued throughout the day and night. Everyone Raven heard seemed to be men. She heard nothing to indicate any other women in the prison beside her. After hours of pacing the floor, Raven slid to the floor, lay down, and fell asleep.

September 15, 1718

The port at La Rochelle was one of the largest Raven's crew had ever seen. French naval vessels, merchant vessels, and local fishing boats were docked along the shore's edge.

Destiny and *Matilda* docked on the far west side of the port. They each draped a sail over their bows to hide their ship's names. It was made to look like they were each involved in repairs. Men were placed at the bows and instructed to look busy repairing the ships should anyone approach.

Pharaoh, John, Pierre, Jeffrey, and Alexander met on *Destiny* to discuss how to rescue Raven.

John started, "Well the first thing we need to do is find out where they are holding her. I don't think it would be wise for any of you Africans to be seen walking around town. It might look suspicious. Jeffrey, Mr. Greer, Isaac, Nathan Coates, Louis Hardy and I will go on shore and have a look around. We'll meet back here this evening to report and decide what we will do."

Pharaoh said, "This sounds good. The rest of us will prepare our weapons and resupply our ships for when we leave."

Jeffrey took Nathan Coates with him, and they were the first pair to leave. Mr. Greer and Louis Hardy were the next group to head into the city, and John and Isaac were the last ones to leave.

Jeffrey and Nathan headed through the center of the city. Jeffrey spotted a tall stone building in the distance that he presumed would be some government office. It was too large to be anything else.

Andrew Greer and Louis Hardy walked down a street on the city's south side. It was filled with pubs, shops, and living quarters for the common people of the town. They planned to ask around about new naval ships that had recently arrived.

John and Isaac walked to the north side of the city. It was an area of La Rochelle where the well-to-do resided. It also held a large Catholic Cathedral. John thought that there might be a priest there who might sympathize with Raven's plight. Maybe they could gain information from him.

Jeffrey and Nathan reached the tall structure and saw by the carving in the stone above the large doors that it was indeed a government office, the courthouse. Guards stood at the door, so they chose to examine the outside of the building, especially around the back.

The first tour around the building offered little clues about where or if Raven was being held inside. As they walked around the back of the building for a second time, Jeffrey noticed that there was a stone half-wall at the rear of the building. It stood three feet high and was erected five feet from the outer wall of the building. They casually walked closer to the stone wall and discovered it was meant to hide small windows near the bottom. Jeffrey was somewhat puzzled and stood there confused, looking for an answer as to why they would build a half-wall here.

Suddenly, Jeffrey heard a cough.

"Did you hear that?" Jeffrey whispered to Nathan.

"What?"

"There it is again!"

Jeffrey realized someone was in the building behind one of the slit openings at the base of the wall. Jeffrey knelt after checking to see if he was being watched. He heard the cough again.

"Someone is in there!" he whispered.

Nathan suggested, "That must be where they are holding the prisoners."

Jeffrey asked, "Yes, but which one is Raven in?"

"I don't know, but it's too dangerous for us to go around calling her name. What should we do?"

Jeffrey replied, "I have an idea. Let's get back to the ship."

Andrew and Louis walked into several pubs on the city's south side, hoping to gain some information. At least, Andrew was hoping. Louis seemed to be more interested in filling his gut with rum. He had more than one drink at each stop they made, and he began to make a spectacle of himself with his drunken and rude behavior. Andrew decided it was useless; he needed to get Louis back to the ship to sober up.

John and Isaac found the Cathedral on the north side. It was the most prominent structure John had ever witnessed. Much larger than the church in Bristol. They entered the front doors and were immediately greeted by the chanting of monks throughout the church.

They quietly entered the sanctuary, which was filled with rows of benches. Around the room's exterior were stained glass windows, each with a picture depicting a moment in Jesus's life. An altar and a pulpit stood on a raised platform in the front. A statue of Christ hanging on a cross was attached to the wall behind the pulpit.

A priest walked into the large room and spotted the men entering. He walked to greet them and spoke his greeting in French.

Isaac raised his hand to halt the priest from speaking, then asked, "Parles vous Anglais?"

The priest smiled and said, "Oui, monsieur, I speak English."

John explained their dilemma, "Father, we are sailors and our captain, my daughter, has been taken prisoner by the French government. We believe she was brought here to La Rochelle. Have you heard any news of her?"

"A woman captain, you say? I don't recall hearing anything."

"She is known as the Red Raven."

The priest's eyes widened as he recognized the name.

"Yes, I have heard of her. She is in our prison, but I was told she was a murderer."

"No, Father. She has killed. But it was to defend the down trodden people of Africa who were being forced into slavery. She is not a murderer."

"What is it you want from me?"

"Do you know where she is being held?"

"Oui, she is in the prison underneath the courthouse at the center of the city."

John asked, "Has she had a trial yet?"

"Oui, she has been convicted and she is to be executed on the 30th."

"What is today?"

"It is September 15th."

John asked, "Is there anything you can do for her?"

"I can pray for her, but there is nothing I can do to intervene. Her destiny is in God's hands."

Before leaving the priest, John noticed the monks in the corner continuing their chants.

"Father, I would like to make a donation to the church. May I ask a favor in return?"

"What is it you need, my son?"

"How many of those robes do you have lying around?"

CHAPTER 37

The night before Raven's execution, forty men left the ship to take their places in La Rochelle before the execution. Thirty-five of them went with John to the Cathedral to visit the priest who was expecting them. The door was unlocked when they arrived, so they entered and stood inside until the priest came to meet them.

John asked the priest, "Father, do you have them?"

"Right inside here, my son."

The priest led the way into the sanctuary, where John and his men found monk robes draped across the benches. John knew that having thirty-five to forty Africans wandering through town would be conspicuous, so he arranged to borrow the robes to hide his men. Under their robes, they could not only hide the color of their skin but also conceal their weapons.

Each man threw a robe and sword over his clothing and then pulled the hood over his head. John then handed the priest a leather bag holding fifty pieces of silver.

"Thank you, Father!"

"God be with you, my son. God be with you all."

The phony monks left in pairs from the Cathedral and went to their appointed locations to wait.

Pharaoh and Jeffrey went to the executioner's home. When they arrived, they saw a light through his window, indicating that the large man was already awake and preparing for his day. Pharaoh knocked on the door.

When the man opened his door, he was surprised to see a young white man and a huge black man standing at it.

"Oui?"

Jeffrey began speaking to him as best he could in the French he quickly learned from Pierre.

"We want to make you an offer."

"What kind of offer?"

"I want this man to take your place as executioner today."

"I make good money killing people for the government."

"How much?"

"They pay me 100 Doubloons." he proudly stated.

"We will pay you £1 to let this man take your place."

The man was shocked because £1 was nearly 3,000 Doubloons. "What? Are you mad? I have never seen that much money!"

Jeffrey took a leather pouch and showed him a handful of gold coins, equaling £1.

"All you have to do is let us have your clothes and your sword. We will take care of the rest."

Alexander and ten other men stayed behind on *Destiny*. Just before dawn, when everything was quiet around the docks, He took his men and quietly sneaked onto the armed frigates at the port. They carried with them over-packed pouches of gunpowder. They stuffed the bags into each cannon aboard the four Frigates by the docks. Then, they packed mud in each tube to clog the channel. They finished their sabotage and made it back to *Destiny* without being discovered.

Just before dawn, six soldiers traveled to the dungeon to retrieve Raven from her cell. They bound her hands behind her back and led her up the stairs into the courthouse. Once in the courthouse, Raven saw a crowd of people gathered around.

Among them were Colonel Michaud and the judge who sentenced her to death.

Then Raven noticed a nearby priest holding a Bible in his hand and praying as she walked by. As he prayed and read from the scriptures, he continually made the sign of the cross from his forehead to his heart, shoulder, and the other shoulder. Next to the priest was a monk who seemed familiar to her. She suddenly realized it was her papa. She gasped until she saw him put his finger to his lips to quiet her. Then he moved his hand to his forehead and finished making the sign of the cross. Raven felt a tiny bit of relief as she turned and walked away.

The guards led her out of the courthouse, then turned left, circling to the side of the building where the platform lay. Walking into the morning light, she saw the crowd sneering, yelling, and throwing vegetables at her. She also noticed an unusual number of monks scattered among the masses. The guards helped her up the platform's steps and led her to a large wooden block at the center. Raven noticed the block was blood-stained, as well as the platform around the block, from many previous executions.

They forced her to kneel and lay her head on the chopping block. They then tied her down so she couldn't move, with a rope draping over her shoulders and secured to the sides of the block.

People from all over the city gathered to witness the execution, standing on tops of buildings around the courtyard. Even children climbed up into trees and rested on the limbs to get a bird's-eye view.

The judge stepped forward and began making a lengthy speech about law, crime, and punishment as the people murmured, waiting for the big finale. The longer the judge droned on, the louder the crowd grew.

Finally, the judge pronounced that the execution be carried out. He stepped aside and allowed the executioner to step forward.

The crowd suddenly grew quiet, waiting for the tall man in the black hood to swing his Saracen sword. He lifted his sword above his head and paused before quickly swinging it down toward the wooden block where Raven's head lay.

Snap! The sword's blade entered the block to the left of Raven's head, snapping the rope holding her down in two. Pharaoh quickly removed his hood, displaying his black face to the crowd, who began screaming and running about, trying to escape the terror of the man with the giant sword. Standing next to the priest, John quickly knelt behind Raven and used his knife to cut her bonds. He handed her an extra sword he had been concealing, and the two began swinging at the guards attacking the platform.

More soldiers arrived from the courthouse to intervene in the escape attempt. They were greeted by thirty-five monks who removed their robes and displayed their swords and pistols. The whole courtyard erupted in battle as the soldiers attacked the phony monks.

The air was filled with the sound of blades crossing as Frenchmen fought against Africans and their compatriots. Occasionally, a pistol shot rang out as one of Raven's men fired at a soldier trying to enter the fight from a distance.

Raven, John, and Pharaoh quickly killed the judge, Colonel Michaud, and the guards on the platform before running down the steps to join the other men in the battle below. It was over in less than ten minutes. Thirty French soldiers and their leaders lay dead. Raven and her men quickly ran down the streets of La Rochelle, ready to fight anyone who dared challenge them. They ran toward the docks less than a mile from the city's center. Ladies would scream anytime they were surprised by the band of running monks wielding swords and pistols.

As Raven and her crew reached the docks, more soldiers challenged them from the naval vessels running toward them, trying to cut them off before they could reach *Destiny* or *Matilda*. However, they were no match for Raven's seasoned crew of marauders. Blades clanged against each other again, and blood spilled as the soldiers were quickly defeated.

Other soldiers fired upon the crew as they ran toward their ships. Six of Raven's men were hit, some in the leg, others in the torso. The companions scooped them up and carried them to the ships.

Raven reached *Destiny* and commanded, "Cast off!"

The remaining crew began freeing the ship from the confines of the dock and lowered the crimson sails to begin flight from the port. As the last man arrived on the ship, the gangplank was lifted away from the pier, allowing the *Destiny* to sail free.

The French were not about to be defeated by this motley crew of bandits. Officers aboard every frigate gave orders to fire upon the fleeing ships with their cannons. The first cannon was lit and exploded on the frigate's deck, sending men flying in all directions. Second, third, and fourth guns were lit, leading to the same result. The cannon tubes exploded, and the cannonballs were expelled from the ruptured tubes only to fall into the water twelve feet away.

As *Matilda* and *Destiny* sailed through the bay, they fired their stern guns at the frigates, sending four-pounders at the naval ships, hitting them squarely onto the decks of each ship. Men scattered to dodge the cannonballs heading their way. Those injured from cannon misfires were helpless to avoid approaching cannonballs. It was complete chaos on the decks of each of the frigates as men fell wounded or dead among the exploding cannon tubes or cannonballs from the opposing ships.

Raven's Destiny sailed away free of damage along with her companion *Matilda*. They managed to disable all four ships in the harbor at La Rochelle, so there would be no one to pursue them.

Raven set sail back to The Robin's Nest, where they could rest and make plans for the future. Four hours after leaving La Rochelle, Jeffrey found Raven leaning against the port rail, already bathed and wearing clean clothes. Jeffrey stood next to her and Captain Billings, who rested on her shoulder. They quietly enjoyed the wind as it blew past their faces, the warm sunshine touching the back of their necks, and the waves slapping the side of the ship.

Suddenly, Raven reached over to Jeffrey and wrapped her arms around his right arm. She pulled him close to her, kissed him on the cheek, and said, "It's good to be home."

RAVEN'S DESTINY

Here's a preview of chapter one of Raven's Destiny

October 20, 1707

Somewhere in the Atlantic

Morning broke to the sounds of insects chirping in the distance, tropical birds singing in the treetops, and the waves crashing against the hull of *Raven's Destiny*. *Destiny* had once been a merchant ship transporting slaves and other goods from the continent of Africa to the Carolinas in Colonial America. She was now used as a pirate ship attacking other merchant ships and freeing them of their trade goods, especially slaves.

Her captain was eighteen-year-old Raven Ashworth, originally from Bristol, England. Raven began sailing the seas at age twelve, disguised as a boy. Her father, John, took her along with him after her mother had died. Raven, then known as Richard, served as Ship's Boy aboard the former ship known as *Destiny,* which Horatio Billings captained. Billings never suspected that Richard was a girl. He took particular interest in training the lad to be a good sailor. Billings found Richard to be a quick learner of the sea and smart as a whip to the business aspects of running a ship. Richard convinced the captain that if he fed the men and the slaves aboard his vessel proper nutrition, they would survive the long, arduous journey through the open seas.

Most captains were losing nearly eighty percent of their slave cargo to disease, starvation, and malnutrition. Richard helped educate Billings that even if it took longer for them to reach their destination, they would make more money in the long run by stopping along the way and replenishing their food stores, especially fresh fruits and vegetables.

Richard seized the opportunity to free some of the slaves along the way by using his hard-earned money to buy their freedom. First, there was only one, Batimkoo, whom Richard had renamed Pharaoh. On his second voyage, Richard freed two more: Caesar and Attila. Then, on the third trip, he freed two more slaves: Nero and Alexander.

Richard renamed all his companions after famous kings and leaders he had read about in books he had borrowed from Mr. Greer, the ship's doctor. After *Destiny* sank during a hurricane, Richard revealed his secret to his men: He was not Richard, but Raven. They and the rest of her crew have faithfully served her in their quests ever since.

Raven awoke groggily from the sound of a screech from the monkey who lay at her head on her pillow. Captain Billings, named after Raven's former captain, was her constant companion. Raven found the monkey lying next to his dead mother on an island in the Atlantic, which Raven and her crew had reached after the shipwreck of the *Destiny*.

As Raven stirred from sleep, she slid out of bed and dressed. She pulled on her white stockings, then pulled on her leather breeches. She slipped on a white linen shirt with billowy sleeves, then added a leather waistcoat. She then buckled on her belt with her sword hanging from it and slid two braces criss-crossed over her shoulders. The braces held two pistols and two knives. She then tossed her long, curly, red locks of hair from underneath her blouse and let them spill down her back. Raven was a beautiful young woman, but men mistakenly thought she was weak or frail. She could outfight most men with ease. She was an avid swordsman and a crack shot with either pistol or long rifle.

Raven stepped out of her quarters, walked across the ship's deck to the officer's quarters, and opened the door to Jeffrey's cabin. Jeffrey Hamilton was a former captive of Raven, who now served as her quartermaster. He was two years older than Raven and had served aboard the *Matilda* as the ship's second mate. *Matilda* was the second ship that Raven and her crew captured after leaving the island that had served as their home for a few months after the original *Destiny* sank. The first ship Raven captured was the *Scarlett Marie*, which Raven and her crew had captured off the coast of their little island by using hand-built dugout canoes to row out and overtake the ship. Once it was captured, Raven renamed the ship *Raven's Destiny* in honor of her former ship.

Raven spoke to her quartermaster, saying, "Jeffrey. Jeffery!"

She then pulled the pillow from underneath his head, struck him with it, and called, "Jeffrey! Get up!"

Startled by the striking of the pillow and shouting of his name, Jeffrey woke up. He wiped the sleep from his eyes as he looked up and saw Raven standing over him as she faced him.

"Good morning." he said.

"Get up! We've lots to do!"

Jeffrey dressed, not wanting to leave the bed just yet. "What's your hurry?"

Raven replied, "We've been hiding here long enough. I want to get back to the seas and find some ships to raid."

It had been only a month since her crew had rescued her from the gallows of the French government after having been captured at Port St. Felix on the southwest coast of Madagascar. Raven's crew left the docks of La Rochelle, and the ships moored there, supposedly in disrepair, as they rescued their captain from losing her head. They had spent the past week at their hide-out, the Robin's Nest, re-supplying for their next voyage.

Raven was down to two ships, *Matilda* and *Raven's Destiny*. *Tryton* had been sunk by the French navy when they captured Raven. Raven's long-time friends and crew members, Caesar and Nero, were among those who were lost when the French frigate sank *Tryton*.

Their first order of business was to make sure the ships were supplied with ammunition. She wanted to return to Port St. Felix to see her old friend Señor Oscar Alejandro Rivera. The last time she had tried to meet with him, she was captured by French soldiers who had set a trap for Raven using Rivera as the bait.

Raven had three things she wanted to accomplish shortly – to establish her trade with Rivera once again, to establish trading with the people who occupied the mountain she and her men had discovered north of Mbini, and to further explore Lomé in Togo. She once spoke to a man claiming to have more than six hundred slaves at his disposal. Raven wanted to see for herself whether or not his claims were valid.

Raven's ships still carried some of the gold they had traded for on what she referred to as the Grey Coast. She had determined the people there had access to more gold than she had ever seen, and they were willing to trade with her exclusively. She needed to return to Port St. Felix to buy rum and textiles, which her new friends coveted.

Raven was not ready to raid another ship or announce her position in the sea, so she ordered the white sails to be lowered as *Destiny* and *Matilda* sailed west out of the Gulf of Guinea.

Pharaoh and his crew sailed within a quarter-mile of *Destiny* to hear the call from *Destiny* should it be made. From the beginning, Raven and her men had developed a series of signals using conch shells to communicate.

The winds coming from the northwest were cold on this October morning. *Destiny's* sails billowed out, catching the wind quickly and propelling her at twelve knots per hour. They were making excellent time.

Seven days out, Raven witnessed the coast at Port Gentil, where Andre Arsenault once ran a trading post and forge where weapons and ammunition were manufactured. Arsenault's body still hung from a tree near the beach where Raven had left it as a warning to other slave traders who didn't heed her words. Raven had warned Arsenault to refrain from slave trading, allowing him to continue the manufacturing of his guns, cannons, and ammunition. However, Arsenault thought Raven's warning to be wanting in credibility. Unfortunately, he and his men learned the hard way not to cross the Red Raven.

Raven remembered watching Arsenault's body sway in the wind as she left him there, choking to his death, with his men hanging in the trees surrounding him. She didn't delight in seeing men die, but she felt it was no more cruel than what they had done to the natives on the African continent.

Raven stood next to her papa as he steered *Destiny* past Port Gentil. John Ashworth caught a glimpse of Raven as she stared at the hanging lifeless bodies. All that was left after several months were the bones and torn clothing hanging from them.

Scavenger birds and insects had removed all the flesh from each body, producing a grizzly site to warn slave traders who might happen upon Port Gentil. Word spread quickly among merchant vessels who were involved in slave trading. The Red Raven was no one to be trifled with, and she and her crew should be avoided at all costs.

John Ashworth was ordered by Alexander, Raven's first mate, to turn the ship southward, sailing toward the Cape of Good Hope. John turned the wheel of the helm twenty degrees southward to steer *Destiny* toward the southern tip of Africa. *Matilda* took its cue from *Destiny* and turned south. The ships continued to sail together throughout the night. The skies were clear, not a cloud in them. The stars shown brightly amid the glow of the full moon.

Fourteen hours into their voyage, Isaac took over the helm. John was now below decks in his hammock. Alexander occasionally climbed to the quarterdeck throughout the night to check their progress. Daktari was in the crow's nest at the top of the main mast. The night winds whistled past him as he stared into the distance. He lifted the spyglass to his face occasionally and searched the distant horizons for other vessels in the area.

Destiny continued to sail five miles off the coast of West Africa. On their twenty-ninth hour, Alexander measured their distance and found they had traveled nearly three hundred miles. A young man, Mtoto Jasiri (Brave Child), who took over the crow's nest for Daktari, called out to Alexander, "Ship ahoy off the starboard bow!"

Alexander climbed to the bow castle and looked through his spyglass. He slowly moved his spyglass across the horizon, searching for the ship. Finally, he saw it—thirty degrees off the starboard bow and about a mile away. Alexander could see three masts but couldn't determine what flag she was flying.

Alexander called out to thirteen-year-old Jeremy, standing on the main deck.

"Jeremy, run and find Raven!"

"Aye, Alexander!"

The boy ran to Raven's cabin and knocked on the door.

"Enter!"

Jeremy quickly opened the door and found Raven and Jeffrey standing at her table, looking over a chart of the Atlantic.

"What is it, Jeremy?"

"Raven, Alexander needs you on the bow castle! A ship has been spotted!"

Raven quickly glanced at Jeffrey and said, "Come on!"

All three escaped her cabin and trotted to the bow castle to meet Alexander. Alexander handed Raven his spyglass and pointed in the direction she should look. Raven slowly moved the spyglass from left to right, searching for the ship. She thought she must have missed it, so she swung the glass back to the left, this time more slowly. There it was!

Raven asked Alexander, "How far do you think it is?"

"I measure it to be about a mile."

Raven replied, "I agree. I still can't make out what type of ship she is. Let's see if we can get closer. If she is a merchant ship and riding low in the water, she might be worth taking."

Jeremy asked, "Why would the ship be riding low in the water, Raven?"

Raven turned to Jeremy and replied, "It means she is probably full of cargo. Could be slaves, could be rum, or maybe even gold."

Jeremy's eyes lit up with intrigue. "Will we capture it?"

"That's the plan! Are you ready?"

"Aye, Raven!"

Raven ordered Alexander, "Ninety degrees starboard. Let's see if we can cut her off or at least get a closer look."

"Aye, Raven!"

Alexander turned back to the quarterdeck and called out to Isaac, who was still at the helm. "Isaac, ninety degrees starboard!"

"Aye, Alexander! Ninety degrees starboard!"

Then Alexander called to the crew on deck, "All hands ready at the sails!"

All the crew scrambled to their positions to receive further orders.

John Ashworth came up from his hammock below the deck and looked around to see what was happening with the crew. He saw Raven and Alexander standing on the bow castle, looking at something in the distance. John moved to the quarterdeck and stood beside Isaac at the helm.

"What's happening?"

Isaac replied, "We've spotted a ship off the starboard bow. Raven wants a closer look."

Excitement rose within John as he heard the news. He enjoyed a good sea chase.

Isaac turned the wheel to the right, and the ship smoothly changed direction as it bounced through the waves of the Atlantic. Raven watched as the horizon changed before her. The sun eventually moved directly in front of her. She watched seven pelicans fly across the bow in a perfect V-formation. She wondered to herself how it must feel to fly. She had always felt a sense of freedom on the seas, no matter which ship she had been aboard. But she couldn't imagine there being a more free way to live than to be a bird and be able to fly among the clouds.

Half an hour later, the distant ship became more visible. Raven checked her spyglass and saw that the boat was *indeed* a merchant's vessel riding low in the water. Raven told Alexander, "Lower the blood sails."

Alexander called out to the crew, "Lower the blood sails!"

The crew set into action, switching out the white billowing sails for the blood-red sails displaying the black raven. *Destiny* slowed slightly as the crew changed out the sails, but their speed increased once the sails were in place.

Pharaoh noticed that the blood sails were lowered and knew that the hunt for prey was afoot. He ordered his crew to prepare their guns and be ready to board the ship that occupied the waters before them.

Raven's crew onboard *Destiny* began preparing their guns as well. Ammunition was running low for the cannons, but they would be sufficient for an unarmed merchant ship. Alexander ordered his gun crew to load the bow cannon. They would fire a four-pound shot across the bow of the merchant ship to warn them of impending doom should they try to run. Few merchant ships ever armed themselves with anything more than blades and small firearms. That's why they were so susceptible to pirate attacks – the pirates needed only to fire a warning shot to overtake the merchant vessel. Crews aboard the merchant ships valued their lives more than the pockets of their employers. Earning sometimes less than £30 per year while serving on board a vessel that many were forced upon in the first place, most men would drop their arms and surrender at the first sign of danger. Some men would even join the pirates to find a more financially stable life among them.

Raven watched the vessel as it approached. Eventually, she was able to read the name of the ship upon its bow: "*Nightingale.*"

Raven was familiar with the *Nightingale*. She was captained by Nicholas Hornsby, a crusty old man notorious for treating his crew as severely as his cargo. He was in the business of hauling slaves to the Americas, but most of his cargo would never make it to its destination. The slaves he carried and his crew often suffered from starvation and malnutrition. If it hadn't been for his loyal officers, Hornsby would have succumbed to mutiny many times throughout the years. However, if any of the *Nightingale's* officers even suspected someone of initiating a mutiny, the man was strung up from the yard arm. Raven would take great delight in relieving Hornsby of his ship.

Hornsby saw two ships sailing toward him. When he took out his spyglass, he saw one of the ships sailing under red sails. He cursed out loud when he realized one of the ships making way for his ship was none other than *Raven's Destiny*. He had never encountered her before but knew of her reputation. He knew Raven was friendly to those he often profited from, namely slaves, and dangerous to those who would profit from slavery.

Thirty minutes later, *Destiny was* just a quarter mile from the *Nightingale*. Raven looked over at Alexander and nodded. Alexander called out to the gun crew on the bow, "Ready one across the bow!"

"Ready, Alexander!"

"Fire!"

The four-pound iron ball whistled through the air as it left the cannon and whizzed past the bow of the *Nightingale*. The shot, meant only as a warning, landed harmlessly in the water ten yards from the *Nightingale*.

A voice from the *Nightingale* called out to its crew. "Raise the sails and come about."

The ship's crew scrambled to work, raising and wrapping the sails against the yard arms of the three masts that towered above the deck. The first mate ordered, "Prepare to be boarded!"

Destiny and *Matilda* pulled alongside the merchant vessel, one on the port, the other on the starboard. Sandbags were draped over the rails to cushion the ships from each other as they were tied together. Raven and Pharaoh's men tossed grappling lines over to the *Nightingale* to pull their ships together. Raven's men scrambled to the trapped ship, brandishing their blades and pistols as they surrounded Hornsby's crew.

Raven swung from a mast line over the side onto the *Nightingale* and landed on their quarterdeck. She landed face to face with Hornsby, who smugly greeted her, saying, "Well, might I presume you are the Red Raven of whom I have heard so much about?"

Michael L. Clark was born in Tacoma, Washington, but grew up mainly in the south. He now resides in Pensacola, Florida.

Clark's debut series was inspired by his many trips down the Natchez Trace. The stops along the Trail mentioned the people who once lived on the trail but gave limited information about their lives. Clark began to wonder about their stories and imagine traveling back in time to live among them and learn more. That desire sparked the idea for his first novel, The Shimmering, which has since evolved into a series of time-traveling Historical Novels.

His fourth novel, Ambush at Horse Creek, is the first of many books he calls The Young Americans series. Each story depicts a young person growing up in a historical situation. Ambush is about a teenage boy who rides for the Pony Express.

His latest series, The Red Raven, is based on pirates who operated during the early 18th Century.

Other Titles by Michael L. Clark

The Shimmering Book 1

The Diary of Gus Childers: The Shimmering Book 2

The Prophet: The Shimmering Book 3

Ambush at Horse Creek

Raven's Destiny: The Red Raven Book 2